GW00689620

a candle or the sun

a candle or the sun

GOPAL BARATHAM

SERPENT'S
TAIL

For Tom King, of the Royal London Hospital

British Library Cataloguing in Publication Data
Baratham, Gopal
    A candle or the sun.
    I. Title
    823[F]

ISBN 1-85242-225-4

'Kissful of Tears', 'Double Exposure' and 'Dutch Courage' have previously been published in *People Make You Cry* by Gopal Baratham, published by Times Books International, Singapore.
The songs 'The First of My Lovers' and 'I Come Like a Beggar', by Sydney Carter, are reproduced by kind permission of Stainer & Bell Ltd.

The right of Gopal Baratham to be identified as author of this work has been asserted by him in accordance with the Copyright, Designs and Patents Act 1988

Copyright © 1991 by Gopal Baratham

First published 1991 by
Serpent's Tail, 4 Blackstock Mews, London N4

Set in 10/12pt Bembo by
AKM Associates (UK) Ltd, Southall, London
Printed in Finland by
Werner Söderström Oy

one

I am at work before anyone else not because I am conscientious or particularly like my job but simply because it is the best way I have of keeping Chuang from ruining my day. Chuang is the general manager of Benson's, the oldest department store in Singapore. I run the furniture department. When I first started with Benson's five years ago, I used to arrive around nine like everyone else. Invariably Chuang was already in the department rearranging the sets we had on display.

I would come in to find him chanting, "Latest statistics has proof that changes is what peoples most want to have." Then, nodding sagely, he would add. "Variety is one of the spices of life, ah?"

When I remained silent, he would ask, "You getting my points, Hernando?"

If there is one thing in the world that really upsets me, it is being called Hernando. I can still remember the horror of discovering, aged five, that I was not just Hernie as I had supposed but Hernando Perera. "Why? why? why?" I wailed, punching my mother's body and kicking at her shins. When she did explain, several years later, I was the worse for the knowledge. My parents, Fred and Clara, had fallen in love while dancing to a tango called "Hernando's Hideaway" and held the tune responsible for all that transpired. Knowing this, I was unable to rid myself of the belief that I had been conceived to the rhythms of a tango and every time someone called me Hernando I was reminded of this.

I had for years agreed with all Chuang's suggestions (hoping the sooner to be rid of him) until I discovered how simple it was to avoid his early morning attentions altogether. I simply arrived an hour before he did, sent for the workmen and began rearranging the furniture displays myself. By the time Chuang came in, the job was almost finished and it required a much braver man than our general manager to order the workmen to redo a job they had just completed.

I take no special pride in running Benson's furniture department and would not have minded Chuang's intrusions except that it took him several hours to decide on the arrangement he wanted, hours during which I was expected to hang around offering suggestions and murmuring approval. Not only did this waste my day but when he finally left I usually found myself no longer in the mood to do what I really liked doing, which was to sit at my desk and dream, occasionally jotting down an idea, an incident or a sequence of words I might find use for in one of my stories.

I don't write many stories, though there are always several buzzing and bumping around in my head, rather like flies behind a window-pane. I usually write when the buzzing gets intolerable or when a plot refuses to unravel itself till I pin it to paper. Once a story has actually been written, I tend to lose interest in it. It becomes an object which I may like or dislike but which has an existence of its own. I suspect that women feel this way about their grown-up children. I could find out by asking my mother, I suppose, except that she probably regards me as a tango come to grief. Had I known how much my stories would come to direct the course of my life I would have regarded them more seriously. On that morning, secure in the cool basement of the furniture department, I could only see them as little indulgences which I used to fill an existence in which not too much happened.

I sent for the workmen as soon as I got in. It was early December and I had arranged, using our latest dining-room suite as the centre piece, a Christmas dinner tableau. I had situated this in the darkest corner of the furniture department so as to heighten the effect of cosiness produced by the artificial fire. Opposite the fire a false window looked on to a painted snow-covered landscape. To increase the effect of winteriness I had lowered the room temperature several degrees and placed rotating fans at strategic spots to provide chilly drafts. Thus I succeeded in justifying the thick carpets and heavy curtains with which I had decorated the room. Early in my working life I had discovered that salesmanship consisted not of providing people with what they needed, but with what was essential to their dreams. I was confident that our dining-room suite, complete with carpets, curtains and an artificial fireplace, would shortly be snapped up by people occupying oven-hot semis in the newer and, as yet, treeless housing estates on the island. The possibility of winter is essential to the happiness of people living in the tropics.

Chuang bounced into the room just as the men were finishing. "Very excellent," he said, clapping his hands. "I think, Hernando . . ."

I gave him a look of such venom that he stopped talking and stepped backwards. It took him a moment to readjust his expression before he again bounced forward clapping his hands.

"Very excellent, Perera," he began. "Chinese say pupil's supremacy is master's reward." He smiled to himself and bowed slightly to acknowledge my gratitude. "The times I spend for you in your junior days, not wasted now, ah. So tiresome I became that sometimes I could not stand, but not wasted, see."

He pranced around the room, nodding approval, rubbing his hands together, a full fixed smile on his face.

"Nothing to do to improve," he said, adjusting the artificial fireplace slightly and drawing the curtains a fraction before he left.

With Chuang gone, I began to settle down. I placed on my desk several design magazines opened at random, a file containing invoices and a pocket calculator. On a pad beside me I jotted down words, phrases and a complicated system of arrows and hieroglyphics by which I plotted the course of my stories. I was now ready to enjoy my dreams, some of which I might write down. Only very occasionally did Ahmad, our senior salesman, disturb me with a request to authorize payment by cheque or to deal with a difficult customer or a VIP.

I resented these intrusions, the more perhaps because I had been working for some time on a character in whose life there were none. I was trying to fashion a man so totally liberated that he had nothing to do with events outside his imagination. Without friends, job, family, needs, his mind was freed to roam where it pleased. My man would hear sounds but have no need to speak. The images that filtered through his eyes he would distil into their essences and with these he would build his visions. Gradually he would shed all the body's demands – hunger, thirst, lust – until he was pure awareness, enjoying consciousness for itself. I leaned back in my chair and closed my eyes. It would be lovely but was it possible? I began wondering. A Hindu mystic, ascetic, the world forsworn, taking to the Himalayas, would hardly have enough around him to make pure consciousness worthwhile. Or would he? Would the past he had forsaken help or hinder?

"Mr Perera," said Ahmad, touching my shoulder, "telephone."

"Ahmad," I said, opening my eyes very slowly then looking sternly up at him, "you are the senior salesman here and quite qualified to deal with all telephonic inquiries."

"But she asks for you by name, sir. Very urgent she says."

"Who says, Ahmad?"

"The lady, *tuan*." Then, getting the point of my question, he added, "She says her name is Su-May, Mr Perera."

"All right, Ahmad," I said. "You get about your work. I'll take the call on my extension."

I was surprised. Su-May rarely phoned. At the outset of our affair a year ago I had been at pains to explain that the last thing I was looking for was a torrid, nerve-racked romance replete with anxious phone calls and unnecessary trysts. She had laughed and agreed. She said she was nineteen and had got over that kind of thing years ago. Our initial meetings had indeed been marvellously light-hearted and inconsequential but somehow, and quite contrary to our intentions, tenderness and passion crept into bed beside us and sweetened our coupling.

I swallowed several times before picking up the receiver.

"Perera speaking," I said in a deliberately well-modulated voice.

"Hern," she said breathlessly, "can I see you this evening?"

She sounded so vulnerably close that it was with some difficulty that I managed to inject a note of irritation into my voice. "God, no, Su-May. My parents are coming over for dinner tonight and you know how upset Sylvie will be if I'm not home early."

"Oh," she said, her voice shrinking. "I'm sorry." Su-May was very sensitive about any suggestion that our affair upset things between me and my wife, Sylvie.

"And you know how I hate you calling me at the office." I could just make out the small but sharp intake of breath and, without my quite wishing it, let my voice soften. "Won't tomorrow do, darling?"

"I suppose . . . but I was hoping . . ."

"Can't we talk on the phone then, Su-May?"

"It's not easy to explain things . . . on the phone."

"Just give me a rough idea what it's about."

"So difficult like this, Hern," she said. "No problem when you are with me and I can touch you. Then you understand but like this it's no good. You know, Hern . . ."

Suddenly I was afraid, and to quell my fear I joked: "I know what this is all about, Su-May," I said, "it's another man, isn't it?" I forced myself to laugh out loud. "You found yourself a nice young man. You want to chuck up old me and marry Mr Right? OK, you have my blessing but you must invite me to the wedding." The silence at the other end of the phone was so complete that I thought we had been cut off. "Su-May, are you still there?"

"Yes, Hern." And after a slight pause, "Yes, my love. Can you meet me tomorrow then, around six?"

"OK, where?"

"Up in Tampines. You know . . . where you used to pick me up when we first started."

"Why there?" I asked, my voice rising. "For heaven's sake, Su-May, don't say you've taken up with that mumbo-jumbo bunch again?"

When we first met, Su-May had been deeply involved with an unorthodox Christian group styling themselves the Children of the Book. I had assumed, obviously wrongly, that our adulterous affair would make it impossible for her to continue with them.

"Hern," she said, her voice very steady. "I never left the Children, you know. Stopped talking about them, that's all." In a voice now almost gay with relief, she said, "See you around six tomorrow." And hung up.

Su-May's call upset me more than I was prepared to admit. At the start of our affair I had seen her often enough in the company of her religious friends, young people in their teens or twenties who bubbled with a vivacity I could not remember. I resented this as much as I did their slim, clean bodies smelling like babies fresh from a bath. They laughed often and without cause, frequently tickling a member of the group slow to join the chorus of giggles. The leader was a lad named Peter Yu whom they jokingly referred to as "The Reverend". Apart from his being a little more intense than his fellows, there was nothing that distinguished him from the other Children, and I had not discovered in what way he was looked upon as a leader. When Su-May was with the group there was an enormous gulf between us. I was excluded from the secret that was the basis of their mirth, and untouched by the wonder they found in each other and the world. I attributed this to the difference in our ages. Today, I told myself, ten years is a long time, the equivalent of a generation, a time-gap that can never quite be bridged. But my explanation never quite satisfied me. Moreover, there was another aspect of the whole business that bothered me. Born a Catholic, I had become a resolute atheist and yet could not, whenever I saw Su-May with her religious friends, help thinking of the lilies of the field who were more glorious than Solomon.

After Su-May's phone call it was impossible to think of my story. The character I dreamed of had, freed from the directives of his body, possessed a sort of biological weightlessness that enabled him to do with his sensations as his imagination dictated. How could I write about such a person when I myself was burdened with jealousy and trapped in doubt? Everything around me brings me back to my situation. A group of schoolgirls gathers round Ahmad, who is slightly deaf. He obviously does not understand what they want. They burst into giggles. I think of the Children. They, too, laugh a lot when I'm around. Perhaps at me. But why? Have I some mannerism, some deformity, some obnoxious secretion of which I am unaware? I pick up a Christmas card with a picture of Jesus on it. It is a young Jesus, a sexual Jesus but a Jesus possessing a formidable gentleness. He reminds me very much of Peter Yu. Suddenly I know what the Children find so funny about me. Peter and Su-May are lovers. Have been for years. But Su-May's affair with me was no infidelity to Peter. Oh, no! She had, in fact, begun it at his instigation, as an act of charity towards an older man terrified of the passing of the years. I had completely missed the point of the exercise. No wonder the Children laughed . . .

By afternoon I had quietened sufficiently to begin thinking of the story again. Perhaps my own bondage told me that my man had to be totally aloof if he was to allow his imagination to respond freely to the promptings of his senses. But how could such a situation come about? Taste, touch, sight, smell competed with one another to dominate consciousness. Linked to these were the body's responses, which were bound to interrupt the process of fantasy. Awareness without strings was only possible in science-fiction, in disembodied brains floating in glass jars. But that was not the kind of story I was trying to write. Somewhere in the back of my mind was a situation I had read or heard about which would solve my problem. What it was I could not for the life of me remember. That evening as I made my way circuitously back home, ambling along side roads flanked by the old houses which I love, I cursed Su-May, Peter Yu, the Children of the Book and everything that had interfered with my exploring a theme that was beginning to interest me.

As I entered my flat, the smell of cooking hit me. My mother was making a prawn sambal. The prawns fried in onions, tamarind and red chillies acquired a burning, all-pervading flavour that simultaneously attacked nose and eyes. The pungency of the confection, however, was only an alibi for my tears. The smell of prawn sambal cooking took me far back into my childhood, to the days when I used to hang about my mother's skirts while she cooked. Now as I stood outside my own kitchen, sniffing the prawns beginning to brown, I wondered why smells often took me to the edge of tears and why they led so often to the days I had spent alone with my mother, days even before Sylvie had begun to be a part of our family.

Abandoned in infancy by her Chinese mother, Sylvie had been left to the mercies of her Indian father, who comforted himself for his wife's desertion with whisky and a succession of mistresses Sylvie referred to as aunts. A year younger than me and living two doors from us, she quite naturally became the daughter my mother wanted but never had. Very early on, the two women decided that Sylvie and I should marry, and I was given neither choice in the matter nor a chance to protest. In adolescence the rowdy games of childhood gave way to erotic ones and, when we finally fell into bed together, it was more an acknowledgement of our changed needs than a consummation of fierce passion. Now in our thirties, we acted like a couple who had a lifelong marriage behind them and, in a manner of speaking, we had. Not that I have any cause to complain. Sylvie, a lovely hybrid, with a laugh that bubbled from deep inside her, was the most companionable of bedfellows and knew me well enough to treat everything about me with a matter-of-factness that only genuine intimacy permits. And, what was more, she talked in mismatched clichés which gave her conversation a jokiness and ambiguity I found intriguing.

As soon as I entered the kitchen, she stopped chattering with my mother and kissed me, putting her right hand against my chest as she always did. (A hundred years ago I had asked her if she did that to stop me getting too close. "It's the currents," she had said. "I make another contact so they can go round and round between us and never have to stop for breath.")

I embraced my mother and asked, "Pa not here yet?" I missed the smell of cigarette smoke that always accompanied my father and was usually strong enough to overcome even cooking smells.

"Ssh!" said Sylvie, touching my lips.

"He's resting," whispered my mother. "Pa's not been too well lately."

"Flu?"

She shook her head, her face suddenly bleak. "Only the good Lord knows what it is, Hern."

"Tell him, Ma," said Sylvie.

"You know the smoker's cough Pa's had for years?" said my mother, her manner as subdued as her voice. "Well, it's been getting worse and recently he's been coughing up . . ." her voice became hardly audible and she paused for a moment before she said, "blood."

"Good God!" I said, forgetting to keep my voice down. "What does the doctor say? What about having X-rays and things done?"

"The doctor says it could be quite serious." Her voice was low and accusing. "He says there are suspicious markings on the X-rays." She nodded slowly several times.

"For heaven's sake, Ma, what does all this mean?"

"More tests and things," she said flatly.

"You know what doctors are, Hern," said Sylvie softly. "They punch a hole in your boat and watch you sinking as your confidence runs out."

"With no straw to clutch on to," I said, laughingly, elaborating on her already incomprehensible metaphor.

"Clever boy," said Sylvie, patting my arm.

"He goes into hospital next week," said my mother, dragging us away from our complex word game. "For more tests."

"Where's he now?" I asked.

"Resting," said my mother.

"In my work room?" I asked, my voice rising.

"No, dear," said Sylvie soothingly. "In our bedroom." She touched my cheek. "You get on with your typing if you must, but shut the door so you don't wake Pa."

Sylvie always referred to my writing as my typing. In part this was disparaging, an expression of her resentment at being excluded from an act in which I so often engaged. Mainly, however, it was proof of her matter-of-factness. Whether or not I was a writer was arguable. A few of my stories had attracted comment but I was, in no sense, established or well known. By talking of typing rather than writing, she was describing an action, not a purpose and was, in her own way, protecting me from my expectations. Comforted by these thoughts, I embraced Sylvie and my mother together.

"I'll be very quiet," I said. "Call me, but only when dinner's on the table."

She did – twice. I was by then so involved in the story that she had to knock on my door and shout, "The food's icing over," before I could tear myself away.

My father, usually garrulous the way retired school-teachers often are, was silent, chewing his food with a thoroughness that betrayed his lack of enjoyment of it.

"Feeling better for your rest, Dad?" I tried.

"A trifle," he said. "Just a trifle."

"Do you have pain with the cough?"

"Nothing agonizing," he said, smiling to convince me. "Just

creaky aches and pains and a feeling of intense tiredness." He smiled again. "So much like sadness."

"They'll have you right as rain soon enough, my sweetheart," said my mother, uttering one of her gutsy little laughs.

"Quite right you are, doll," he said. "As always," he added gruffly. He had on his face a look meant to indicate that, whatever his fate, she could be sure he would see it through with courage.

My parents Fred and Clara Perera had met, fallen in love, lived and would die in the spell of the films and music of the 1950s. Even as they talked, I could see my mother rehearse the moment when she finds out that father's disease is incurable. "How long has he, Doc?" she would ask. The doctor, grey-haired, his face lined with the suffering-he-has-had-to-share but nevertheless retaining its kindliness, would say with a wisdom that transcends mere personal experience, "It is not the number of days we have left but the use we make of them that matters." She knew she would be smiling and brave to the end so that Father would never know that she knew. And my Father would, right up to the bitter end, remain his gruff, kindly self, sneaking grimaces of pain but only when he thought Mother wasn't looking, sparing her the agony of knowing. Yet deep down each one knew the other knew and their pretence was but another aspect of their love. Then suddenly would come the news: there had been a terrible mistake, a mix-up of X-rays. The nightmare is over and staring into each other's eyes they find the happiness-ever-after as the camera zooms out, leaving two figures alone but blissful in a landscape of unending green.

"Right as rain they'll have you," said my mother, reaching out for Father's hand. "Just you wait and see."

My parents left after dinner and I returned to my writing. I was more than halfway through and the story was by now telling itself, incidents racing ahead of the words I had for them. At each pause in my typing, Sylvie called to ask if I had finished. I answered with a fresh clatter of activity on the machine. Her intrusions, though mildly disturbing, moved me to write faster. After a while she stopped calling out.

The aroma of my mother's cooking had started me off on the tale of a man who had lost all his senses except his sense of smell. The sensations that came to him through his nose made no demands on him. Instead, each carried with it a fragment of his past which, undistracted, he relived in its original intensity. The man I wrote about was very old and I called my story "Roses in December". By the time I finished, the traffic and other city noises had died away. It was early for the birdsong that, swelling as it did from the concrete heart of Singapore, awoke me every morning but the breeze that preceded daybreak was beginning. This came from the sea as a steady cool breath on which were superimposed shorter, sharper bursts. A little like applause, I thought, clipping together the typewritten pages.

two

"You gotta mean problem, man," said Samson Alagaratnam, leaning across my desk. "A real humdingeroo with spikes on." Sam had bulging, slightly bloodshot eyes which lent a spurious intensity to everything he said.

I was a little light-headed from staying up to finish "Roses in December" and was experiencing the lethargic relief that comes upon me when I complete a story or manage an overdue bowel movement.

"Have you seriously considered the possibility of your being right, Sam?" I asked.

"Listen, Hernie-Bernie," he said, eyeing me severely, "you just quit the joke routine, will ya?"

Samson and I were childhood friends. Even as a schoolboy Sam had yearned to be part of what he saw as the established order of things. The headmaster of the mission school we attended was a fundamentalist Christian who invariably found that heathens lacked the qualities he sought in prefects and captains of football teams. Sam had defied his illiterate Hindu parents and embraced Christianity, choosing for himself the name of the Old Testament strongman. On graduation, he had joined the civil service and had rapidly become a highly-placed official in the Ministry of Culture. He also taught Third World studies at the university and was considered an authority on English literature originating in Nigeria, Bangladesh and, most recently, Papua New Guinea. He frequently, if inconsistently, adopted the idiom and accent of a disc jockey. Samson had, initially, adopted this manner of speech to be, as he put it, "trendy". The pursuit of the contemporary was, however, not its only purpose. It had become a habit with which he disguised the intentions of his words, and the nastier these were the more colourful did his affectation become.

"All right, Sam," I said. "What have I done wrong?"

"You think you're cool, don't you?" he said. "Swinging outside the main scene, like?"

"Sam," I said. "You make me feel like a chimpanzee ostracized because of herpes."

"You are," he said solemnly.

"A herpetic chimpanzee?" I asked.

"No. Ostracized," he said, unsmiling. "Use your quotient man," back to his DJ voice, "no columns in the papers, no flashes on TV and you don't ask how come."

"Should I?"

"Turn on your headlights, boyo," he said. "Your stories make waves on the BBC, you group into anthologies of Asian writing, yet back in homesville you're Mr Unknown. How come, man?" he asked, his voice rising. "Ask yourself, how come?"

"You tell me, Sam."

"We roll it that way, man. Nothing heavy, mind you. Just a whisper here, a nudge there. Sluice it among the media boys that the big brass don't love Hernie Perera because Hernie Perera don't love the big brass." He grinned. "It's like you got bad breath, man, and nobody will get near you till they know you're chewing double mint."

"Good God," I said, genuinely surprised. "What have your people got against me?"

"You don't swing with the group, man," he said lugubriously. "You make single tracks, you wax one-sided discs, you –"

"I don't quite understand what you're –"

"You're not even a member of the Singapore Guild of Writers, Hern," he said, lapsing into everyday speech. "My ministry people don't get a chance to look at your work or advise you about it. The first time we see your stuff is when it's published in some foreign magazine." He shook his head several times, then placed a hand on my shoulder. "We are here to guide, Hern. To help you get your thoughts into the proper social context." He squeezed my shoulder. "We would never interfere with the actual craft of writing, mind you. You say things in your own way. The artist must remain free."

"Look, Sam," I said. "I'll join the guild for your sake, if nothing else. You're president and you're an old friend." He patted my shoulder, and I continued. "And as for my stories, you're welcome to read them before they get published. You can have the one I just finished last night."

"Man, oh, man!" he said, beginning to jive around my desk. "Now you've got an upbeat number. No," he waved both hands about wildly, "don't tell me what it's about. Let mammy's Sammy guess." He screwed up his eyes and pressed his knuckles into his forehead. "It's about the cool way we've jazzed up worker-management relations. Right you are, man. All swinging sweet sounds with no discords." He stared at me, his eyes bulging towards mine, then shook his head. "No. It's more romantic like, yeah? Ah geddit, ah shore do. Multiracial harmony's the beat, right? It's about an Indian chick slurping with a Chinoise guy, right?" I must have shaken my head, for he said, "Wrong." He held up both his hands and said, "Two strikes down. I surrender, Hern. What's it about?"

"Smell," I said.

"Smell!" he said, his eyes suffused and bulging intimidatingly. "My God, Hern!" Then, outrage making him relinquish his disc-jockey affectation, he continued, "there are a million things to write about in this multiracial, culturally plenipotential society that retains tradition without losing flexibility. There are our leaders. Merely to recount their historic struggles would be an epic. And you write about smell!" He shook his head, silenced by incredulity.

I am not attached enough to my characters or my plots to feel obliged to defend them, but I felt some kind of explanation was necessary. "Well, Sam," I began, "it's really about an old man and how smells –"

"Hern," he said, holding up his hand, "not a word more. You really need guidance, you know." He gazed slowly around the room. "Look at all this junk you've got up." He pointed at my Christmas tableau. "I feel so ashamed."

"I'm sorry, Sam," I said, doing my best to look downcast.

"Man, oh, man," he said, composure returning. "You sure don't savvy, do you?" I shook my head and he continued. "You're in Dullsville, man. Sure as God made little green apples, you're in Dullsville."

"Oh, dear, oh, dear," I said, working a look of contrition on to my face.

"You're my oldest friend, right? I know you better than you know yourself, right?"

I nodded twice.

"You want out but don't know how, right?"

I nodded again.

"Now hear this and hear good." He held up a hand to pre-empt interruption. "You quit this scene, hear? Just pack it in and vamoose. Right? Then get in and get in good with us, the nation's writers. No ifs, no buts, no attap huts. Hear?" He grasped my wrist. "You do just that, and Sammy here will see you're in the cookie where the cream is."

"I'm not clear, Sam . . ."

"No worries about bread, man. You get bread and butter and jam."

"Meaning?"

"Meaning, dumbo, recognition by the writers' guild, good paid jobs from the ministry and something . . . an optional extra at the university." He stopped, scratched his head thoughtfully, then continued: "No problem, man. You can lecture in creative writing, prose style."

"But I've no experience . . ."

He held up a finger. "No attap huts, remember. All this plus, plus . . . you know."

"What?" I asked.

"We'll help out with any little problem that stops the flow of creative juices." He grinned coyly. "You need a flat. Shazam, we find one. Girlfriend needs job. Alakazam, she's situated."

I laughed, "When do I start, Sam?"

"No time like show time, man," he said, prodding my chest with his thumb. "Culture Week zooms close. You could fly with us that trip. Just call, then check-in, man. Call and check-in," he said as he left.

With him went the elation I had felt on having a story completed. However, I could not blame Sam entirely for that. I was beginning to worry about my meeting with Su-May. From our talk on the telephone I felt sure that this was going to be disagreeable. I had to be ready to deal with anything her mood threw up: tears alternating with bitter jocularity, recriminations juxtaposed against happy memories, accusations inextricably bound to cajolery. But how could one contend with the vagaries of reality? If a plot went awry I could, with bathos, whittle away sharp corners, smooth, with alliteration, the ungainly contours of events. If a story took a wrong turn, it was possible to move backwards and forwards, massaging away painful bumps with analogy, rubbing down unsightly excrescences with onomatopoeia. Whatever I did, this evening was, however, going to be unalterable and in the final analysis unaffected by apologies or recantations. The moving finger did not write. It acted, and actions could not be erased. Su-May's actions, I knew, tended at the best of times to be unpredictable. I had great difficulty in following her train of thought, and her manner was on occasion so strange it appeared somnambulistic. I suspect this is what attracted me to her a year ago.

It was around Christmas. My tableau was an adoration: magi, shepherds and a multiracial group of urchins. The magi were draped in short lengths of curtain material Benson's was pushing that month; the shepherds wore a new line of Italian sandals from our shoe department; the urchins looked uncomfortable in expensive kiddie clothes the children's department was trying to get rid of before they became unfashionable. It was the time of the year when people drifted through the store, idly looking at things they did not want or could not afford. It was the season for vandals and shoplifters, and I had warned my staff to be on the look-out for them.

It was Ahmad who drew my attention to her. "That girl, Mr Perera," he said. "No good, I think."

I had worked with Ahmad long enough to trust his intuition, and asked, "Which one, Ahmad?"

"There, Mr Perera," he said, indicating the corner that housed the Christmas tableau. "Three times she come today. Yesterday evening also." He lowered his voice, "Always look at you, Mr Perera."

A slim, long-haired girl stood staring at the tableau. She leaned slightly forwards on long legs, with her rump sticking upwards, awkwardly, the way a young animal's does. I was flattered to think that my artistic efforts engrossed her so.

"She hasn't touched anything, has she, Ahmad?"

"No," he said. "Just look-look, then go away."

"OK, Ahmad," I said, "I'll deal with her."

I walked quietly up behind her and said in a loud voice, "You seem terribly interested in our Christmas decorations, young lady."

She turned slowly, not in the least startled, and smiled. "I was wondering," she said. "Just wondering."

"What," I said in as officious a voice as I could manage, "may I ask, were you wondering?"

"Every time I pass through the big shops at this time of the year, you know . . ." Her smile broadened.

"You wonder," I said, smiling against my will. "But you haven't told me what about."

"Are you in charge here?" she asked, suddenly serious.

"Well, I'm the manager. Why?"

"What happens to all the decorations, after?" I must have looked puzzled, for she quickly added, "After Christmas, I mean."

"Which ones?"

"These," she said. "The wise men, the shepherds, the holy family."

"Well, we get rid of them after the festive season."

"Chuck 'em out, you mean," she said, and smiled slowly.

"Yes."

"Can we have them when you've finished?" A fresh smile overtook the one fading from her face. "We could put them up in the kids' wards next year."

Having secured my attention, she let it all come out. Did I not agree that Christmas was a time for children, particularly those who were sick? She was a nurse. She felt terrible when she saw the meagre decorations in the children's wards. But things were so expensive. Yes, the staff raised the money for the decorations and hospital staff were so badly paid. She was sure that if I listened really hard this time next year, I could hear the voices of sick children raised in excitement at seeing the decorations Benson's was going to throw away. As she talked, her smile varied. It was sad, joyful, pleading, hopeful, desperate. It had rhythms, cadences, harmonies. I listened. Finally I agreed, not only to let her have the decorations after Christmas, but offered to have them delivered to the hospital at Benson's expense. When she accepted, it was I who felt grateful.

"I'm always thirsty," she said. "Talk too much."

I took her to tea and began the kind of affair I did not think myself capable of.

Right from the outset, I was not unaware that Su-May manipulated me. But she did so with my connivance, the way a lady guides an inexpert dancer across a ballroom floor. Perhaps in the very manner my mother led my father in that fateful tango to which I owe my origins. Whatever my thoughts were now, there was one thing I had to admit: knowledge of the way Su-May did things had never before upset me. But the situation had suddenly changed. The phone call was pure machination. Not telling me why she wished to see me was a ploy to build up my anxiety and increase my vulnerability. If she let me anticipate the worst, she would be able to make me accept anything short of it.

I remained touchy and difficult for the rest of the day, my mood reinforced by minor irritations to which at other times I would have been insensitive.

Normally, I didn't mind the seven-mile drive up to Tampines which took me through a part of Singapore that had resisted change. Today, I was irritated by the slow and erratically moving traffic. By the time I parked my car outside the house where the Children met, the tension of my mood was such that it could only be relieved by a fierce quarrel or prolonged lovemaking.

It was dusk as I entered the garden surrounding the house. It had rained earlier and the dripping of leaves mingled with the noises of insects beginning their nightly chorus. The house itself was a simple structure with a rough cement floor and a roof of corrugated-zinc sheets. In its thin wooden walls were several large windows, and all that took place inside could be observed from the garden. As I made my way nearer one of the lighted windows, squelching over wet leaves and crunching, to my disgust, the occasional snail underfoot, I realized I was trembling slightly. About a dozen young people sat around the room on benches and low wooden stools.

Su-May was perched on an up-ended wooden crate, strumming a guitar. She held her pale, delicate face to one side and looked down at the instrument she cradled, her long hair falling across its strings. She looked infinitely vulnerable and disturbingly like the Virgin gazing at her sleeping child. My heart was so filled with tenderness that I found it difficult to breath. My hand touched the low window-sill and I held on to it for support. There was a moment of absolute silence and Su-May began to sing:

"Oh, my loves have been many
But the loving was for One,
For the same light can shine in
A candle or the sun.

And the bells will be ringing
On a high and holy hill
For the first of my lovers
And the last."

Her voice was sweet, but surprisingly strong. There was about it an uncompromising clarity, and the few chords she strummed on the guitar added interest and counterpoint without disturbing the purpose of the melody. She saw me framed in the window, but sang on without the slightest change in her manner.

"To the end and beginning
Of the loving that I know,
To the end and beginning
My candlelight will go.

And the bells will be ringing
On a high and holy hill

For the first of my lovers
Or the last."

There was a tiny patter of applause when she finished, and she said in my direction, "Jump in, Hern." Then the Children closed in and she was surrounded by excited voices.

"Where did you find it, Su? The song, I mean."

"She wrote it, silly. Right, Su?"

"Not poss. I've heard it somewhere."

"I found the song," said Su-May slowly, "in a record called 'Lovely in the Dances'. There was this old guy at Benson's, eyes all over me, with hands to follow. You know what I mean?"

There was a chorus of laughter. I knew she meant old Lingam. He worked in the record and tape department and had a reputation for being a dirty old man, but I felt resentful and was unable to shake off the feeling that I was somehow included in her description.

"Shined up to the old letch for a bit and got him to play the track several times. Then, when he wasn't looking, took the song-sheet that was inside the sleeve."

There were delighted squeals from the Children. Peter Yu walked up to Su-May, put out a hand as though to squeeze her shoulder but let it rest instead.

"Please be careful about this sort of thing, Su," he said in a voice that was very soft, but, because of its depth, totally without sibilance.

"I am, Peter," she said, placing a hand over his. She turned to where I stood. "You kids know Hern, don't you? And if you haven't actually met him, you've heard me talk about him."

The group burst into wild giggles and seemed inclined to crowd around me until Peter Yu held up his hand.

"I think Hern wishes to talk to Su alone," he said, turning towards me with a look so neutral he seemed almost unaware of my presence.

"As you say, Reverend," said Su-May, laughing into his face.

The discovery that Su-May had been discussing me with the Children angered me and completed my sense of isolation, and though she took my hand as she led me towards a damp wooden bench in the garden, I felt quite alone.

I was not going to reveal this to Su-May, so I said, "I hope you haven't brought me all the way here just to tell me you've been stealing from Benson's?"

"Oh, you mean thing," she said, slapping my face lightly. "We only pinch little things, and mostly we've left Benson's alone." She added, laughing, "Out of respect for you."

She led me to a seat but did not say anything, and for a while, the garden was totally still. I sensed rather than heard the drip from the leaves. The damp from the wooden seat seeped silently into my trousers. I wondered how I would explain the stain to Sylvie.

"You know, Hern, I've been thinking about things . . . like wondering about us and all."

"And?" I prompted.

"And I guess Peter and the kids are right about us."

Su-May had an exasperating way of making a point, but I knew that if I showed the slightest impatience or anger at her discussing me with the Children, she would shut up altogether.

So I said, "I see. And how were they right?"

She sighed deeply. "Well, we kinda shouldn't go on, you know. Hern," her voice was urgent. "I told the kids you were sure to understand."

"Of course I understand," I said, keeping a firm hold on my voice. "But before you go on, let me assure you of one thing. You must be very clear that this affair of ours is hurting nobody. You are not taking anything away from Sylvie." I let this sink in before continuing. "I'm an ordinary chap and can only discuss things along common-sense lines. I am sure that Peter Yu," I paused to allow myself a derisive laugh, "your Reverend, will be able to enlighten you on the theological objections to adultery and what punishments should be meted out to those unfortunates who break the seventh commandment. I believe head-shaving and stoning are prescribed."

"I don't know what you're going on about, Hern," said Su-May, breaking into a laugh. "Peter has no moral objections to our carrying on."

"Then what," I asked, pulling myself together, "does he object to?"

"It's sort of agreed that the group stick together. You know . . . find friends among ourselves."

"I see." I laughed bitterly. "So that dear Peter has no competition. I seem to notice that there is a preponderance of girls in the group."

"Oh, Hern, it's not like that at all," she sighed. "It might be better for you too, you know, Hern." She sighed again. "Not to get too close, I mean."

I looked towards the house. The Children moved across the lighted windows, pausing occasionally to look out into the garden. I was convinced they looked in our direction. It was too dark for them to see us clearly, if at all, yet I felt spied on. And somehow I couldn't avoid the feeling that they were waiting for a signal from Su-May.

"Su-May," I said, "can I see you some time this week?"

"You know, Peter . . . well, all the kids really think it will hurt less. . . . It's true, isn't it, Hern?" I could sense her moving nearer. "The pain will be over more quickly with a clean break." I put my arm around her shoulder and she said, "I better go back to the rehearsal."

"Rehearsal?"

"Yes. We're putting on an act for cultural week. Must get back." She stood up. "Really must."

I stood up and she came into my arms easily. We had been lovers for a year and the compliance of our bodies could not be easily erased. Her kiss was wide-mouthed and warm the way a lover's should be, except that there was a slight saltiness about it. I recognized tears – whose I was unsure, though tears I felt were in order. It was not possible to generate this kind of love without sadness nor to end it without a feeling of betrayal.

Over Su-May's shoulder I could see the Children – shadowy, flitting about the windows. We were in the dark they could not see us, yet they seemed to be watching, waiting for something to happen. Somehow this mood of expectancy spread across the damp darkness and seeped into me.

It stayed with me as I reversed out of the garden, and though I drove around for several hours the mood would not be left behind. The feeling of expectancy had its basis in memories, flickering in the back of my mind, vague as the shadows of the Children crossing the tail of my eye. Try as I might, I could not relate them to some definite event from the past. Finally I gave up and drove home.

Sylvie was asleep. As I lay beside her, exhausted but restless, it all began to come back. The hot afternoons at Sunday school, listening to Mrs Ong, the plump, maternal teacher who chronicled with breathless enthusiasm violent tales of sin and equally bloody ones of salvation. It was Mrs Ong who first told me of a darkened garden and the kiss of betrayal. Hers had been a simple, if uncharitable, tale. Perhaps there were more generous ways of considering the goings-on in Gethsemane. I began thinking of them. To lull myself to sleep, I arranged my thoughts into a story. My tale was more about love than deceit, a love so intense it could only find expression in tears. In telling it I was not unkind to Judas. I liked to think that this reflected the charity I felt towards Su-May, whom I now regarded as a betrayer of my love. I did not know then that I would once more feel betrayed in that garden in Tampines and that it was not Su-May or the Children but I who would ultimately be guilty of treachery.

I knew that sleep came easier if I actually set up the story in the way I would if I were writing it, so I began mentally to type it out. By the time I reached the last page I had become quite drowsy and was almost asleep when I typed the title, "Kissful of Tears", in bold capitals.

kissful of tears

From the very beginning, they asked me, not once but again and again, what it was that was so special about our leader. It wasn't that they were curious about why people were drawn by the thousands to him. They simply wanted to be able to recognize and arrest him. You would have thought this would have been easy enough. After all he travelled all over the place and he taught openly. But, strange as it seems identifying him had proved a real problem to the authorities. Why, this year alone they had taken in six men, each of whom claimed to be the leader. Funny, isn't it? The special police actually executed one poor wretch. And, just when they thought their troubles were over, the incidents began all over again in another part of the country.

I clearly remember the morning I first met him. I was lounging against a tree by the market-place, watching the housewives haggling, and wondering if they did the same in bed with their husbands. Yes, I spend a lot of my time watching the goings-on at street corners . . . and day-dreaming. My mother complains bitterly about this. "You should get a job, Ju," she grumbles. "Earn some money. What good's a son to a widowed old mother if she has to work her fingers to the bone just to keep body and soul together?" And, believe me, once Mum starts on this tack, very little can stop her.

I was just beginning to doze when something woke me sharply. It took me a while to realize that the whole street had suddenly gone quiet. I could see the housewives still bargaining, but their voices were hushed and their gestures less violent. At first I thought it must be a raid by the special police. These raids are common, the cops sweeping through crowded places looking for freedom fighters (they call them subversives, of course). And you know what the police are like – ready to pick up any layabout they can find if there's no one else suitable. I stood up quickly, got ready to run and found myself looking straight into his face.

An ordinary face, it was. Soft perhaps, with gentle doggy eyes in which I could see myself quite clearly. He smiled and nodded, agreeing that the reflection I stared at was truly my own and in that same movement he called me to him. I left the tree and joined his group. There wasn't anything unusual about them – Sy, Jim, Tom, Andy – and we shared no great secret. Then why did we follow him? I don't know. Honestly, I don't.

"What's so different about his brand of subversion anyway?" asked the deputy chief of the special police. "Why, even squabbling rebel groups want to join him." People in his line of work tend to answer the questions they ask and the deputy was no exception. I would have laughed but controlled myself. Guys like the deputy have no sense of humour and, what is worse, turn quickly to violence.

So I said, "He talks about a universal brotherhood and –"

"Ah-ha," he interrupted. "Wants to get all the subversive groups under his leadership."

". . . and love," I added limply.

The deputy scratched his bald head. "Now, that's a bit puzzling." He frowned for a while, then suddenly brightened. "I see, I see. Wants his followers to know he's not against a bit of fun and games, eh?"

"Not quite . . ." I began.

"Anyway," he snapped. "Who cares? What we want to do is to nab the bastard." He laughed and turned to his lieutenant.

"You know they say he's actually a bastard – illegitimate, I mean."

The young man laughed and the deputy continued, "Getting a positive ID has been a real pain in the arse. The bastard," he chuckled again at the word, "seems to be everywhere and everybody. Zeus wept, you wouldn't believe the number of chaps who claim to be him! All ordinary enough blokes." He shook his head. "Refusing to admit, even under intense interrogation, that they are just Joe Blow the cobbler and not the great leader." He turned to me. "You really think the festival is a good time to get him, do you?"

"Yes, sir," I said. "We'll be having dinner together and the best time to pick him up will be immediately after this. Just ask your men to keep close to me and there'll be no mistakes." It seemed a good time to bring it up so I added, "Could you pay me in gold, sir?"

"Gold?" he said, looking sternly round the room. "Why gold? Don't you trust our currency?"

"It's not that, sir," I wheedled. "But it's my old mother, sir. She says these are troubled times and gold is the only thing you can trust." I looked abject. "You must understand, sir, we will have to move to another town if my part in all this comes out."

Gold, the deputy said, would be hard to get at such short notice, so we finally settled on silver. I hope I got the exchange-rate right. Mum would be really mad if I was short-changed. She was planning to buy the house at the bottom of the street. The one with the biggish garden and its own well. At last, she said, her boy was going to be able to give her something she had wanted all her life – a house of her own. I was happy at the thought.

Most people were booked out for the festival but Sy (trust him!) finally found us a joint a little out of town. It wasn't a classy place, mind you, but at least we had a room to ourselves. Sy always insists on a private room. Feels more comfortable, I guess, as he usually drinks too much and often falls asleep during the meal.

Dinner over, someone suggested a walk in a nearby garden. A good idea, since most of us had eaten and drunk too much. I looked around as we left the place. There were a few blokes hanging about looking pretty liquored up. They certainly didn't look like members of the special police. Anyway, none of them made a move to follow us.

The leader seemed a little agitated and went off by himself as soon as we reached the garden. The rest of us dozed, lying on

the grass or propping ourselves up against the trees. There was
no sign of the special police. Well, perhaps they'd changed their
plans. Even arrested someone else claiming to be the leader. Yes,
that must have been what had happened. I was glad and at
peace.

When the leader returned he was wonderfully calm and we
all began walking slowly through the still, dark garden.
Suddenly we were surrounded by men carrying torches. These
they thrust into our faces. Their light was hot, blinding.

"Which one is he?" they shouted, shoving us about. "Which
one's the great revolutionary leader?" I heard the sound of a
slap. "Come on, come on. We haven't got all night, you know."

Any one of us there could have betrayed him: Sy, a coward
always, but especially so now that the effect of the wine was
wearing off; Tom, the sceptic and sophist who would find, later,
some justification for his action. But I was the one who had
taken the silver . . .

I looked across at the leader. There was no way the police
could distinguish him from the rest of us. No, it wasn't he who
had become like us. It was we who had become like him. A
great love welled up inside me. I walked over and took his face
in my hands and kissed him. There was no way of knowing
whether the tears I tasted were mine or his.

Then I was thrown to the ground. I heard the sound of clubs
landing on flesh and the leader scream as a bone snapped. After
this he was fairly quiet, only moaning occasionally as a blow fell
or a boot found its mark. The moans became fainter as they
dragged him away, but my body continued to hurt as though it
was still being pummelled, and I am certain that the tears that
streamed down my face were not produced by my eyes alone.

three

I awoke to find Sylvie snuggling into the curve of my body. As soon as she realized I was awake, she turned her face to mine, stared at me with black-bright eyes and very gently began running her nails across the front of my chest. I ran my hands between her legs and we made love. It never failed to surprise me that an act seemingly designed for mishaps could become so unendurably perfect. As I lay in her arms, basking in the warmth of this thought, the phone rang.

"Hern?" It was my mother. "Your father, Hern. He's very ill. He's haemorrhaging."

"What do'you mean, haemorrhaging, Ma?"

"It's been going on from early morning, Hern." She stopped, either to let her words sink in or to gather strength to go on sighing deeply several times, before continuing. "At first it was just streaks he was coughing up. Then, oh, God, Hern, it came up in big chunks. Just like strawberry jam it was, Hern."

"What have you done, Ma?"

"An ambulance is coming over, Hern. To take him to Mount Elizabeth Hospital." She stopped again to sigh. "Dr Lim has arranged for a specialist. Right away, he'll see him, Hern. Right away. It's that bad. Don't forget to tell Sylvie, now."

"Don't panic, Ma," I said. "Sylvie and I will be at Mount Elizabeth in an hour."

There is a dynastic grandeur about the foyer of Mount Elizabeth Hospital which made my father's room appear dingy, and he, forlorn in it. He was propped up in a narrow bed, breathing rapidly, his eyes bright and frightened. I had never seen my father look like this, and I embraced him more out of embarrassment than anything else. There was a clayey dampness about him, as though his body was already beginning to resemble the earth to which it would shortly be returned.

Clara, my mother, sat on the bed beside him clinging to his hand, which from time to time she patted absent-mindedly as though it were some dumb animal in need of comfort. A fit of coughing seized my father and he began to expectorate a tenacious, rust-coloured phlegm. This my mother, using sheaves of Kleenex tissues, helped him deposit into a shiny and wonderfully clean-looking steel mug, which had been placed on his bedside table. Her manner was generally one of solicitude but she periodically shot him looks of intense animosity that would have bewildered an observer who did not understand her as well as I did.

It was not that Clara Perera was unprepared for Fred's death. I am certain she would have, in her dreamings, rehearsed the moment of his passing several times, viewing it as the climax to the romance that had been their life. But he should have looked pale, not grey; weary not shit-scared. If he had to cough blood it should have been bright red and it should have gushed out of his mouth against his will even as he lay dying on her lap. Clara could then wipe (ever so gently, mind you) the blood from his lips with a spotless, white lace handkerchief extracted from her bodice. But Fred chose not to play the game and this business of bringing up sticky brown mucus was disgusting.

"Well, what does the specialist think is the matter?" I asked, as cheerfully as I dared.

"Cancer," said my mother in a stage-whisper.

"Now, now, my sunflower," said my father, mustering the remains of his composure and patting her cheek.

"That is somewhat the less optimistic of the proffered diagnoses." He lingered pedantically over the Greek plural.

Irritated, I asked, "Can we skip the hearts and flowers?"

"Now, now," he said. "If everyone reacts and, might I add, over-reacts, emotionally, any possibility of viewing this problem," he pronounced it prob-lem, "rationally will be lost." The old Fred Perera was rapidly reasserting himself. "To be quite honest, getting everyone over so hastily wasn't my idea at all, but you know how women are about a bit of blood, son." He winked at me conspiratorially. "It issues out of their bodies monthly yet the sight of it on someone else throws them into a state of disarray." He chuckled and pinched his wife's cheek. "But I wouldn't change the way you feel for all the tea in China, my little sunflower."

He turned to me. "Now there's something I have to get on and discuss with my son here . . . alone." He raised his hands to forestall protest. "Nothing for you two to bother your pretty heads over, so run along now and don't get your tail feathers ruffled." Laughing, he shoved Mother and Sylvie towards the door.

For a while he was silent, catching his breath. Then he said, "It simply isn't cricket, what you're doing." I shot him a puzzled look and he added, "To Sylvie, old chap."

"I don't quite get you, Dad."

"Don't you indeed." He had to pause for breath but screwed up his face and pretended he was collecting his thoughts. "It has come to my ears that you have a . . . um . . . romantic liaison with a young woman . . . that is a young woman other than Sylvie." He paused, panted for a bit then asked sharply, "How say you?"

"Guilty," I said slipping easily into a game of my boyhood in which he acted the judge severe and I the terrified miscreant.

He smiled, pleased that I remembered. "Unfortunately I cannot sentence you to a month without television or withhold your weekly allowance. Looking at things quite dispassionately, I must face up to the fact that I am quite impotent to do anything to correct the situation."

"Dad," I said. "Please don't let this bother you. Not now. I promise. . . ."

"Assure, Hern. You mean assure," he said in a matter-of-fact, slightly weary voice.

"I assure you that nothing is going to come between Sylvie and me." I thought of saying that an affair on the side freshened a marriage, but I caught his eye and stopped myself in time.

"I am not unduly worried about the practical side of things, my boy. Not at this time of my life." His face became bleak. "What bothers me is the justice of the whole thing. What you are doing, Hern, simply isn't cricket. How can love, honour and respect sleep in the same bed as duplicity?"

"Try not to excite yourself, Dad," I said, reaching out to squeeze his arm.

He shook off my hand. "You listen to me, young man," he said, beginning to pant again. "I don't want any nonsense from you. I am not a man who subscribes to this newfangled morality," he laughed bitterly, "immorality really, that you young people think you have discovered." He was breathing very heavily now.

"As must be pretty clear to all and sundry, I'm a very sick man. Probably a dying one. I want to extract a promise, not an assurance, a promise from you." He stopped and fiddled with the bedclothes in an effort to pretend he was not breathless. "Promise me sincerely and solemnly that you will break off your relationship with this young woman, who I understand is a nurse. Promise this will have immediate effect. If you find that impossible, you must do the decent thing and tell Sylvie about the whole affair." He held up a hand before I could protest. "That I'm afraid is the only honourable solution to the problem. I did not, mark you, say the easy solution but what I propose is indubitably the only way a gentleman would conduct himself if he ever got into a situation such as this." He smiled, revitalized by his eloquence.

I promised. His face took on an expression I had not seen on it since I was a little boy. He shook my hand solemnly and I feared he was going to ask me to cross my heart when crossing my fingers would have been more in order.

"I am tired and want no further discussion on the subject." He allowed himself to flop back on the pillows. "Now, I would be obliged if you would call in the ladies."

"Well," said Sylvie brightly, as I ushered the women back into the room, "what's next on the menu?"

I said, "I'll have to be getting back to the office." My father's disclosure had made it urgent that I talk to Su-May. "Chuang must be wondering what's become of me. And," I added as an afterthought, "Ahmad can't handle things himself."

Noticing my restlessness, Sylvie said, "Not with the Christmas rush and all that, I guess."

"Mr Chan, the specialist chappie, says that some time this afternoon he'll do a bronchoscopy . . ." my father began.

"A what?" asked Sylvie.

"From what I understand, they slip a lighted tube down the windpipe, get a good look at the tumour or whatever and take a little piece of it for examination under the microscope." He looked bravely matter-of-fact about the whole thing and Clara squeezed his hand, then held it, nodding approval.

"By tomorrow whatever it is that ails me will be brought out into the light of day. Oh, yes," he added, "he will also be removing a small gland from my neck."

"I'll run off to the office then," I said. "And drop round when I finish this evening."

"Ma and I will just hang around," said Sylvie.

My mother smiled and held her hand. Sylvie, in turn, reached out for Father's. They formed a happy, smiling circle. I couldn't help feeling my presence was superfluous.

I returned to Benson's to find an anxious Ahmad peering out into the street. He said that Chuang had already been in twice. He had brought with him a Chinese gentleman. He told Ahmad that he needed to speak to me, that big changes were about to take place at Benson's, and these would begin in the furniture department. He had apparently been most impatient and, not finding me in the department, had stomped about muttering to himself. I could picture him generally upsetting Ahmad, poking about things as though he expected to find me tucked between two bales of crinoline. In his gentle way, Ahmad had tried to ascertain the nature of these changes, but Chuang had merely "ah'd" several times and trotted off.

Normally even the slightest hint of having to make alterations in my daily routine would have worried me to a frenzy. Today, Ahmad's news produced only a rumbling anxiety that formed, as it were, a backdrop to the main action of my life. I did not look on changes at Benson's as cosmic aberrations premonitoring disaster, the thunder and lightning preceding the entry of the witches. I ignored the signs and dwelt instead on a plan I had hit upon to prevent Su-May's defection.

My father's disclosure had convinced me that my disquietude in the garden had not been unfounded. It was clear that I had been betrayed. It was equally clear that one of the Children was responsible. What I planned to do was simple and elegant. There is, when you look at things objectively, an order that runs like a thread through events. Once recognized, it can be utilized. Su-May worked at the General Hospital, the largest in the city, and getting her on the phone was usually difficult. Today I got through without trouble.

"Hern," she said, "it's so lucky."

I knew her well enough to be unpertubed by that kind of opening remark and said, "Oh, good," and waited.

"Sister has gone off with Matron and left me in charge of the ward." Finally she explained what was lucky. "I can use the phone for as long as I want."

"Su-May," I began, then added, "my darling Su-May," and paused. "Something awful has happened." I hesitated for a bit, then said in a lower voice, "Somehow my father has found out about us and," I let my voice falter, "he's also just found out that he's got cancer." I said this in a rush, letting my voice peter out.

"Oh, God," she said. "How horrible, Hern. When did all this happen?"

"This morning."

"How did he find out – about us, I mean?"

"Well," I said. "We've been extremely discreet about things."

This was true. If we met in the store itself it was always after office hours when we used the flatlet that Benson's kept for visiting executives. I made sure on these occasions that the building was absolutely empty before letting her in by a side door beside the main entrance. At other times, we met in a secluded bungalow belonging to a man called Sheng, a furniture buyer who was often out of town.

"How could he have found out then?"

"There's only one way, darling, You think about it for a minute."

"I don't know, Hern. Please, I don't know."

"Through your friends, darling. Through the Children of the Book. They are the only ones who know and they would like to break us up."

"No way, Hern," she said and laughed. "You know, maybe you'll never understand us. The kids, I mean, and people our age. But it's different for us." I was mortified and cleared my throat several times to indicate this, but she carried on: "Sure, the kids don't like my going with you. Sure Peter thinks we – the group – should stick to itself. But we're about understanding, Hern. And concern. The kids don't want to blackmail me into chucking you up."

"Su-May," I said, keeping my voice unnaturally even, "I have never been convinced that religious sects are above trickery and deceit. But you must believe what you want to believe. I ask a favour of you, though." I let my voice drop, "Don't . . . till I've got over what's going to happen to my father . . . don't talk about leaving me."

"Poor, poor Hern," she said gently. "Is the diagnosis certain?"

"Almost," I said, elated at the turn in the conversation. I lowered my voice further with an effort and continued. "He's been coughing blood and there is a gland in his neck. The specialist is doing a biopsy. We'll know for sure sometime tomorrow but I don't think there's much hope." I dropped my voice to a whisper. "Can I see you soon, Su-May?"

"Oh, Hern," she said." It's so difficult, but how can I say no."

I let my voice brighten. "Will you come to Benson's in the evening, or would you rather meet at Sheng's bungalow?"

"Oh, no!" she snapped, hardening. "I want to talk, that's all."

"Su-May, at a time like this, what else d'you think I had in mind? I think we should still keep our meetings discreet. Just because Dad knows, doesn't mean I want everyone –"

"Sorry, Hern. Sorry." Her voice was soft again. "Oh, dear," she said. "Oh, dear."

"What's up now?"

"Tomorrow's no good. I can't see you. Or the day after."

"See me the day after that, sweetheart. On Friday."

"Hern," she said, "I can't stand thinking of you by yourself . . . worried. . . ."

"Don't worry, nurse," I said. "The patient will survive till Friday. But only just."

"At Benson's. A little after six."

I put down the receiver and leaned back in my chair.

The unlikely juxtaposition of my father's cancer with his discovery of my affair with Su-May had been particularly fortunate. It gave me not only an excuse to call Su-May but provided me at the same time with an instrument to unleash the affection I knew she had for me. It's funny how misfortune, even misfortune with which one is not personally concerned, forces us to rearrange our lives along more compassionate lines. The cable car disaster was a perfect example of this.

Shortly after my affair with Su-May began, Chuang had a managerial brainstorm and insisted that I review all our existing stock and investigate new designs better suited to state-subsidized housing estates. This meant I had to work not just overtime but often through the night, for, as always, he wanted everything in a great hurry.

At that time ours, like many love affairs, had reached a stage where we had to get more involved than we originally intended or accept breaking up altogether. Like most lovers we compromised and agreed not to meet for a month. This was largely my idea and Su-May looked on it as a ploy I was using to terminate a relationship with which I was beginning to tire. There may have been some truth to this for I was not displeased at the prospect of a month free from emotional strain.

Late one evening an oilrig which was being towed to sea hit the lines of a cable car system that links Singapore to an offshore island. Several cars crashed into the sea but two were left dangling over the ocean for several hours till rescue by helicopter was possible. Su-May had been on duty when the survivors were brought in to the emergency department. She was aghast at the mental condition of people who, having seen the occupants of the cars ahead fall hundreds of feet, had themselves to wait hours fearing that even the movement of their heartbeats might be enough to precipitate them to a similar end. She phoned the store several times in the course of the evening and, despite our agreement not to see each other, came round as soon as her shift was over.

I have never seen anyone in the condition Su-May was in. She was tearful and trembling, jumping at my slightest move. She wouldn't sit still, but insisted on walking around the room tearing up bits of paper she had fished out of the wastebin. She sweated profusely, which was something she never did even in the throes of making love. I was alarmed at her condition, and said so.

"It's nothing," she said. Then kept repeating, "You should have seen those people. Poor people, poor, poor people. . . ."

I took her to the upstairs flat of Benson's to quieten her. She needed to lie down. Soon we were in bed together. I had unintentionally made a commitment.

I am certain that when Su-May came over she had no intention of manoeuvring me back into the affair. Horrified by what had happened to a group of strangers, she had turned to me for comfort. Her grief found my sympathy. But tragedy, even remote tragedy, so stimulates the flow of compassion-juices that they dribble out and stain everything around them. People use this effect for personal ends in much the same way that stockbrokers capitalize on calamities.

Leaning back in my chair, I realized that this tactic (for such it was, conscious or not) in human relations could well be the basis of a story. It would have to be a moral tale, admonitory and heavy with social significance. Perhaps even an allegory, marching to its foregone conclusion. Samson would approve, and, though this would not be my main reason for writing, I saw no harm in pleasing him.

I began poking around my head for a plot. Normally a casual observation, an incomplete train of events, a whimsical thought, is all I need to spark off a story. I have, with some difficulty, managed to discern a moral message in some of my stories, but the messages are often conflicting. This was the first time I was writing to prove a point, the first time I was allowing fable to spring from moral rather than the reverse.

"Just because you're sick with unhappiness," said Sylvie, entering our flat ahead of me, "you think you have the right to rock the boat so everyone else wants to vomit too. Right, Hern?"

"I don't know what you're going on about."

"The way you treated Ma this evening," she said, turning on a light. "I know this cancer thing is driving us all under, but that's no reason for snapping off Ma's head every time she poked it above ground."

"Did I?"

"Didn't you just." She came up close against my side and tilted her head against my arm. "Fancy telling her that the beach where she and Pa spent their honeymoon was under several tons of garbage, and," she laughed in spite of herself, "that even the brand names of the French letters they would skid on had changed since their time."

Sylvie was right.

I had arrived at the hospital earlier that evening to find my mother perched on my father's bed, holding his hand and gazing into his eyes. He gazed steadily back into hers, unafraid. On the right side of his neck, a tiny piece of sticking-plaster marked the site of the biopsy. It was his badge of courage. They were clearly in the middle of a Fred-and-Clara-Perera-face-death-together sequence.

"Honey," said Clara.

"Yes, bunch," said Fred.

"You remember the beach where we spent our honeymoon?"

"Pantai Cinta Brahï," he said, rolling his head around with the words, though this caused him to stretch the wound on his neck. He grimaced. "The Beach of Passionate Love. How can I ever forget, sweet?"

"Heart," she said, "Can we go again when it's all over?"

"Wonderful, pet," he said. "We will, in exactly the same way we did the first time round. Namely, by bus."

"Stopping at the rest-houses on the way up," she said, half asking, half remembering.

"Indeed, my pet. Indeed," he said, patting her hand. "All the way up the east coast of Malaya."

They began to talk of river-mouth villages, undiscovered bays, unspoilt beaches. As they talked, Clara's body seemed to migrate into bed until its upper half lay on the pillow beside him, her hands fluttering over his body, toying with the buttons of his pyjamas.

"Mother," I said, hoping to stop the disgusting goings-on in what I was beginning to see as my father's death-bed, "Sylvie and I will leave if we're cramping your style."

Sylvie, sitting silent in the corner of the room, glared at me, but Clara Perera was undaunted. She turned upon me a look so coy it was almost sly, and said, "It's all right, Hern. I don't think your father is up to anything . . . yet." She giggled. "I hope not."

"Mother," I said, my disgust evident in my voice, "will you stop behaving like a love-sick nymphomaniac."

"Now, now, my boy," said my father, disentangling himself momentarily from Clara's attentions. "I will not, in any circumstances, have you being unkind to your mother, still less downright offensive. Moreover, you may not be mature enough to quite appreciate," his voice softened, "how unrealistic you are being."

"Unrealistic?" I said, indignation rising in my voice. "A middle-aged woman, who happens to be my mother, starts acting like a teenager on heat, and I'm the one who's unrealistic. I can't believe this."

"Perhaps, my love," he said, turning to Clara, "the lad doesn't yet realize that the creature that lives inside each and every one of us doesn't ever grow old. In fact, it changes very little, if at all, with the passing of the years. Only its outer covering," he smiled wryly to himself, "its integument, the façade it presents to the world, only that does. And the world around it."

Clara gazed into his eyes, all adulation. She knew that Fred, her Fred, was saying something terribly clever and important.

He continued, "I used to think, when I was much younger of course, that this business of growing old outside but not inside was one of the really tragic things about life. But now I am convinced, yes, firmly convinced," he smiled beatifically on Sylvie and me, "that it is one of the most joyous, if not *the* most joyous, thing about it."

I turned on the kitchen lights and got myself a glass of water. Yes, I had been unkind to my parents. What was worse, I knew why I had been so irritable.

I had spent all afternoon working out plots to fit the theme that I had labelled "The effect of unrelated catastrophes on individual human relations" without any success. Normally, once triggered off, the events that make up a story tumble from my head, out of my control. Though I might begin with a facsimile of someone I knew, the characters that people my tales are strangers who speak in voices I do not recognize. But with my theme in hand, things simply refused to happen. What was worse, when I listened to my characters talking, they all spoke with one voice: mine.

"Hern," said Sylvie, speaking directly into my right ear, "I'm so bushed. I think I'll just shower off my tiredness and collapse."

I finished the water I was drinking, then said, "I'd like to work on a story for a bit."

"You go to your room and type as much as you want," she said. "But make sure you keep the door shut." She laughed. "Sometimes your typing wakes me up and I think it's gunfire."

In the quiet of my room things got worse. Instead of a story forming around the theme I had in mind, another began trickling out. The creature inside us doesn't change, my father had said. How right he was. At thirty, I realized that I am what I have always been, will always be. The child is not father to the man, he is the man and persists in the dotard. This thought contained, simultaneously, the seeds of compassion and despair, the potential for tragedy and for laughter. It could only be one thing: the truth. With increasing force, it nudged the skimpy plots I had fashioned around my "unrelated catastrophes" theme out of my head, replacing them with a new story. I began typing this reluctantly; but by the time I was ready to sleep, I was halfway through it.

four

As soon as Chuang walked in, I realized that this was not one of his routine tours of inspection. His movements were that of a marionette, full of someone else's purpose. The sing song tones in which he, like many Chinese-educated persons, spoke English were strident and I thought I detected a touch of aggression in their cadences.

"I am hoping you will take what I am going to say in the genuine spirit, Perera," he began.

I looked up from my desk, surprised.

He continued, "You are Singaporean too. It is clear to all Singaporeans that, like crystals, we must be tough, but flexible. The third Minister for Defence and Commercialism soon, cried out for Singaporean to be like good-quality panty-hose. We must stretch and stretch but never tear. Otherwise how can we fight our enemies from outboard or," he added darkly, "inboard?"

He spoke as though he were a medium, some itinerant spirit having taken over his vocal cords, and my mind slipped back some twenty years. At the bottom of the road where I lived as a little boy was a small Chinese school. Every time I passed, I saw classrooms of little schoolboys in identical white uniforms intoning, in unison, the words of some Chinese sage. Their teacher (had he not mastered the teaching of the ancients this way?) made them repeat words and phrases again and again, tapping out rhythms with his ferrule, his ears pricked for unacceptable, if slight, variations. Thus had wisdom percolated down the ages. In Chuang's manner this morning was the conviction not merely that he spoke the truth but that he spoke the truth over which he had been give proprietary rights.

"Remember, Perera," he said, "flexibility is strength."

"I always thought unity was . . ." I began.

"And unity is strength too," he said triumphantly. "Yes, my friend. As ancient Chinese scholar once exclaimed, a bundle of twigs getting knotted is strong as log of wood." He smiled round the room. "Correct, Perera, my friend?" he said. "The board, Benson's directors are united. Benson's must adopt more Asian image."

"Meaning?" I prompted.

"Higher productivity," he said. Ignoring the bewilderment on my face, he continued, "We must flung out false Western values leading to moral decay, unemployment and social welfare. No more imitating falsity. Right here in furniture department," he waved his arm expansively, "we install traditional Asian values. Soon we sell antique Chinese furniture –"

"But, Chuang," I interrupted, "antique Chinese furniture is too expensive for most Singaporeans and jolly difficult to come by."

"We manufacture cheap," he said.

"You mean imitation antique furniture," I suggested.

"Modern Chinese antiques," he snapped. "Singaporean-manufactured, by skilled Chinese carpenters."

"Oh," was all I could manage.

"Here we recommence true Asian spirit of co-operation and co-prosperity. Vanquish cut-throat competition from Manila, Jakarta and Thailand." He leaned conspiratorially towards me: "You are the first to behold the good news. We have under-the-table joint venture with Teng's. By next month, even, we stock Teng's latest antiques." He rubbed his hands together and beamed at me.

I am not proud of my work and am quite cynical about the aesthetic standards of department stores. Nevertheless Teng's disgusted me. From its mock pagoda front to its faintly ammoniacal latrines, it epitomized all that was nasty about things Chinese. The look of distaste on my face must have been obvious, but Chuang, intent on whipping up his enthusiasm, failed to notice it.

"You will find collaboration so happily with their furniture manager – Rex."

"Rex who?" I asked.

"Ah," he said. "You are already known. Good. But," he smiled confidentially, "one correction. You must say his name rightly. Z-H-U. Rex Zhu." He smiled (I thought inscrutably) and went on. "Rex Zhu has business diploma in America but birth and upbringing in Hong Kong only."

I knew the type and hated the man already. He would be one of a breed of smooth young men who sported bright bow-ties and alligator shoes. He would have spent just enough time in an obscure American college to have learnt to roll his r's slightly, but would have difficulty containing his sibilants and disguising his truncated vowels.

"When does this co-operative effort begin?"

"Ah, already you are impatient to start. Highly positive, highly positive. But be patience, my friend, which the Chinese poets say is the parent of virtue." He patted my shoulder. "Next week meeting," he proclaimed as he left.

The implications of what Chuang had said were not lost on me. Collaboration with Teng's indicated more than a simple sinophilia. It meant modernization, capitulation to the mass market. Soon, my haven on the ground floor of the oldest departmental store in Singapore would be invaded by predatory housewives in hot pursuit of bargains, by bushy-tailed honeymooners selecting soft furnishings to feather love-nests, by Australian spinsters seeking orientalia for drawing-rooms in Perth. Even worse, I would be beleaguered by systems analysts, advertising consultants, marketing experts. . . .

I saw it all coming, yet couldn't find the energy to be afraid. A large part of my mind was focused on my story. I was listening to voices, watching intentions becoming events, inventing phrases in which to trap them. I was halfway through "Homecoming" and I couldn't wait to get back to my typewriter, tap the keys and watch letters form words, words sentences, sentences paragraphs; to type a page of dialogue, then, turn it on its side and see the skyline of a city; to decorate with commas, colons and question-marks. Impatient, I avoided looking at the office clock, hoping that my indifference would tempt it to sneak forward a bit, and stared instead at a brochure on my desk. When Ahmad shook me awake, it was just after three.

"Missus," he said, pointing to the telephone.

"Hern," said Sylvie, in an alarmingly calm voice, "Dr Chan the specialist wants to see us in the hospital today. Can you get off work early?"

"I'll leave right away," I said. I was anxious to finish my story. Whatever the specialist had to say, it couldn't take more than an hour.

I met Mother and Sylvie in a side room of the ward and, shortly after I arrived, we were joined by Dr Chan. The specialist was a small man, smooth-faced and looking younger than his years. He used medical terms freely and directed his remarks exclusively to my mother. His clipped, Singapore accent interfered greatly with his efforts to speak in a slow, deliberate manner and the effect he finally achieved was that of a requiem gone wrong.

"When the malignant process is widely disseminated, as it is in Mr Perera's case, the long-term prognosis is unfavourable." He shook his head slowly to disclaim any responsibility for his patient's plight.

My mother, looking confused and frightened, asked: "What does all this mean, Doctor?"

"Cytotoxics," he said, looking sternly at her. "With the presence of metastases in the liver and cervical lymph nodes," he glanced at Sylvie and me as though daring us to challenge him, "metastases proven by biopsy, mind you, there is certainly no place for radical surgery or radiotherapy."

"Hern," my mother appealed to me, her eyes glistening with bewilderment.

"Is my father's case terminal, Doctor?"

"Terminal?" he said, turning the word round his tongue as though unused to its taste. "Terminal?" He cocked his head to one side and looked into the distance. "I think I see what you mean, but these crude, lay terms never give you the true picture." He smiled at my mother, a benediction. "We don't think like that any more. I would say that Mr Perera's disease is advanced. I would say that it is more than a single-organ problem. I would say that had he come to me earlier I would have been able to do more for him. I would say that, as things now stand, my therapeutic options are limited."

"How long has he got, Doc?" I snapped.

He ignored me and, continuing to address my mother, said, "Terminal is an ugly word. An unnecessary word. Let us together, Mrs Perera, look on the bright side of things. I have proved the diagnosis. I am now going to offer him the best treatment modern medicine has." He smiled, acknowledging, in anticipation, our gratitude.

"Can we expect my father to live for a few years," I persisted, "or does he have a few months, or, perhaps, even just a few weeks left?" He held up a hand but I continued, "From what you just said, I understand the cancer is pretty widespread."

"In cases like this, madam," he chanted at my mother, "you must at all times be prepared for the ultimate eventuality."

"You mean Fred might die suddenly . . . and quite soon?" said my mother, her eyes round with fear.

"To think of his survival in years would be unrealistic. To talk in terms of weeks would be unduly pessimistic."

"What shall I tell Fred, Dr Chan?"

"We leave that sort of thing entirely to the next-of-kin," he said, putting his hands together. Mass was over. "Mrs Perera," he said, leaning forwards and shaking my mother's hand.

He glanced at me, and my mother said, "My son, Hern."

"Mr Perera," he said shaking my hand. Then, turning to Sylvie, he said, "Your daughter, I guess. So much like her mother." And, shaking her hand, he murmured, "Mrs Perera."

God, I thought, this self-centred bastard – too stupid to realize automatically that two Mrs Pereras cannot be mother and daughter, even if the tremendous difference in their looks had not made this unlikely – was the person who was going to preside over my father's dying. A flood of tenderness washed over me. I put an arm around my mother and drew her close. She leaned on my shoulder for a bit, then I felt her stiffen and draw away. Standing very straight, she first extracted from her handbag a tiny lace handkerchief and with it she began meticulously to dab her eyes. Then she drew out a silver compact and began making minute repairs to her make-up. A change had come over her. At first I failed to understand what was happening. Then I did.

The church is hushed and the lighting low. In the background an organ plays. The coffin at the altar is simple but well made and of an expensive black wood. Its edges are trimmed with silver. Real silver. There are little murmurs as Clara Perera, unsupported and alone, walks slowly up the front pew. Under the fashionable hat her head is held high and her eyes, behind the black lace veil, are dry. As she walks by, people whisper one word: "brave". She takes her place in the front and looks at the coffin, unafraid. The organ is replaced by a choir. The singing lifts up her heart and warms it. Strengthens her faith. Yes, Fred and Clara will meet again. Death's parting is but temporary. The singing reaches a climax. It's the conclusion of the Mozart Requiem. "Agnus Dei", lamb of God. No, that's wrong. It's not "Agnus Dei" that she hears. It's "Crying in the Chapel."

"Come along then," said my mother. "Let's go tell your father what's been happening." She held her head high, her chin turned slightly to the left. She had to be sure that her better profile appeared in the final close-up.

"Well," said my father as we trooped into his room, "what had young Dr Chan to say? Now, remember that Fred Perera is only interested in the truth, the whole truth, and nothing but the truth."

"Everything is going to be all right," said my mother, sitting down on the bed beside him.

The outright lie stunned me into silence. I had not expected her to come out and tell Father that his condition was terminal, but I expected her story to have, at least, a foundation of truth to which we could add as his condition progressed, so that, in time, he would realize himself that the end was not far.

Before I could say anything, she continued, "They are going to give you this brand-new treatment and you'll be as right as rain. As rain, d'you hear?" She laughed and tossed her head girlishly. "Just think of the worry we went through for nothing."

My mother's behaviour puzzled me, but only momentarily. Clara knew Fred was dying. She had already rehearsed his funeral. She had decided she was going to be brave and she was going to be brave alone. No one, not even her beloved Fred, was going to share her moment of courage. Her jaw assumed its upward tilt and there was a faraway look in her eyes.

"But what did he say was wrong, my darling?" asked my father querulously. "And what about the gland in my neck? What did that show?"

"A rare virus," said Clara.

"It's cancer, isn't it?" said my father in a toneless voice.

"Oh, you silly-billy-kins . . ." Clara began.

But he cut her short. "It's cancer. I gathered this quite easily from the bits and pieces of conversation I garnered while they were in the process of doing the biopsy." He looked at us all and smiled, his upper lip fluttering between tears and a show of courage. "From what I gather, the disease process began in my lungs, then spread to my neck and – correct me if I'm wrong – my liver."

"Oh dear, oh dear!" said my mother, deflated.

"Dad," I said, gathering myself together. "You're right. But I gather from Dr Chan that nowadays, with the latest drugs . . ."

He held up a hand. "There's no need for all that, Hern. I'm fully cognizant of the fact that I am dying of cancer." He looked at the three of us and managed to smile a little more resolutely. "I near my journey's end and soon must shuffle off this mortal coil." He reached across for his wife's hand. "Yet I feel no older, not a single day older, than when I began it. The skin wrinkles, gets mildewed and discoloured and begins to smell a bit, but the inside remains the same." He paused to breathe. "There's a light burning in each and every one of us, and it continues to burn, undimmed, till the moment it is finally extinguished."

Clara looked at him unblinking, her eyes alight with genuine adulation. She was not quite sure what Fred was going on about, but intuitively knew that a heroic pose had been struck.

"Oh, Fred," she said, "you are so brave and so lovely."

"Whatever happens, my pet, we'll take that honeymoon trip up the east coast." He forced a lecherous look to cross his face.

Sylvie gazed at them, entranced, her eyes overly bright.

I looked at them and thought that in half an hour, an hour at most, I could be back home and at my typewriter.

Back in my room I realized my story "Homecoming" existed by default. I had begun by trying to illustrate something I thought experience had taught me and been distracted from my theme by a chance remark of my father's. As I wrote, memories my grandmother had shared with me crept in. Pulled this way and that, my narrative was distorted. What finally appeared was quite different from what I had intended. It seemed disfigured, and yet I was reluctant to disown it. Finally I decided what I would do. I would keep it secret. I tucked it away in a drawer, away from my other stories.

five

"It's really half-and-half, you know," said Su-May, her eyeball almost touching my nipple. "Can't make up its mind whether to stick its head out like mine or draw it in."

As always, her scrutiny was insatiable. She frequently made detailed inspections of my anatomy, inspections which alternately flattered and irritated me. Right now I was charmed. After three hours of conciliatory love-making, it was difficult to be otherwise.

I stroked her hair and said, "Perhaps it's just tired."

She looked up sharply. "It's 'I suppose' time, isn't it? Don't bother to say anything. I know." She began rummaging about for her clothes.

"Su-May," I protested. "I don't quite understand –"

"You understand very well, Hern. As soon as you're fed up with me it's: 'I suppose it's getting late . . .', 'I suppose you must be getting hungry . . .', 'I suppose we should think of surfacing.'" She affected a rich, fruity voice the better to mock my mannerism.

"I suppose you're right to . . ." I began and we both burst out laughing.

Su-May's was a giggle, and she hid her face behind her hand when she laughed but not well enough to conceal the stricken look that crossed it. The child had been told it was bedtime. The party was over. I longed to take her into my arms and tell her that this was not so. It wasn't "I suppose" time at all. We would lock out the world, stay in the flat on the top floor of Benson's for ever. Nothing would change: her nipples would always be soft translucent buds; the curve of her belly, like that of her cheek, would remain slow and smooth, her navel making the shallowest of dimples in it; my passion would continue undiminished through the tunnel of the years. I longed to tell her all this but I didn't. In a story I would happily have trampled on truth in the interest of my plot, sacrificed fact for fabrication, discarded aspects of reality that refused to conform to the shape of a sentence. Yet now, when all that was human in me demanded I mollify the truth, inventiveness deserts me. Lacking the courage to lie, I change the subject.

"What does Peter, the Reverend, feel about your coming here tonight?"

She stopped unravelling her underwear. "How come you think he knows?"

"Guessed. Doesn't he?"

"Yup," she admitted without ill humour. "Pete knows. In fact it's a funny thing."

"What is?"

"He wants to meet you, Hern."

"What on earth for?"

"I think, to talk," she said, screwing up her face.

" 'Better a known friend than an unknown enemy,' he said, I think."

"Full of aphorisms, your Peter," I said. "No wonder they call him the Reverend."

"Such a stupid head I am," she said. "Can't remember what aphorisms are. Anyway, will you?"

"Will I what?"

"Meet Peter, silly."

"Can't see that it will do me any harm."

"He really wants to, you know." She looked at me steadily for a while, and when I said nothing, continued, "I'll ask him to phone you at the office so you can work out a convenient time."

"Oh," I said. "So you won't be there."

"No, silly. Pete wants to talk serious with you. Also, you'll get to know each other better if I'm not around. Feel freer, like."

"Anything you say, sweetie."

"I say, pass me my bag. It's on your side of the bed."

Su-May usually appeared with a large canvas bag, the kind

squash players carry around. I had once asked her what it contained. A change of clothes, so she could get out of uniform after work, and all the bits and pieces a nurse needed on duty, she had answered. I rolled over and picked up the bag from beside the bed. I was surprised at its weight.

"What do nurses wear to work these days?" I asked. "Lead shoes and iron underwear?"

"Heavy, yah?" she said, moving it with obvious difficulty to her side of the bed. "All sorts of things I have to carry in it, you know."

For a moment I thought she had been stealing from Benson's but as I watched her dress, her skin flushed and damp, her long hair a little straggly and in need of brushing, the pulse at her throat reminiscent of her heart beating against my chest, the thought left me. I pictured her lugging her bag along dark streets, shifting it from hand to hand, hurrying, afraid of who or what might be behind her, and was filled with tenderness. It was my fault that she had to leave. I should somehow have contrived to make it possible for her to stay. I reached out and ran my hand across her back as she buttoned her blouse. No, I must never give up this girl, whatever my father said, whatever Peter Yu argued was the morally correct thing, whatever tricks the Children of the Book got up to. My determination was not based on self-deception. I saw Su-May for what she was: a naïve, somewhat silly girl; her conversation so superficial that she sometimes seemed hardly aware of what she was saying. She enjoyed moments simply for themselves with an enthusiasm that was totally uncritical and pointlessly optimistic. But I suspected that these were qualities inseparable from an innocence that was irrepressible and, in a sense, indestructible: an innocence I could not remember ever having possessed.

"I love you terribly, Su-May," I muttered.

"I know, Hern," she said, managing a weak smile. The weight of the bag made the veins of her forearm stand out.

"Shall I help you with that thing?"

"No need, Hern." She grinned, then bent over and kissed me. "As we both know, I must go my way and you must go yours."

Whenever we used the flat at Benson's I insisted that we leave separately. Su-May would let herself out by a side door beside the main entrance. This latched on the inside and required no key. I myself left by the back entrance, which was always locked but to which I had a key. I argued that leaving the store by different routes would make it impossible for anyone to see us around Benson's together or to guess our secret meeting place. Both of us enjoyed the cloak-and-dagger aspect of our affair. However, there was, as always, more than one reason for my actions. The front entrance of Benson's opened on to busy Orchard Road. Just past the entrance a blind man had a small newsstand. Like everyone else, I felt obliged to buy something from him whenever I passed, and to avoid doing so had given up using the front entrance altogether. I also disliked the main Orchard Road, crowded with tourists and teenagers, and preferred to walk home along back streets fronted by old shop-houses in the process of demolition.

I got dressed slowly, still in the spell of Su-May's love-making. This was broken the instant I realized I did not have the key to the back door with me and would have to follow Su-May out of the front entrance. I waited fifteen minutes, giving her ample time to get away, before I left the flat. It was late and Orchard Road was deserted. The blind newspaper-vendor had long gone, leaving on the pavement his wooden table and the little packing-case on which he sat. Hanging over one side of the table was a rough newspaper poster, the kind on which headlines are scrawled. It said: HELP YOURSELF. On the table itself were stacks of typewritten sheets held down by the bricks the blind man used to secure his newspapers and magazines. I took a sheet, more from curiosity than anything else. The appearance, in a large city, of a clandestine pamphlet would not be cause for great interest. But this was Singapore, where the most trivial publication required a special permit from the Ministry of Culture and where contravention of this regulation was dealt with swiftly and severely. I was conscious of an excitement, a sense of doing something dangerous and illegal, when I did help myself to one of the typewritten sheets. In the bad light of the street I could just make out the capitals scrawled across the top which said STREETPAPER. The typescript that followed was blurred and difficult to read. I folded the sheet and looked around me several times before I slipped it into my pocket and began walking home.

Sylvie was asleep when I got in. I was glad of this, not because I feared her recognizing traces of another woman on me, but for a reason indefinable and in some way related to the streetpaper, which I unfolded and placed carefully on my bedside table. I had been uneasy from the moment I had picked it up. Even a long, hot shower did not quite rid me of this. When I finally slipped into bed, I checked to see that Sylvie was asleep before picking up the streetpaper. My hands trembled. There was nothing written across the top except the date, 16 December, and the word STREET-PAPER. I began reading.

You are unhappy and you dare not admit this to anyone. Certainly not to your masters in the government. After all you have no right to be unhappy. Your masters provide you with good housing, safe streets, good hospitals, schools for your children and pay you enough for three square meals a day and a colour TV. Your masters may be right. You are wrong to be unhappy. Look at the people in the countries around you. Diseased, starving, living in slums. Yet in some ways they seem happier than you. Why?

Ask yourself why this streetpaper is necessary. Because, my friend, our masters control every newspaper and every magazine on this, our wonderful island paradise. And every movie, TV show and tape-recording is censored before it gets to you. But why should this make you unhappy? After all, you've got all you really need. Because, my friend, you are a man, not a dog. And men must be free to talk, to write, to contact other men, to organize themselves into groups. Groups they choose themselves, not groups ordained by our masters like the Peoples Consultative Committees and other Residents Committees. Men who are not free to do this are no more than animals. You have been made into dogs. Your masters kennel you in neat boxes, doctor your females, control litter size according to pedigree and tell you what names you can give your pups. It is no wonder you are unhappy and ashamed. In your own eyes you have become animals. In exchange for – necessities?, comforts? – you have allowed your masters to take away your most precious right. Your right to talk and mingle freely with your fellow men; your right to control your destiny. You have known this for many years, my friend, but you have been afraid to face it, afraid because there was nothing you dared do about it. And you are right to be scared. Criticism is punishable unless you first get their permission to criticize. So you are careful how you talk. If word got around that you were anti-government you might not get your annual wage increase or the promotion you were expecting. Somebody would be found more suitable than you for the government flat you were about to move into. So you keep quiet and walk with head down, for deep in your heart you feel no better than a dog. But lift up your heads and your hearts, my friend, for you are not alone. All around you are people who do not want to be dogs any more. They want to be men again. They want to reach out freely to other men.

But how can we do this safely, you ask?

I will tell you.

Sylvie stirred beside me and rolled over on her back. I looked to make sure she was still asleep. Her mouth was slightly open and she snored gently. On her upper lip were minute beads of sweat. The slip she wore had ridden up to her waist and her legs had fallen apart. In the orange shadows of my bedside light she looked vulnerable and irresistible. I was distracted by a momentary twinge of lust but pulled down her slip and continued reading.

We can communicate safely and freely by streetpapers like this. Make a carbon copy of whatever you have to say and destroy the original. That way the police can't trace the typewriter you use. Then make photocopies of the carbon copy. Do your photocopying at several different places so no one gets suspicious of you. Think where you want to leave YOUR streetpaper. Bus-stops, shopping-centres, car-parks, hotel lobbies. Any place where people gather. Watch these places. Find out when they are deserted so you can leave your pile of streetpapers there safely. If you plan to work in groups, trust only relatives or close childhood friends. If you follow these rules there is nothing to fear. There aren't enough secret police in Singapore or in the whole world to stop you. Do not be afraid. You have more friends than you think and to be a man is your God-given right.

P.S. When you have read this, pass it on to a friend or leave it where someone else can pick it up to read.

I do not see myself as a person involved in moral problems, and

polemical writing of any sort tends to put me off. Nevertheless I
was troubled by what I had read. Not that I was personally affected
by the issues the streetpaper raised. I have never felt inhibited by
the censorship prevailing in Singapore, nor have I felt the urge
for mass communication. However, the possibility that other
people might miss what I did not require was not something that
escaped me, and in a strange way I began almost at once to
yearn for something I had never needed. The more I thought about
it, the more convinced I became that the streetpaper was, in its
crude way, right: Singaporeans were denied essential freedoms
and I, who had never had anything in common with the mass of
people around me, was beginning vicariously to share their
deprivation.

I slept easily.

Sylvie woke me early to say, "Dad turned bad last evening." She
put a cup of coffee beside me. "Been throwing up like a volcano in
high spirits."

"Oh, God, why?"

"It's the drugs he's on," she answered. She looked at me darkly
for a moment before she grinned. "The latest thing, as the specialist
informed us, in cancer treatment. You've got cancer and you feel
bad. They give you something that makes you feel worse. You
stand the drugs for as long as you can. Then you plead with them to
stop the drug and give you back your cancer. So they stop the drug.
You feel better and are dutifully grateful to your doctor."

As we walked to the hospital Sylvie became more serious. My
father was reacting very badly to the anti-cancer therapy. He felt
exhausted and nauseated all the time. His hair was falling out in
clumps. His gums bled. His teeth felt loose. I had not seen my father
for three days and was shocked at the change in him. His face was
thinner and in a strange way darker, but it was the darkness of a
shadow, not a pigment. This made his eyes seem larger and
unnaturally bright. In their depths I saw glimpses of that mixture of
terror and resignation that only total despair can produce.

He was throwing up his breakfast when Sylvie and I walked in
and we waited in embarrassed silence for him to finish.

"It's just the cytotoxics," he said, as my mother dabbed his face with a towel soaked in cologne. "These anti-cancer drugs attack well-nigh everything en route to the cancer cells." He smiled, overcame a spasm of nausea, then continued: "Anyhow, there's no gain without pain, I suppose, and I guess I'll have to get used to the idea of losing a little before we finally win through." He ran a hand wearily through his hair and stared ruefully at the clumps that were uprooted in the process.

Sylvie and I spent the rest of the weekend at the hospital. There was nothing we could do to help, yet infected by my father's lethargy we could not find the energy to leave. After several false starts we abandoned the idea of conversation and busied ourselves, avoiding each other's eyes. My father vomited frequently and despite my mother's efforts with the eau-de-cologne ("Believe me, dearest, sweet smells do really drive the blues away") there was no escaping the odour of putrefaction that hung expectantly about the room. After a while he stopped trying to hide his fear, which was obvious behind his dull, but somehow transparent, eyes. Confronted with Fred's terror, her thoughts frequently interrupted by having to attend to her husband's needs, Clara Perera was unable to alight on a fantasy and finally surrendered to the unpleasant reality around her.

Dr Chan, the specialist, dropped in twice.

The first time he said sternly to Mother, "These untoward side-effects tend to occur with the newer cytotoxics. Quite idiosyncractic they are too. Quite idiosyncratic. They in no way indicate the response of the malignant process to the therapy. Nor," he paused to readjust the grim look in his face, "have we evidence that they bear the slightest relevance to the ultimate prognosis."

He left before we could recover from our bewilderment.

My father seemed to have stopped vomiting a little when Dr Chan visited again. This time the doctor seemed in a buoyant, near lyrical mood.

"Good," he said. "The winds of change are here. I see fair weather ahead. The monsoon is over." He was dragged away to operate on an emergency before he could elaborate on this forecast.

With no plot to occupy me, I turned my thoughts to the

streetpaper. Perhaps the writer was correct. The average Singaporean was indeed unhappy and incomplete because his freedom to communicate was severely frustrated. Deep down he felt ashamed at having given up a basic right for a few paltry creature comforts. Birthrights had been sold for messes of pottage but never before without the loss of an intangible which humans value. It was funny that in all my poking around for plots I had never thought of this as one.

On Sunday evening my father's condition improved dramatically. "It's been a long haul for you two young people," he said, his eyes alive with relief. He managed a laugh. "Give your mother and me a little time alone, will you?"

As we walked home along Orchard Mall, I studied (I think for the first time) the people around me. The Mall is a broad, tree-lined promenade which gets crowded on Sunday evenings, and there were enough people about for me to observe. Surely I would find in their faces evidence of pain and humiliation, stigmata of excommunication from their species. Not too much seemed wrong with the teenagers bouncing out of McDonald's, and the elderly, walking dogs or grandchildren, seemed content enough with their lot. Sylvie and I stood waiting for a traffic light to change. Suddenly, beside us appeared three young men. Their faces were drawn and expressionless. They seemed lost and looked about them nervously. The lights turned green but I did not move, wanting to study them a little longer. Then the oldest of them grabbed the other two and shouted, "*Hayaku*, Narika, Miro, *hayaku*." They were Japanese tourists. Thirty thousand of them visit Singapore every month.

As soon as we got home I slipped into the bedroom and picked up the streetpaper. I began rereading parts of it and didn't hear Sylvie enter.

"Hey," she said, "you've got one."

"Oh," I said, startled to find her in the room. "You picked up one too."

"Yup," she said. "Outside the market."

I began tearing up the streetpaper.

"No. You mustn't do that, Hern."

"Why not?"

"You're supposed to pass it along. So more people get to read it."

"I see," I said. "And what did you do with yours?"

"You know the waiting-room in the hospital?" She grinned. "I slipped it in among the magazines there. Clever, right?"

six
___

"Affirmative twice," said Rex Zhu, his face quite bland.

We were halfway through the set lunch, of which he ate little, examining every morsel he consumed with extreme suspicion. I was by now beginning to get used to "affirmatives", "negatives", "nixes" (strong negatives), "checks" (confirmations), and even beginning to think of things ranging from A to Zee.

Rex looked at me through thick rimless spectacles. It was difficult to be sure whether the highlights confronting me arose in his eyes or his lenses, an uncertainty that conferred an inhuman dimension to his gaze. He said, "The whole caboodle's gotta go."

"You mean we'll have to physically alter the place as well as employ new staff."

"Hernie," he began, then asked for the third time, "you don't mind my using your first –"

"Please," I protested, holding up a hand.

"Specifics then," he said, raising a manicured finger. "Expansion into available space." A second finger went up. "Total renovation." A third finger joined its fellows. "Complete staff overhaul."

"What do we do with our present staff?" I asked, turning to Chuang.

Chuang began to answer my question but, before he could, Rex put a hand on his arm and said, "They get laid off."

"You mean we just sack them?" I asked.

"Yup," he said. "Critical for total image change," He put his fingertips together. "Problem," he said. "No direction in sales thrust. Solution," he glared at Chuang and me, the lights in his glasses dancing madly: "Stratification. Stratification, that's the name of the game. Apartment space availability predicates our strategy, which must have just three prongs. We have all the advantages."

What he proposed was clear enough. The majority of Singaporeans lived in state-built flats. These, depending on size, location and design, fell roughly into three categories. Everyone aspired to a better flat, and knowing simply where a person lived told you not only the kind of furniture required, it told you the type of flat aspired to and the kind of furniture needed in the future.

"Van one," Rex said, hitting the corner of the table with the side of his hand, "market research unnecessary."

"Van?" I asked.

"Advantage," he explained, spinning round to glint at me. "Van two," he continued, striking the table twice, "sales promotion conceptually uncomplicated. Van three, only minimal personnel training required. Neat." He clapped his hands several times and bowed in several directions, simultaneously the applauder and the applauded.

Chuang, who had been dumfounded by all this, asked, "And Chinese antiques, Mr Zhu?"

"Error, error," said Rex in a flat computer voice. "Correction, correction," he continued, smiling blandly. "Van four. Cultural preferences identified and easily accommodated." He clapped his hands twice. "Question-time."

"Ahmad, my assistant, will find it a bit difficult to cope . . ." I began.

"Top priority for you, Hernie," he said, pointing sharply at me: "replace that deaf senior citizen."

A waiter plonked three ice-creams in front of us. Rex turned, half-rising as he did, and seized the man by the arm.

"Low-cal?" he snarled.

"No, sir. No, sir," said the man, almost dropping the tray in his alarm. "One hundred per cent full-cream imported American, sir."

Rather than laugh, I made hurriedly for the gents. By the time I got back, lunch and the meeting were over.

I returned to Benson's depressed. Oddly enough, Chuang

seemed in a similar mood. I expected him to follow me into the furniture department, pointing out how and where we could put into immediate effect some of Rex Zhu's suggestions. Instead, he left me at the front of the store, muttering something about having to rush upstairs to his office to get on with his "hurry ups".

I was glad of this. It would have been too much simply to march in with Chuang and tell Ahmad and the four middle-aged spinsters we called salesgirls that we would shortly be dispensing with their services. Sitting at my desk, I avoided catching their eye as they pottered about and, strangely, they too seemed intent on avoiding mine. I was reminded of the times I have been invited to select the fish for dinner in Chinese restaurants that keep their stocks swimming about in large glass tanks for patrons to inspect. On such occasions both fish and I seemed to avoid each other's eyes. It was not possible that the fish guessed what would happen if they caught my attention, and yet . . .

I looked at one of our salesgirls idly polishing a corner of a table scratched in transportation and at Ahmad moving slowly around the room adjusting price-tags so they could the more easily be read. There was no way that this lot would cope, even if given the chance, with the changes Rex planned.

"Feedback is success," he had pronounced. Then, suspecting that an aphorism of such profundity required elaboration, added: "Productive enterprise depends on balanced servosystems. Monitoring who, when, what, why . . . And," he smiled at Chuang, anticipating his agreement, "yes, sir, staff orientation. Personnel immersion in sales strategy is mandatory. Meaning?" he glinted at my bewildered general manager inquiringly. "Cor-rect," he continued, not waiting for Chuang's reply. "Yes, sir. We need whole-staff seminars, tracking product movement. Movement, mark you, not just profits and loss. Balances based on turnover. All impossible without in-depth systems analysis and whole-scale computerization. The works. The whole god-darned works. And all moving by January two."

No. Ahmad and the girls would never manage, even if I succeeded in persuading Chuang to keep them on. But why should that worry me? After all, distasteful as I found the choosing, I had never refused the fish when it was fairly cooked and served. It was not Ahmad's fate that worried me but my own. I could not survive in the kind of world Rex Zhu was creating. My best plan was to get out before my own collapsed. Then, at least, I could keep intact the memory of long afternoons at my desk, afternoons untroubled by customers or the need to justify slow-turnover-product-space-occupancy, afternoons that would return to me whenever I smelled new leather or furniture polish. If I stayed I would not merely see Rex Zhu destroy my world; I would see him dismember my dreams and, seeing this, I would deny myself the possibility of roses in December.

I had to act quickly. Rex planned to begin reorganizing at the start of the new year; whatever I might think of him, there was no doubt in my mind that when Rex Zhu said January two he meant the second day of the year. It was Monday the 19th of December. I had just under a fortnight.

I did not doubt that Samson Alagaratnam would find me a job. He would be glad to, especially if in doing me a favour he compromised himself ever so slightly, proving to himself that his most recent affiliations had not necessitated the destruction of his loyalty to old friends. He could continue to see himself as a good chap who always had time to stop and help a friend for old times' sake.

I had no objection to becoming a hack in the Ministry of Culture, to joining the Guild of Singapore Writers, to accepting a sinecure at the university or any other pay-off that Sam needed to maintain his image of himself. No great principle was involved, and even if there were I would not have been terribly bothered. I am not one who attaches great importance to principles. Yet I did not call him. Three times I picked up the phone and dialled his number, each time hanging up before the connection was made.

I did not deceive myself. I knew exactly why I hung up: I was expecting a reprieve. News would suddenly come through that the planned collaboration between Benson's and Teng's had been called off. There had been disagreement at high levels. Things could continue as they were and Hernie Perera could live happily ever after. I cursed myself for my folly, for being truly the son of Clara Perera, but I waited for the reprieve and became more depressed and irritable with every hour that passed without news of it.

I was still in this mood when I made love to Sylvie that night. It was an unsatisfying, corrosive exercise that left us unhappy and irritable. This kind of experience was rare in our marriage. As we lay silent in the dark, our bodies chilling even more as they dried, I looked for the words to apologize. I thought I should tell her of Rex Zhu, of the changes about to take place in Benson's, of my troubles that day, of the reprieve that never came . . .

"I'm sorry, love," said Sylvie, reaching out to touch my thigh. "Choked on my pride swallowing my pill this morning, and have been in a foul mood ever since."

I put my hand over hers. "It's all right, darling."

There has been in our generally happy marriage one source of discontent. From the outset, Sylive had wanted children, and from time to time expressed resentment at having to take contraceptive pills. I had difficulty in understanding this, for she had no great maternal instinct, nor did she picture ours as a conventional marriage in which children were essential.

Then one day, quite out of the blue, she had said, "Hernie, you and me, we swirl around like snowflakes and when we are gone, there'll be nothing."

"Nothing?"

"Yes. Nothing to say we've been and gone. Nothing to remember us by."

"Perhaps we can arrange for a commemorative stamp to be issued or even coins to –"

"That's not funny, Hern," she said. "Think about it. I am very serious."

This had been fairly early in our marriage. With the passing of the years, her tactics had grown more subtle. She reared fish, whose every spawning was a rebuke in my direction, but adamantly refused a pet dog or cat. I think she feared I might look upon the animals as a substitute for a child, though this was not the avowed reason for her refusal.

Once at a party I heard her explain, knowing I was in earshot, "No, we don't have any pets. I couldn't keep them and not allow them to breed. I think they too need to leave something behind when they go."

We lay still, our unspoken thoughts drawing us closer. Then Sylvie said, "Ma's been talking family again."

"Oh."

"She says it's not for herself but for Pa. He's a little better now and has started thinking about things." She began stroking my hand. "He knows he hasn't long to go. No future. To go on walking even the little way he has left, he must know the road continues."

"Look, Sylvie," I said, "even if I impregnated you instantly, I honestly don't think Pa would live long enough to see the result of our efforts."

"True, Hern." She laughed. "But also true, you don't have to walk on a road, you don't even have to see it to know it's there." She paused. "A map will do."

I could feel her smile in the dark as she pressed against me.

I met my mother the next morning in the foyer of Mount Elizabeth Hospital. It was early and there was no one about. In that grand empty room we felt like conspirators and tended to whisper to one other.

"You put Sylvie up to it," I said.

"Yes," she hissed. "Children are good for everybody."

"I have enough trouble at the moment without getting into this sort of thing."

"Bubble trouble," she snapped. "What do you think I have, with your father so ill?'

"You can talk," I said. "You won't have to bear the child."

"That's the easy part," she muttered. "I'll help with the hard part, looking after the child."

"You know Sylvie would never let you do that."

"Then she can't grumble, can she?" she said, tossing her head.

I pleaded. "Things are not the same with a couple once there's a child around, Ma."

"Correct. They're much better." Then suddenly her manner changed. Her face became soft and her shoulders slumped forwards. Her upper lip trembled slightly. "You young people don't understand. You really don't, do you? It's so important for us to peep into the future before we go."

"You're not going anywhere, Ma."

"True. Too true. But Pa is." Her whole person became hard and resolute. Clara Perera, the matriarch, was going into the future alone. She looks into the next decade. She looks into the next century. She sees grandchildren, great grandchildren, even great, great grandchildren . . . the thread stringing together beads of existence. "Come on," she said, her voice suddenly loud and business like. "Let's go upstairs to your father. He gets terribly upset when I'm even a teeny-weeny bit late."

My father seemed better and was very pleased to see me. I assured him I would return later and left before my mother brought up the subject of grandchildren.

I arrived at Benson's to find a commotion going on outside the main entrance. Several policemen in dark blue uniforms mingled with the early morning crowd. I was just in time to see two leading the blind newspaper seller into a police car.

"What in heaven's name is going on?" I asked a young shopgirl with a familiar face.

"Subversion," she whispered, obviously enjoying the excitement. "Communist subversives, Mr Perera," she added by way of explanation.

"Who, the blind newspaper fellow?"

"Yup," she said, nodding slowly. "Spreading anti-government propaganda."

"But that's impossible," I protested.

"Who knows?" she said, with a disclamatory shrug of her shoulders.

Inside the furniture department, things seemed normal enough. A few workmen were putting the final touches to some alterations I had made in the Christmas decorations. I gave the decorations a quick look before settling down at my desk. There were the usual bills and invoices for me to check. A pile of furnishing magazines had come in the post. It was among these that I found the streetpaper.

It had on it the day's date, 20 December; three days after the first streetpaper had appeared, someone had bothered to publish again. I wondered if it was the original writer or some person responding to his appeal. Though I had seen the blind newspaper seller arrested and was in full view of my staff, I was not nervous. I wasn't, of course, prepared to be seen reading the blasted thing, but the hand with which I folded it was steady. I was about to tuck it into my pocket when I looked up and saw Edith, the oldest of our salesgirls, watching me. She flashed me a quick knowing smile, then looked down. What the hell, I thought. I was impatient to know what was in the streetpaper. I might as well read it here as at home.

The first streetpaper was great. It really was. Now we know how we can reach each other. Especially us kids. Would you believe it, we can at last talk the way we want to. No need to put out any shit about how much we owe our leaders or any crap about respecting the mouldy old farts who do everything to stop us having fun. Yeah, man, this is it. No big brother watching you like in the community centres. You can tell it like it is. OK. So let it all hang out but for real, dirty underwear and all. And we sure know what is complaint number one. Where do guys go when they finish school? NS, National Service, Nasty Shithole. And what happens there? Maybe you guys in school still don't know. You get tortured, man; yeah, and buggered. True, fella, you get raped by the tough boys. It's OK for guys who liked to be arsed . . . but if you don't? Those toughies will still stretch you sphincters. So you heard they build up your bodies, did you? Seen before-and-after pics, like? Sure, man, but press-ups are much sweeter with a chick underneath. But, boy, oh, boy, have they got it in for sex. No good clean boy–girl fun, even on the movies.

I stopped reading and looked up, the streetpaper still in my hands. There was a minor commotion going on in my department. A Christmas decoration had come adrift and Ahmad had persuaded Edith up a ladder to adjust it. The other girls stood around tittering as Ahmad encouraged Edith up yet another rung. Finally she reached the top and I thought I noticed her knees trembling a bit, but the look she shot across the room at me was far from nervous. It was decidedly conspiratorial.

I was upset by Edith's look because it confirmed what I had for some time begun to suspect: control over my life was being taken out of my hands. By no stretch of the imagination could I be considered a political agitator. I was totally uninterested in the kind of thing the streetpaper chap was going on about. What was worse, his style disgusted me. Yet I must have been one of the first people to pick up the streetpapers distributed by the blind newspaper man. And had I not arrived this morning at the very moment of his arrest? And now, right in my office, in the heart of the world I had so painstakingly put together, a shopgirl who would not normally address me directly, smiled at me secretly because she thought she and I shared a cause.

I had been vaguely aware of this loss of control for some time. I suppose it all began the day Chuang had come into my office with Rex Zhu while I had been out. That was a sign. Had I been more perceptive or less intent on designing strategems for Su-May's recapture, I would have seen it as such. I hadn't, of course. And, whatever the state of one's awareness, it is the "of course" that produces the feeling of inevitability. Cassandra, gifted with foresight and damned never to be believed, was not so special. Her powers, like so many of those we reserve for gods and heroes, are fairly commonplace.

My apprehensions increased when I noticed Edith trying to catch my eye. I began to get a feeling of acceleration, which so often accompanies that of inevitability; that somebody else is in control of the car and is driving much too fast. However dispassionately I looked at things, there was no doubt that events in my life were speeding up: Su-May's threat, my father's cancer, the changes at Benson's, Sylvie's demands and now the streetpaper, which I was sure would soon begin to play a part in my life.

I picked it up and reread portions of it, finding it as offensive as I had the first time round. There was something about its style that was familiar, that reminded me of someone. I scratched around my head for a while; then it hit me. Samson. Samson Alagaratnam. But Sam could not, by any stretch of the imagination, be the author of the streetpaper. He had struggled hard to get where he was, and was not only a devout believer in all the government's policies but was said to be concerned with the less savoury aspects of governmental affairs. Thinking about him reminded me that I should not put off phoning about a job.

A sweet-voiced girl told me that Sam was at an important meeting. I left my name. An hour later I called again. He was still at the meeting, the sweet voice informed me. Would I please not call again. She promised to get him to phone me as soon as he could. I waited. Just before lunch the phone rang. It was Chuang's secretary to say that he would like a word with me in his office after lunch. Five minutes after hanging up I decided to go upstairs at once, rather than delay finding out what Chuang had in store for me. There is a dignity about meeting one's fate head-on, which I am sure is the basis of tragedy.

Long lines of Christmas shoppers waited for lifts. I climbed the five floors to Chuang's office. His secretary, normally in a reception area outside his room, had obviously gone to lunch and I paused beside her desk to catch my breath. The door to Chuang's office was ajar and I heard voices.

". . . slow; slow now, Mr Rex Zhu. All staffs, including Perera too?"

"Check," said Rex Zhu. "Phase out all personnel in furniture department by March one."

"Too fast, too fast," Chuang protested.

"We have contractual clearway?"

"Not that," whined Chuang. "Got other considerations. . . ."

"Forget them."

I tiptoed out of the room.

It was nearly four before the sweet-voiced girl from Sam's office called. Mr Alagaratnam, she informed me, would be on the line in a minute.

It was exactly sixty seconds before Sam came on the line.

"Man, oh, Hernie baby," he said breathlessly. "This sure has been the meanest, pussy-footin', twenty-eight-hour day of my life. But things are blowing big, baby. Real big."

"Oh," I said. "What's happening?"

"Hernie," he said reproachfully. "This thing is so top secret I don't even talk to myself about it. But soon the balloon goes up, up, up, up, up. . . ." He stopped out of breath. "Now you didn't call just to hear my sweet tone on the phone, did ya?'

"It's about the job, Sam," I said. "I'm thinking of leaving Benson's and you said there might be something. . . ."

"That's good thinkin' and groovin' movin', man," he said. "Let's see what we can dig up from the cook-book for you."

"Anything that has got to do with writing, Sam."

"On the button, baby. Right on the button." He paused. "How does deputy editor of *Reflections* sound?"

"Reflections?"

"Yeah, man, *Reflections*. What we push out every month for the slaves, man, for the government servants. Directional stuff, like, and aids to attitudes. News flashes from ministers' speeches, swinging campaigns, neat slogan contests. All cool stuff, man."

"I don't know much about these things, Sam," I said. "And deputy editor sounds a bit big. Who's editor, anyway?"

"Man, Hernie. You is sometimes real dumb. Who d'you think fella? Sam's your man."

"Anything you say, Sam. If you think I can manage. . . ."

"You stir that pot till it cools, Hernie, and when you get stir crazy," he paused to guffaw, "there's *Limbo*."

"*Limbo?*"

"Sure, baby. Creative arts and all that jazz. All paid for by oil money. Cute sticker, *Limbo?*"

"I don't quite get it, Sam?"

"And just as well, 'cause it ain't heaven and it ain't hell." He laughed. "Punny money there too, man, like a swinging West Indian beat." He began singing. "Limbo, limbo, limbo like me. Limbo-o, limbo like me."

"I could work with that too?"

"Sure as Tampax is worn on the inside, man. Swing aboard as associate editor."

"And the editor?"

"At your service, baby. At your service."

"Things have become quite urgent, you know."

"I guessed, and mammy's Sammy don't forget friends he knew from diaper days. No, sir, I gotta long memory for old times. A whisper to the deputy minister and we're set for take-off. Cigarettes out, safety belts on."

"Can I give Benson's notice then?"

"Sure thing, man. You quit now and climb aboard with us when the year turns. By culture week in June you'll be running so smoothly they won't hear your tyres on the road."

Sam's call did nothing to placate me.

Changes were obviously taking place in my life, and as I walked home that evening I had to remind myself that change and disaster were not the same thing, that the appearance of a vague pattern in one's life did not justify fatalism, that even zealous fatalists did not see life as a chain of catastrophes. I walked slowly, muttering these thoughts to myself, but the feeling that I was not just moving but being rushed along some pre-ordained path towards a precipice just would not go away. Talking to Sam had, in a way, made things worse. Added to my impotence was now a distinct feeling of guilt that I found impossible to understand. I was in no way responsible for the fate of the staff at Benson's. It was clear from the conversation I had overheard in Chuang's office that I, like them, was a victim of what might be looked upon as progress. If I hadn't let down Ahmad amd my salesgirls, who or what had I betrayed by joining Samson's outfit at the Ministry of Culture? Certainly not my literary talents, which at best were slight and were hardly served by my job at Benson's. But the feeling of helplessness and betrayal stayed with me, and the best I could do by the time I reached my flat was to convince myself that, while I had accepted the thirty pieces of silver, the object of my betrayal had yet to be revealed to me.

The flat was in total darkness and I turned on the lights to find Sylvie curled up on the sofa, her eyes red-rimmed and dull, as though weeping had leached them of their brightness. She did not bother to look at me. Sylvie only became like this when she was faced with a situation so bleak that looking for any hope in it simply drove her to greater depths of despair. (She called this: "Trying to take away the taste of a bitter medicine by swallowing more of it.") On the rare occasions when I have seen her this way I have been moved to pity and have tried to comfort her. Today, engrossed with my own pain, I was estranged from hers. I sat beside her but stared straight ahead.

Several minutes passed before she said, "Pa's refusing further treatment."

"God, why?" I said. "I thought he was just beginning to look a little better."

"I can sense how he feels, Hern," she said. "First you tell him he's got incurable cancer. When he's had the living daylights scared out of him, you fill him full of sickening poisons. Then everybody's surprised because he won't co-operate."

"But the cytotoxics are his only chance. He'll be finished without them."

"It's not equations, Hern," she said wearily. "They don't balance anyway. Ask yourself whether a slightly longer miserable life is prefable to a shorter, less uncomfortable one." She turned lack-lusture eyes towards me. "It's no-good a question, is it?"

"So what's he going to do?"

"Go on that holiday with Ma. That second honeymoon you were so nasty about."

"Oh," was all I could say.

Sylvie turned and looked at me but did not move any closer. "Hern," she said. "I choke on the thought. I simply can't swallow the idea of Pa's giving up the ghost like this. He was always so strong. Just look at him now, a hollow brick with all the stuffing knocked out. It's all over for him, you know." She paused. "And Ma."

She began to cry, her body convulsed with sobs. But her eyes were dry, her grief unconsummated. I should have reached out to her, touched her, showed her that, even though I couldn't, I wished to participate in her sorrow. Finally her sobs were reduced to an occasional whimper and she was able to speak.

"Pa brought it up again, you know. And I don't think Ma put him up to it."

"What on earth are you talking about, Sylvie?"

"The baby," she said. "Us having a child."

"I thought we'd –"

"I know, I know," she said tonelessly. "I just thought I'd mention it in case it comes up when you see Pa." She looked at me and tried to smile. It was a twisted grimace. "I'll get into bed and see if I can get some sleep. Why don't you go and do some typing?"

It seemed a good idea until I sat in my room and found my head empty of plots. The noisy turmoil of my life had stopped the buzzing in my head. After several empty hours, I got into bed beside Sylvie. We slept in snatches, our restless bodies touching each other occasionally and quickly rejecting the contact. The silence was complete.

seven

As soon as I got into Benson's the next morning, I sent up my letter of resignation. With this act of severance, I thought I had taken hold of my life again and felt immediately better. At least, I felt better until I got the phone call that one of the girls put directly through to me. I was taken by surprise. The line was bad and the caller had a particularly soft voice. It took me a while to realize it was Peter Yu. Not only did Peter tend to whisper, he paused in the wrong places. I wondered if he was doing so to disconcert me.

"There's something I would [pause] like to long [pause] see you about. I [pause] think it would be [very long pause] of interest, [pause] of importance to you, Hern."

"Look here," I said, "I simply can't imagine anything . . ."

"Sorry. I'm sorry. I've given [pause] quite the wrong [pause] impression. I'm not [pause] trying [pause] to threaten or bribe you. Can you see [pause] me today?"

"I'm very busy with the Christmas rush and all that, you know."

"Just [long pause] for a few minutes. After lunch."

"Where?"

"The McDonald's across the road from Benson's."

I knew I was a fool to let him get his way, but to refuse to see him would have seemed too much like cowardice. I decided to have lunch at McDonald's, thinking that familiarity with the terrain would give me an advantage in battle.

I was uneasy from the moment I entered. The place was crowded. Fried-food smells hung about it like stale incense in a temple. Beneath this I could feel the sweaty, feral excitement of the teenagers who surrounded me. Crouching in groups, faces greasy and pimpled, clothes stained and damp, they gibbered at each other, incurious of anything outside themselves. I watched and was satisfied. They justified the hostility I felt for Peter Yu and people of his generation.

I saw him before he saw me. He stood framed in the entrance and stared around the room. He looked weak, easily crushed. I had forgotten how thin he was and how pale. His skin was so delicate that around his eyelids and cheeks it was transparent, the veins showing through like those of a new leaf held up against the sun. He seemed tense, a little unsure of himself. Then he saw me. I raised a hand slightly. He smiled across the heads of the teenagers bent over their burgers. Somewhat against my will, I smiled back.

Peter walked over to me and, putting his hand on my shoulder, said, "Get you another coffee."

I had forgotten what a soft voice he had. Soft but so deep that there was no sibilance about it.

"No need to," I said. "There's still plenty here."

"In case. Anyway," he said. His hand still on my shoulder squeezed it a little.

I was surprised. Normally, familiarity of this kind rather offends me. I was far from offended. In fact, I derived a curious warmth from Peter's touch.

"All right," I said. "And thanks."

He was a while at the counter and by the time he returned several of the teenagers had departed, taking with them some of the hostility I felt for people of their generation. My feelings for Peter Yu had, in a matter of moments, altered a good deal. For one thing, my animosity had disappeared. This was partly due to his personality. He seemed so fragile, so in need of protection, that it was impossible to hate him. But there was something else. Something stronger than pity had displaced my ill will: curiosity. I could not wait to find out what sort of a person Su-May's lover was. (Why does one always think of the other fellow as the lover?) I drank up the remains of my coffee and fiddled impatiently with my empty cup.

Peter put a steaming plastic mug in front of me and said, "You're wrong to believe that one of us spoke to your father." He sat down. "Quite wrong."

"Well –" I began, then was unable to think of quite what to say. Peter and the Children were my most likely suspects, but confronting him with this was proving more difficult than I had expected.

"But we," he grinned and prodded my chest several times with his finger, "can understand why you should think that."

"No matter," he shook his head. "Whatever else all," his open palms made a circular movement in the air, "of us believe in, hold as a group to be the truth, it is that love can never be misplaced. Nor can it ever be immoral. Affectionate contact," he smiled sweetly, folded one palm into the other and squeezed his hands together, "never needs to be justified. Shaking hands and making love are ends in themselves." He paused, waiting for me to say something.

The encounter was not going the way I envisaged. For a start, even Peter's manner of speaking seemed different from what I remembered. On the phone he talked jerkily, interrupting in inappropriate places the flow of words. Face-to-face, I was not merely unaware of any discontinuity of his speech but was impressed, even overpowered, by the fluidity of his communication.

At a loss for words, I bent over my coffee cup, taking tiny sips and staring into the steam. Seeing that I was not going to speak, he continued.

"Any loving act is good. Must be. Nothing, no intention, no ulterior motive can make it wrong or evil."

I looked up from my coffee, smiling. I understood why Peter's speech seemed so wonderfully fluid. As he talked, he pre-empted or embellished words with facial expressions, and hand and body movements. Watching him speak I was unaware of interruptions, for he filled them with gestures that added to his meaning.

He continued, "We really," he rapped his forehead with his knuckles, "believe this to be true."

"Is that a belief or a hope?" I asked.

"I can never seem to tell them apart," he said, raising both palms in surrender. "Can you?"

He looked at me wide-eyed, his face open, and waited for my

answer. It took me a moment to grasp what he was getting at.

"It wasn't just convenient for me to think that one of your lot told my father about Su-May and me," I protested. "It wasn't simply what I wished to believe. It just seemed that you would be the people who would most benefit by breaking us up. Who else would have done it?"

"I don't know," he said, his face expressionless. "We are not a detective agency."

I felt anger stir in me and said, "But you don't deny that you and your . . . your group urged Su-May to break things off with me?"

"That we," he nodded abjectly, "did."

"After all your big talk about love, you seem quite prepared to destroy a loving relationship." My anger fed on itself and I continued, "Because, adulterous or not, that's what Su-May and I have. You, a good Christian type, were prepared to destroy the love of two people for purely selfish reasons."

"What you say is the truth." The veins under his transparent eyelids had become more prominent and his eyes were beginning to redden. He rubbed them with his knuckles, the way children do when they are about to cry. "Yes, the truth and the more painful to bear for being so."

"So you don't deny," I said, pursuing my advantage, "that you tried to get rid of me so you could have Su-May to yourself."

For a moment he looked stunned. Then his face cleared, brightened. He laughed and touched my shoulder, almost coyly. "Oh, dear, oh, dear," he said, shaking his head several times. "Try to be honest without saying too much and you're sure to screw things up."

"What the hell d'you mean by that?"

"That you've got it all wrong."

"You mean there's nothing going on between you and Su-May?"

"That's not," he said, shaking his head very slowly, "what I meant. What I was trying to say is that we don't let jealousy live with us. Except for very short spells and even then," he smiled, "only on a day-to-day basis."

"Then why –" I began.

"We agreed when we first," he locked his fingers, "grouped that we would try not to seek close relationships with outsiders.

Very," he looked down, "sad, isn't it, for Christians who believe so totally in universal love to start talking of insiders and outsiders?"

"Why make such a rule?"

"We thought we had reasons. Certain," he shrugged, "things that, for the moment at least, we should keep to ourselves."

"What things?"

We both saw the absurdity of my question at the same time and laughed. Still laughing, he reached across and put his hand on mine. "I'll tell you when we next meet," he said.

I felt lighter, relieved of my anger, and asked, "When will that be?"

"Why not be with us on Christmas Eve?" He leaned back and looked at me, his eyes strangely affectionate. "We gather in the afternoon. Come with Su."

As I walked across to Benson's I felt a kind of gladness that I had never experienced before. It wasn't relief. Relief is emptiness, a temporary draining away of fears, ill humours, suspicions. What I now had was fullness, not a sense of satiety, but a welling up of something inside me that made me want, if not to sing out aloud, at least to hum under my breath. It made me want to reach out and touch the people who stood beside me at the pedestrian-crossing opposite Benson's. I didn't. But when the lights changed and we hurried across, I was grateful for an arm, a leg or a shopping-bag that bumped accidentally into me.

I arrived in my office to find Samson Alagaratnam stomping impatiently around my desk. He looked on the verge of an apoplectic attack and I asked, "Is something the matter, Sam?"

"Some weirdo threatens to put out all the lights in the carnival and this cat asks," he put on an exaggerated English accent: "'Is anything the matter, sir?'"

He was pulsating with indignation. I forced him into a chair and indicated to Ahmad that we were not to be disturbed.

"What's happened, Sam?"

"You mean you don't know?" He stared at me, his eyes bulging fiercely out of his head as though better to detect any dissimulation on my part. "It's filthy vibes, man. Someone's putting out filth, making the kind of waves that can pull us all under."

"How is that possible, Sam?"

"With this kind of shit." He whipped out the streetpaper I had seen the day before and placed it on my desk. "This shit-paper is all over town."

"I know," I said, trying to sound unconcerned.

"One thing we know, sure as we know that chicken pox ain't the clap, and it's this: some mangy cat and his groupies started pushing this muck, and now every skunk in town is going to give his balls an airing."

"Have you got the culprit?" I asked, thinking of the blind newspaper man.

"Not the main cat, man. Not the main cat," he said almost in a whisper. He slumped in the chair, even his eyeballs seeming to recede into their sockets. "We pick up some bloke – worse, some chick, on info we get and try to make them sing. Not scream out loud. Just croon."

"You mean you torture these kids, Sam? Beat them up, use thumbscrews?"

He grinned. "These ain't the Dark Ages, man. We got electricity." He let his body quiver rhythmically. "We load sixteen tons and what d'we get?" He held up his hands in despair. "F– all. Forget about energy conservation. We pump all that juice into some cat and what d'you think he says?"

"I haven't a clue, Sam?"

"He tells us that he is Mr Big." He looked at me appealingly.

"But?" I prompted.

"But he can't be, man. This ain't no one-man band. Behind the main scene is some production, man. One cat in control and a lot of kits helping. And you know one thing about all the cats we've bagged, Hernie?"

"What?" I obliged.

"They ain't got the cool, Hernie. Style's all wrong." He shook his head. "Told the deputy minister this and what does he say? We gotta find the culprit. And soon." He rolled his eyes heavenwards. "Says the man up top wants these streetpapers stopped, but yesterday, man. Yesterday." He sighed at the injustice of it all and was silent.

"Anything more about a job for me, Sam?"

His whole manner brightened. "Yup. There we have ignition,

man. Click, click, click and vroom, it will be blast off, baby. But we gotta do this right. All official like, geddit? Kill any talk of favouritism dead, dead, dead, *si*?"

"Sure, Sam. What'll I have to do?"

"Check this form then sign it. We've already filled it in for you." He smiled mysteriously. "All facts and figures in place, right, man?"

"You seem to know a lot about me. How is that, Sam?"

"How come, he asks, how come?" He laughed. "Piped straight out of our whiz-brain computer. Neat, man, real neat." I nodded and he continued, "Now hit us with a sample of the merchandise."

"One of my stories, you mean?"

"Just it, man. But," he leaned over and grasped my arm firmly, "not the one about farts."

"Not farts, Sam," I protested. "Smells."

"Listen, Hernie-Bernie. Don't farts have smells?"

"Not always –" I began, but he would not be interrupted.

"Anyway, they don't interest us. Give us something real solid to impress Mr Numero Uno."

"Mister who?"

"The Deputy Secretary of Culture. Punch through a real mean message, man, and you'll zap Mr One."

"I've got a few possibles lying around. I could bring one round to your flat this evening."

"Sure thing," he said, standing up. "See your face around the place. Back of nine, be on time."

Sylvie wasn't in when I got home. This was lucky, for I was able to get down to choosing a story for Sam. Flipping through my pile of stories I realized how distant I had become from them. Not only had I forgotten the words I put into my characters' mouths but I seemed to have lost even the purpose of those words and had to discover it anew in the context of my narrative. It was a nice feeling. I paused sometimes to smile, sometimes to bite my knuckle. I was moved by my people, these strangers who had once been part of me but were now my grown-up children.

It was going to be difficult to find a story for Sam. On top of the pile was "Dead Certain", a tale that explored the most gentle of erotic expressions: necrophilia. A little below this was "Eyes

Only", in which I had examined the aesthetic reactions of a cannibal to the human body. Would he look upon Michelangelo's David as a banquet, feel short-changed by Venus De Milo, or would he be moved beyond carnality? My stories were indulgences. They were my designs for experiencing an inaccessible world in the only way possible: with words. They were discoveries, not parables. It wasn't going to be easy to find among them something suitable for Sam.

Finally I settled on one called "Double Exposure". I flipped through it and found it trite and dull. Then I began to think of how I had come to write it. Sylvie and I had just moved into our flat. New to high-rise living, I was struck by how it offered intimacy and aloofness at the same time. I didn't, of course, dare talk to my neighbours, still less spy on them, but I wondered what they would say if I offered them some of my thoughts, or how I would react to some of theirs. My head buzzed with hypothetical conversations all day. I read "Double Exposure" again. Remembering how it had come to be and my early troubles with it, I began to warm a little to my tale. It had been written a long time ago and I had grown distant from the person who had written it but it contained, unquestionably, something that was a part of me. There were times when my commitment to the goings-on in my head was so complete that contact with reality was unnecessary and, even, irksome. This characteristic I did not regard as an asset; not, that is, till the nightmare that was to fill all my conscious moments began.

Just as I was putting the sheets of typescript together, Sylvie came in.

"Hern," she said, "Pa upped and walked out of the hospital today."

"What about the special anti-cancer treatment?"

"Told that horrid little specialist where he could put that." Her face became prim and affected, the way my father's did when he was about to make a pronouncement. " 'Your medicaments, my dear fellow, are hardly suitable for the nether end of a water-buffalo, let alone a fellow creature in pain.' Really told him, Pa did." She grinned happily. "It was great to hear Pa talk that way again."

"But what happens now?"

"He swans off on that second honeymoon with Ma." She shrugged. "You know how it is. Keep out the future with the past."

"And then?"

"And then, whatever." She seemed annoyed with me. "The crystal ball I use suffers from voluntary shortsight."

"Where's Pa now?"

"At home and they want to see you before they leave on that trip tomorrow."

As we drove to my parents' home, I told Sylvie what had been happening at Benson's, that I had put in my letter of resignation and that I hoped to get a job with Samson in the Ministry of Culture. She was silent but had a hand on my knee throughout.

"I've got to see Sam later this evening to drop off one of my stories."

As I reversed into the driveway of my parents' house she said, "Life's a smokescreen. Never can tell what's for the best." She took my arm. "I think that Samson is a nasty and can't say I'm thrilled about your spending hours in your room typing, but still . . ."

My mother let us into the living-room which, like the rest of the house, was cluttered with oddments of the most unlikely sort. A papier mâché Buddha sat nonchalantly cross-legged below a print of a wild-eyed Cardigan leading the Light Brigade on their last disastrous charge. Washington pointing the way across an icy Delaware inadvertently indicated the bosom of the Virgin exposing a sacred heart. Rosewood tables huddled in dark corners already occupied by wrought-iron garden seats that had belonged to my grandmother. I never entered without feeling that the room had once been visited by beings who had passed on, leaving behind haphazard evidence of their passage. This feeling was heightened by my mother's use of extremely low-wattage light bulbs, which seemed permanently on the point of going out.

"Pa's in the bedroom," said my mother, leading the way.

My father lay in bed in his street clothes, unaware of how incongruous he looked. He was terribly short of breath, almost gasping, and seemed to have withered away from his clothes. There was in his eyes a wild devil-may-care look that even the dim lighting could not hide. I seemed to have seen that look somewhere recently, then I remembered: it was the look in Lord Cardigan's eyes as he led the men of the Light Brigade to their deaths at Balaclava.

As though his thoughts were in resonance with my own, my father began, "Mine not to reason why, mine not to make reply . . ." He stopped, and managed a spluttered laugh. "You see, my boy, I obey the dictates of my heart, not my head." He gazed fondly at Clara.

"You're off tomorrow, then," I said.

"At the first light of dawn," he said. "The very first."

"Just like we did the day after the wedding," said Clara, a faraway look in her eyes.

"Yes, ma'am," said Fred. "It's going to be just like it was. Taxi up to Mersing, then up the east coast of the peninsula by bus. Whenever possible, that is."

I knew the type of taxicab that ran the eighty-odd miles between Singapore and Mersing. They were antiquated vehicles whose drivers knew little and cared less for the rules of the road. Their attitude, combined with the unpredictable internal (though not always entirely so) combustion processes of the vehicles they drove, made rides in them bumpy enough to disrupt the innards of a person unafflicted by cancer or cytotoxic drugs.

"Marvellous," I said. Then, catching Sylvie's eye, quickly added, "I'm sure you two will have a really marvellous time." I reached out to grasp my father's arm and was shocked at how much of his shirt sleeve I had to squeeze before I reached it.

"Good news for all," chirped Sylvie. "Hern's getting a government job. He's on his way to see Sam Alagaratnam about it."

"I'm glad to see you getting on, Hern," said my father. "Yes, indeed. Seeing you getting on in the world is really a sight for sore eyes."

"You run along whenever you wish, darling," said Sylvie, "I'll catch a cab home."

I kissed my mother and, as always, shook hands with my father. There was an uneasy finality about our actions that I did not like at all. My father was dying but he was doing it all wrong. Death should come upon one in a noisy, brightly-lit house full of baby-smells, children's laughter and the murmurings of lovers. Then a man could make his exit touching, almost sampling, the future he was not going to share. I understood why my father was so anxious to see Sylvie pregnant. What he asked was very small indeed: a tiny fragment of the future to clutch on to as he entered the tunnel of darkness. I started the car and, putting aside such thoughts, slipped it into gear.

I drove around aimlessly for a while, needing time to think before facing Sam. It wasn't fear of what he might say about "Double Exposure" that bothered me. While rereading it had made me dislike the story a little less, I was certainly not proud of it or particularly attached to it. Nor had I any grandiose notions of my literary abilities, or reservations about selling myself. Why then was I so troubled?

Sam lived in an area of luxury condominiums some distance out of the city. This entire district was surrounded by highways on which there was a steady stream of traffic at all times. As I drove round and round the area, I became aware of a single, dim, square headlight in my wing mirror. I made a left turn, which took me back to a road I had already crossed. The light did the same. I ignored it, increased speed and drove round in a huge circle. The motor-cyclist remained with me. In Singapore one is followed only by would-be kidnappers or by the police. I was not rich enough to attract the former and couldn't imagine what there was about me that could be of interest to the law. I have a habit of getting involved with minor distractions when confronted with problems I cannot solve. Rather than let this happen, I turned down my mirror slightly and went back to thinking about Sam.

Once I accepted Sam's job, I was sure I would have to do things I found distasteful. In my writing, I would support causes of which I disapproved, distort reality if my masters wished, suppress truths inimical to their purpose. I suppose this loss of self-respect is what distressed me. It must be something that all whores grappled with. Every prostitute must learn to disentangle temporarily the act from its association. It was simple. I would do the same. But, for the fourth time, I drove by the entrance to Sam's apartment.

Words were more to me than a part of my body which I could

put up for hire and from which I could be temporarily dissociated. They were the instruments with which I explored the world; my organs for tasting and testing it, smelling and sounding it, palpating and plumbing it. With them, I sensed the world and grasped it. They were my antennae and my tentacles. And by joining Sam I was betraying them.

I knew that I must find in words themselves a solution to my problem, or at least some form of compromise. The analogy with prostitutes was a good one. There must be prostitutes who were wives and mothers, who ran families, loved their husbands. Their salvation must lie in an ability to separate in their minds acts which were physically identical. There was a word for what I was thinking of. I entered a box junction to make a right turn and it came to me: compartmentalize. Yes, that was what I would have to do. Compartmentalize my life. I turned into the entrance of Sam's block of apartments. As I did, I saw briefly in my wing mirror the square headlight as motor-cycle and rider flashed past.

I stood outside Sam's door a moment before ringing the door-bell. In my left hand I held my story, with my right I thumbed through its pages slowly, one by one. My head was bowed. I am an atheist, not a Catholic. In my fingers were sheets of paper, not beads. Yet somewhere in the distance I could hear a voice murmuring, "Holy Mary, mother of God, pray for us sinners now and at the hour of our death."

double exposure

As soon as he was awake, Alaga jumped out of bed and rushed to the back room of his flat. The sun hadn't quite risen and powdery puffs of mist clung to the streets that ran in the valleys between high-rise buildings. Most of the windows were dark but the light in her bedroom came on the moment his watch pipped six. She was always on time, woken he was sure by an alarm. The large glass doors slid open and she stepped out on to the little balcony beside her bedroom. She was wearing, as he knew she would be, maroon leotards. It was maroon on the odd days and navy on the even days of the week.

He had been watching her for six months but could not claim to know very much about the girl. This was not surprising. Alaga had never found it necessary to find out about people in their entirety. He was, like many lonely people, content with glimpses of a life and was able, driven by an unerring compassion, to fashion situations from these with which he could involve himself. Getting involved in her early morning exercises called for little effort on Alaga's part. Simply watching her made him breathless and exhausted.

As always, she began with the breathing routines. Standing on tiptoe, her feet widely apart, she inhaled deeply, raising her arms slowly till her palms touched over her head. The thin cotton of her leotards, stretched as tightly as her skin, clung to the curves and creased itself into crevices of her body. She was about a hundred metres away but even the uncertain morning light could not hide the serrations of her ribs, the tiny but

distinct points of her nipples. Her arms were well-rounded,
smooth, creamy. Her hairless armpits, he was sure, would give
out the friendly, sour-sweet smell of overnight sweat. He
thought of fruit-flavoured yoghurt and inhaled deeply. She held
the posture and Alaga held his breath. When he felt he was
about to burst, she began exhaling slowly. Alaga released his
breath in a rush and waited for her to begin her exercises.

He remembered how at first these had puzzled him. They
demanded great strength and muscular control yet possessed the
mysterious rhythms of a ritual. He did not think they were the
kind of thing to be found in the usual books of physical fitness
and was baffled till quite by accident he saw the end of a
television programme on yoga. The next day he bought a book
on the subject.

He watched her getting into the *rajasana* posture. Sitting on
her heels, she leaned backwards until her elbows touched the
ground. Then, supporting herself on their points, she grasped the
backs of her thighs. Tensing her stomach muscles, she gradually
raised hip and thigh, thrusting her pelvis upwards towards the
newly-risen sun. It was impossible to hold the final position for
more than few moments. Alaga could sense the tightness of the
posture, understand why it was called the diamond, share the
trembling pleasure of muscle and tendon stretched to their
limits. Her head was thrown back and her long hair trailed on
the floor. Her breasts were flattened so completely that even her
nipples disappeared into the tautness of the pose. The deep
hollow of her belly emphasized the thrust of her pelvic bones.
Her legs were strong but shapely. Nice legs, thought Alaga, to
have around one's waist . . . or neck.

Yoga over, she bathed and dressed. Then she came out on to
the balcony again and stood there looking around, breathing
deeply, enjoying the air freshened by the sun. He knew she
would smell of soap and talcum powder; that the lipstick, freshly
applied, was thick and a little numbing on her mouth.

In the evenings he watched her do *pranayana* breathing
exercises, after which she would shower and get into bed, snug
in a pool of warm yellow light. At times she read. At others she
would lie daydreaming, making idle patterns in the air with her

hands. She always kept the big glass doors open and he watched over her till she was ready for sleep. Then she would pull the doors together, draw the curtains, turn on the air-conditioner and, finally, turn off the light.

It was as he watched her lying in bed one evening, dreamy and receptive, that Alaga started offering her his thoughts. Sadness, he told her, was a deserted beach at sunset, the tide going out with the sun; happiness, the moment one shared with a shooting star; comfort, the knowledge that death could turn the stuff of our bodies into the scent of frangipani in the graveyard, the freshness of the sea-surf, the promise of the morning breeze. She laughed when he spoke of his collection of pornographic photographs, photographs on to which he had stuck the heads of famous people; Imelda Marcos accommodating Henry Kissinger; a weird and colourful threesome of Maggie Thatcher, Martin Luther King and Ronald Reagan. Yes, he was sure she laughed, covering her mouth with the back of her hand. Touched by her laughter, he giggled a bit himself.

At times, it was clear that something troubled her. She would put aside the book she was reading and toss about in bed, or wander restlessly around the room, spending long periods in the one corner of it that was outside his range of vision. He wondered what was in that corner. Thinking back, he remembered that she occasionally turned towards that corner even in her calm, dreamy moments and seemed to cock an ear in its direction. But what on earth could she be listening to? She got her music from the tiny red radio on her bedside table; Alaga could tell from the rhythmic bobbing of her head whenever she had it on. And no flickering lights originated from the corner to suggest that a television set was housed there. He was baffled.

He hated her periods of agitation. They so interfered with what he had planned to tell her. Instead he was forced to offer her peaceful thoughts: the stillness of the jungle after a rainstorm; the look of an infant peering into its grandmother's face; the silent covenant between the farmer and the earth. He would persist even when she grew uncontrollable, padding about the room like a newly-caged animal, and staying for longer and longer periods in the corner, where his thoughts could not reach her. He persisted because he knew that in the end he would win. She would return to bed and lie quiet in the warmth of her bedside lamp. Shortly after getting to bed, she would close the doors, draw the curtains and turn on the air-conditioner. In minutes the light would go out. He knew her breathing would be quiet and regular as she fell asleep and Alaga, too, would feel tired and a little drowsy. . . .

One evening she was more disturbed than he had ever known her to be. It was a Tuesday and she should have washed her hair but she didn't. Instead she tossed around her bed fully dressed, jumping up now and again to pace the room. Nothing Alaga offered appeared to help her. Then she went into her corner and did not emerge. He willed her out of it, but nothing happened. He begged, offering her all the secret thoughts he had stored in the corners of his mind. She didn't respond. Then his phone rang.

Alaga cursed. The phone was in the living-room, and answering it meant he would have to leave her on her own for a while. He had no friends or family and wondered who could be telephoning him. A wrong number, perhaps. He ignored it, but the ringing wouldn't stop. It interfered with his thinking.

"Is that Mr Alagrajah?"

It was a woman's voice, husky, foreign-sounding. He would have liked to talk to her but was impatient to return to the girl.

"Yes," he said. "Whom am I talking to?"

"You don't know me," said the voice. "My name is Shan, but I prefer to be known as Shanti. Shanti means peace, as you may know."

God, thought Alaga, a crackpot and at a time like this. "Look," he said brusquely, "I'm terribly busy." And hung up.

He returned to his back room.

The girl was pacing the floor now. He could feel her restlessness. She hurled herself on the bed and rolled over and over, pounding the pillows with her hands then with her head. He offered her every image of quiet he possessed, but it was very late in the night before she closed the glass doors and turned off the light.

His telephone was ringing as he let himself into the flat the following evening.

"Prince Charming," she said. "Peace."

"It's Shanti, I suppose," he said. She was a crackpot but persistent and he did not try to conceal that he was pleased to hear from her again. "Peace and Shanti I can understand, but what's the Prince Charming bit about?"

"Your name, silly."

"My name?" He puzzled over it for a bit. "Alaga" was Tamil for beautiful and "rajah" was a ruler. Then he got it. "Clever," he said. "And really quite nice. You're a Tamil scholar, are you?"

"Oh, no," she said. "Just a few words here and a few words there. And a dash of Sanskrit." She paused. "But I'm crazy about India, and anything Indian really."

"You're not Indian yourself?"

"No." She sounded sad. "I'm a Singaporean Chinese. My name is really Lu Shan, but I think of myself as Shanti."

A real odd-ball, thought Alaga, but he said: "Quaint, very quaint. Have you been to India?"

"Several times. Have you?"

"Never," said Alaga.

"It's a marvellous place," said Shan. "I first went ten years ago, just after finishing school."

So she was in her middle-twenties, Alaga reckoned, as he asked, "What's so wonderful about India?"

Shanti told him.

She spoke of a land of contrasts and contradictions, a land she had first visited when she was little more than a girl. She talked of the thread of Hindu culture that ran through and united it, but was forever weaving tapestries on the side, which were as beautiful as they were at variance with the main pattern. She waxed long on a religion that identified in its gods, Brahma, Siva and Vishnu, the primary forces of consciousness, change and preservation, then gave them a thousand names and human faces so they were the more easily worshipped. She told him of how she had travelled the land, often on foot, of how she had been warm beside a lingam of solid ice in a Himalayan cave.

She spoke of Kannya Kumari, where the land ended and one could see sunset and moonrise on the same horizon, and seeing this had come to understand that pain and solace, frustration and fulfilment were possible in the same moment.

Alaga was fascinated by what she said but couldn't avoid noticing that she mixed short Singapore vowels with sighing Indian ones, bit off her consonants while rolling her r's, and it was this that made her speech sound foreign.

She paused, out of breath, laughed at herself and said, "I'm sorry. Once I get started I never know when to stop."

"Not at all," said Alaga. "I'd like to hear more."

"Can I call you tomorrow, then?"

"Sure. About the same time."

"Thanks," she said. "Goodnight, Prince Charming."

"Peace," he said, laughing into the phone, pleased at his new-found jocularity.

He wandered about his flat before going to the back room. He was afraid that his absence might have upset the girl, but he need not have worried. She was lying in bed holding up a book. She wasn't reading, though he could see she was untroubled. It wasn't very long before she drew the curtains and turned off the light. The next morning she did her yoga with a vigour that made Alaga sweat. She held the diamond and camel postures and ended with the *vrksasana*, or tree posture, which necessitated standing on her head.

In the evening Shanti called and talked to him about Indian temples. By the time she had finished and he could get to the back room the curtains were drawn.

The pattern of his days was now fairly established. In the early mornings he saw the girl through her yoga exercises. In the evenings he talked to Shanti. By the time he and Shanti had finished, the girl was usually in bed. He sometimes feared that his long conversations with another person might disturb the girl, but this did not seem to be the case. In fact she appeared generally calmer. It had been a long time since she had padded around restlessly or tossed about her bed. Perhaps, thought Alaga, the more vigorous yoga exercises she appeared to be doing kept her more tranquil.

Shanti and Alaga talked every day and Alaga began to feel that he knew her quite well. Not that she told him details about herself or discussed her personal problems with him. On the contrary, by a tacit understanding reached early in their relationship, they avoided talking about their day-to-day life. This, peculiarly, increased the degree of their intimacy and gave them a freedom that was impossible even in the closest of ordinary friendships. As their relationship grew, Alaga felt increasingly the need to tell Shanti about the girl. With this need was born the idea that Shanti and the girl were in fact the same person.

The thought was so bizarre that he first refused to acknowledge it. It was all this chat about Vishnu having "countless visages and countless eyes, countless astonishing forms" that was going to his head. He tried to put it out of his mind but could not. An idle thought became a suspicion; the suspicion a certainty. But even certainties needed to be tested and he would have to do this without exposing himself.

He could have asked her the direction her bedroom faced, the colour of bedsheets she favoured or the time she had gone to bed the previous night, but this kind of inquiry would have sounded unnatural in the normal course of their conversation. Then he thought about yoga. He knew he would have to be very careful.

"What do I think about yoga?" she repeated. "Why, I'm all for it."

"You don't find any contradiction," he asked, "between Hindu asceticism and yoga, which is so terribly physical?"

"Not at all," she said. "The *Gita* brings them very nicely together." She began chanting: "The body is my chariot, the five senses are my steeds, the intellect is my rein, but I AM THE CHARIOTEER."

"Do you practise yoga?" he asked, ashamed at his duplicity.

"Every morning," she said. "As soon as I get up."

"You do?" he laughed. "Where?"

"On my bedroom balcony. Why?"

"Nothing." Surely she would notice the tightness in his throat when he asked, "I guess you have to get into a special outfit for yoga, like they do for Tai Chi?"

"Not at all," she said. "I do my yoga in leotards." She laughed. "I'm quite vain really. Maroon leotards on Mondays, Wednesdays and Fridays. Navy on . . ."

This should have been enough but it wasn't. Leotards were worn commonly for yoga exercises and maroon and navy were the most popular colours. And where else could one better exercise than on a bedroom balcony in the morning? He had to meet her to be sure.

"Do you feel we should never meet?" he asked.

"Yes."

"Why?"

"I don't know," she said. "I'm just afraid it will spoil things."

"I'm not a hunchback or a harelip, you know," he said.

"Oh, I'm sure you're quite handsome, Prince Charming."

"And I'm certain you're beautiful." He thought of the strong, shapely legs, the porcelain arms, the clean armpits, the long black hair tied up or flowing free. "You must be," he said, a tiny rasp in his voice.

"I'm not bad," she said and giggled.

Every time they talked he brought up the subject of their meeting.

"Aren't you happy with things as they are?" she asked. "With just talking to me?"

"Not quite," he muttered.

"Why?"

"I would like to picture you as we talk. To know whether your eyebrows go up or down when you say 'Why'."

"But surely that doesn't matter," she said.

"You may consider such things to be *maya*, but illusion or not, they matter to me." He introduced a pleading note to his voice which he hoped disguised the threat. "I find it more and more difficult to talk to you without imagining you at the same time, Shanti."

"I see," she said and sighed. "I'm so frightened we'll spoil everything."

"I tell you what," he said. "Why don't you arrange to be

at some place where I can see you without your seeing me?"

"Oh, no," she laughed. "I'm curious about my Prince Charming, too."

Finally they agreed to meet in the coffee-house of a hotel. They synchronized their watches the evening before, decided on the exact table, described the details of what they would be wearing. They both knew all this was unnecessary.

He watched her from behind a pillar as she came in. She was lovely. Beautiful arms, a perfect face, her long hair in a pony-tail, which she tended to toss.

He stepped forward and she said, "Alaga?"

"Lu Shan," he said.

They shook hands. It was awkward but there seemed to be no other greeting they could use. He was surprised to find himself ordering beer. He didn't like alcohol.

She wasn't late, but for want of something to say apologized. "It's difficult to get a taxi at this hour."

He agreed. "It's never easy in town these days."

They laughed, resigned to the problems of city dwellers. She pulled out a crumpled pack of cigarettes which looked long-neglected, then fished around in her handbag for a lighter. It was out of gas. He lit her cigarette from a book of matches on the table.

"They're bad for you," he commented.

"I know," she agreed. "But so difficult to give up." She was seized with a fit of coughing because she had tried to talk and smoke at the same time.

It wasn't, they agreed, the best coffee-house in town.

"The service is slow."

"And the food's not really worth waiting for."

"But expensive."

"It's conveniently central, I suppose.

"And therefore always crowded."

"*Ciao*," she said as they parted.

"Will I see you again?"

She shrugged. "*Que sera*," she said, turning on a coy half-smile.

Back in his flat, Alaga paced up and down his bedroom

looking for the source of his discontent. He was not disappointed by her looks and he knew that she was quite attracted by his. There had been awkwardness, of course, but what could one expect from a first meeting? And it was natural to pretend a bit.

It was getting dark and a bit stuffy so he drew open the bedroom curtains to let in the last of the daylight. Opposite was a new block of flats, which was just beginning to be occupied.

A girl sat at a dressing-table brushing her long blond hair. she struggled with the ends where the knots were, then smoothed the whole with slow strokes. Alaga saw her hair begin to glow. He looked closer and wondered whether it was true that blond hair threw off sparks when it was brushed.

In the bedroom of a nearby flat a girl thumbed through a directory. She looked under S. S was for Siva. Siva the destroyer, Siva the creator, Siva the god of change.

She found a name that she liked. She looked shyly across the room. In the corner hidden from the big glass door a telephone sat on the floor and looked back at her . . . invitingly.

eight

"Neat and sweet, your little treat," said Sam, looking up suddenly.

He had for the past half-hour been going through my story. He had thumbed through the pages, held them up to the light, looked at them side-on, smelled them, flipped through them rapidly from front to back, and then from back to front.

"What treat, Sam . . . ?" I began.

"Now Sammy ain't the boy to say no to a compliment and," he waved the sheets of paper around, "I sure got me a bare-arsed one staring me right in the face."

"I don't quite get you?"

"You can play baby-bottom innocent with me, Hernie chile, but I savvy who our hero gets his moniker from." He tapped his head several times.

"Oh, the name Alagarajah, you mean."

"Sure, baby. As close as you can get to Alagaratnam without scraping paint from the boat's bottom." He jerked his head obliquely several times and winked wildly. "But still a very nice com-pli-ment, Hern, very nice indeedy." He took a long draught from his glass of whisky.

I sat on a deep leather settee in Sam's large and luxurious living-room. There were several thick carpets on the floor and more hung on the walls. They muffled both sound and light and made me feel I was participating in an underwater film sequence. This effect was heightened by the illumination, which came from hidden sources in the ceiling and was dim, except for a bright sliver of light emerging from Sam's half-open bedroom door on the far side of the room.

As soon as I had come in Sam had snatched "Double Exposure" from me and pressed into my hands, as though in exchange, a half-full glass of whisky.

"Whisky," he said.

"I don't want to be difficult Sam, but I'm not very fond –"

"Royal Salute," he declared, indicating an elaborate, deep-blue porcelain bottle on the table. "The best money or love can buy, so don't you be shy. With ice," he added, popping two cubes into my glass.

He had then flopped into an odd-looking chair opposite me, turned on some mechanism which caused it to vibrate gently and set to work on my story. He drank heavily as he read and had refilled his glass three times in the space of fifteen minutes.

"Apart from my little compliment to you," forcing myself not to smile, I managed to look convincingly sheepish, "what do you think of my little story?"

"Remember, Hern, I said we wanted you to punch through a real mean message and, sure as truth hurts yore arse this –"he flipped quickly back to the title-page – "this 'Double Exposure' of yours just ain't sharp enough. I hear you, man. I sure do, but Sammy's a literary freak, baby. A word wallah, a dicto prickto." He took a large swallow of whisky. "Now, your man-in-the-street," he laughed and drank more whisky, "your Mr Low Ai Kew, he won't get it. He needs it single wavelength and laser bright. No double-talk, no double-think. Like no allusions, man. Just straight down the line. I get your message, baby. I get it loud and clear: Peeping Toms don't get girls. Right? I get it, I get it. But your Low Ai Kew, he can't get it no more than swallowing spunk can get a girl pregnant.

Earlier that evening I had decided to organize my life, to sequester it such that the contents of one compartment did not leak into another. Many people did this. In fact, everyone, to some extent, must. Living would be impossible if one didn't. Each compartment had its dimensions and its rules. I had accepted that I had to get used to Sam's ways, even when I disapproved of them. I had steeled myself to the idea of my work being misinterpreted and misused. But I had not prepared myself for total incomprehension.

It was a few moments before I said, "I see," and reached for my whisky. I took a larger sip of it than I intended, choked, and had a fit of coughing that brought tears to my eyes.

"You see and see good, bright-eyes," said Sam, leaning forward, his eyeballs bulging. They seemed larger and more protuberant than usual, the veins that crisscrossed their whites swollen to the point of rupture. I stared fascinated, taking in their tiny details, incapable of looking away. Then something very odd began happening. Sam's eyes seemed rhythmically to become larger, then smaller. Large, small. Large, small. Large, small. I couldn't believe it was actually happening: Sam was trying to hypnotize me. He was practising some obscure technique of persuasion he had picked up in the course of his work. But that was impossible. The thought was too absurd for words. I had simply drunk more whisky than I was accustomed to and had been upset by Sam misunderstanding my story. Yes, I was tired, unhappy and slightly drunk. I shook my head and leaned back against the settee. Now Sam's whole face seemed to advance and recede. I shut my eyes. I had to make sure that what appeared to be happening was not doing so entirely inside my head. I opened my eyes and the truth hit me. Sam had, without my noticing, altered the mechanism of his chair so that, instead of gently vibrating, he now oscillated bodily backwards and forwards.

I leaned further back, removing myself as much as I could from the effects of his chair, and said, "You tell me exactly what you want, Sam, and I'll do my best to deliver."

"Snap," he said, drifting backwards. "Did I say, your average man, Mr Low Ai Kew, won't understand your stories, Hernie? Why, even my supremo . . ."

"Your who?"

"My supremo, man, the deputy minister," he explained curtly. "Why, even my supremo won't read your vibes, baby. Lookit, man," he switched the chair back to its vibratory motion, "the supremo's a five-sided square when it comes to books. If he gets through the title credits of *Dallas*, boyyo, he's had a hard day's night reading."

He stared around the room slowly, stopping to peer into its darker corners as though looking for eavesdroppers. He seemed uneasy, afraid he had said too much. Finally his eyes wandered back to the table and came to rest on the bottle of whisky. He picked it up and pointed it in my direction. I shook my head. He filled his glass.

"You keep what I say to yourself, you hear. You keep it to yourself and you keep it real tight. Tighter than a polecat's arse."

"Sure, Sam," I nodded.

He tapped my story. "Some instant small-print changes needed here." He sipped whisky. "Knocking Martin Luther King is fine, man, sweet as a sundae. But squeezing the piss out of Dr Kissinger and First Lady Marcos," he shook his head, "that's taboo, man, a no-entry zone and as out-of-bounds as the reverend mother's twat. See why, Hern? They's our buddies, man. That's why. And," he held up a finger, "rule one in our outfit: we don't knock our buddies. But," he shrugged, "no sweat. We'll change that to some old shit-softie like Gandhi or Mother Theresa." He chuckled at the thought before continuing, "One more thing, don't make my funny-bone tingle, man."

"And what's that, Sam?"

"The title, Hernie, the title. Don't dig it no more than I dig my grave." As though to emphasize his disapproval, he altered the mechanism of the chair so his head jerked from side to side.

"Oh. What's wrong with it?"

"Too confusing, baby. Mixed-up like. Could be sugar, could be spice. Could be things that ain't too nice." He fiddled with a dial on his chair and his head began to bounce and wobble the way an Indian dancer's does. "You and I, Hern, we geddit. But we're word turds, man. For us it's slam, bam, I understan'. Peeping Tom sees girl one from back-room window. Zap, single exposure." His head jerked once sharply. "Then Peeping Tom sees girl two from bedroom window, zap — ahrap, double exposure." His head jerked twice. "But will Mr Loh Ai Kew and," he rolled his eyes heavenwards, "the powers that be, figure it out? No way, Hern. No fist-fornicating way."

"What d'you think we should do, Sam?"

"Get yourself a new song title, man." He put up a hand. "Hold on to your heartbeats, boysies, Sammy's creating." His head wobbled silently for about half a minute, then he screamed, " 'Peeping Doesn't Pay'. Geddit, baby? Alliteration and all. And will it slip smoothly into our crime-prevention programme? Like a red-hot dick into a creamed pussy, it will."

"You've lost me, Sam," I said. "What has crime prevention to do . . .?"

"Get off your tortoiseshell, buster, and buy yourself a skate-board. Crime doesn't pay. Geddit?"

Before I could, the door to Sam's bedroom opened and a girl walked out.

Her entrance was less surprising than her beauty. She was South Indian and dark, darker in fact than most Tamils, but there was a redness underlying her skin which gave it a burnished quality. Even in that dimly-lit room, its radiance was evident. Her eyes were black but bright, almost unnaturally so. Scintillating, they made highlights against the glow of her face. The most striking feature about her, however, was her mouth. It was unpainted and a darkish orange, full and soft, perfectly shaped yet pliant. Slightly open, it hinted of sweet, secret places within. She was wearing a short white bathrobe. Her hair was turbaned in a bright green towel.

"Nuit, meet my –" Samson began.

"Anuita," she said firmly. "My name is Anuita."

"I dig Nuit better," laughed Sam. "Swings more easily with *nuit d'amour* and Frenchie things. But this here crêpe Suzette licks," he guffawed and slapped his thigh, "yeah, man, she sure licks anything. She licks anything French, I mean." Choking on his mirth, he wiped the tears from his eyes. "Yeah, Hernie baby, she'll blow you to kingdom come and come again so many times, you'll feel like somebody pulled the pillow out of your pillowcase."

"Hello, Hernie," said Anuita, smiling at me across the table. "I know so much about you, it feels like we've met."

I shared that feeling. There was something terribly familiar about her and I could not fathom why this should be. I had certainly not seen her before. I would have remembered if I had. Memories of this kind of beauty are not easily mislaid.

My bewilderment must have been obvious because, laughing,

she said, "I feel I know you because I handle your file at the office and you know me because we've talked on the phone."

Of course. This was the sweet voice that answered the phone whenever I called Sam at work. I looked up and smiled acknowledgement. She smiled back, opening her mouth wide, revealing small, white teeth and behind these the richer, darker reds of her throat. There was something about her mouth that was soft and warm, comfortable and safe. There was also a sweetness about it that I could almost taste. Perhaps it was simply the sweetness of her voice: honey poured into my ear dripping on to my tongue. She came round the table and before sitting on the settee beside me offered me her hand. I had a wild urge to lick it.

"Nuit . . ." Sam began, then, quickly correcting himself, said: "Anuita is one of Sammy's little discoveries." He nodded several times. "Screw me blue if just two years ago, night-of-love here was not just a simple-as-a-pimple messenger-girl, fetchin' and carryin', carryin' and fetchin'. You name it, she got it: the post, memos, the coffee, the blame . . . And her background? Ess-eff-ay." He snapped his fingers three times. "Out of school with one O-level, father buggered on the booze, mother buggered on the streets.

"Then bright-eyed Sammy spies her in his headlights." He drank up the whisky in his glass. "Hey, presto! One touch of his magic wand," his head wobbled lewdly and he winked several times, "and Cinderella's walking shoes grow stiletto heels. She stops moving her sweet arse from office to office and parks it in my secretary's chair. She got talent, Hern. She got one big talent. She sure knows what Sammy wants."

Anuita leaned forward, picked up the bottle of whisky and poured a generous amount into Sam's glass. "Teamwork and co-operation, Hern. That's the name of the game. You scratch my itchy spots and I'll scratch yours."

"I see, Sam," I said. Then, trying to sound more enthusiastic than I felt, added, "I think I am beginning to get a clearer picture of things."

"Up, up, up," he shouted suddenly. I was looking around the room for whatever it was that required us to be on our feet, when Sam continued, "The hour's up, man. One is all I get. One measly hour is all the orthopædist allows me on this gizmo. Says I'll shake my spinal joints loose if I go on longer." He turned off a switch and the chair shuddered to a stop. "Anuita will give you the lowdown on how the office swings while I grab me a shower." He stood up and downed his drink. "I'll dig out some stuff I punched out on the night of the full moon." He grinned. "Inspired, like. Show you the kinda line we put out at the ministry." He turned to Anuita. "Swinging guy is our Hernie, but needs to be more on the ball and up the beat."

He left the room.

Alone with Anuita, I was a tangle of conflicting emotions. Looked at coldly, she was no better than a whore. Rather worse, in fact, for the circumstances leading to her prostitution were less compelling than those which led most women into the trade. Moreover, the extent of her subjugation to Sam and the degree of humiliation she accepted was certainly more than the average street-walker would tolerate. Nevertheless, she attracted me very much. And I was certain my feelings were reciprocated. I began to see her more as a victim than a predator, one whose plight was not unlike my own. Perhaps she too had compartmentalized her life. Perhaps there were areas of it I could come to share.

She smiled, holding her mouth open for my inspection, before saying, "I'm just trying to think if there's anything about you that I don't know."

"What on earth do you mean by that?"

She laughed, throwing her head back. Her bathrobe fell slightly open and the smell of her body reached me. It was a strange fragrance, complex and tantalizing: a mixture of flowers and sweat, pollen and dew, incense and old wood. A rush of memories clamoured for attention. With an effort I shook them off and concerntrated on what she was saying.

"You're on our computer, Hern." The sweet voice changed to the monotonous falsetto of a robot but her eyes continued to laugh. "Hernando Perera. D.o.b: 2 November 1953. Parents: Frederick; Clara née Klass."

"Very good," I said, looking straight down her neck. She leaned slightly forward, acknowledging a compliment as she allowed me a better view of her breasts.

"See. There's nothing I don't know or remember. Samson didn't mention memory among my talents. I'm what goes between him and the computer." The laughter left her face and she added, "I'm also what goes between him and the mattress. I'm very convenient too. He doesn't have to remember what buttons to press. I come on to spoken instructions."

Embarrassed by these revelations, I took a tiny sip of whisky and said, "Samson seems to be able to handle quite a lot of this stuff."

"He drinks a lot," she said flatly. She wrinkled her nose. "But I don't touch it. The smell makes me sick. But then, Sam has his reasons. He's worried."

"What about?"

"You must have heard about these so-called streetpapers that are turning up all over the place."

"Yes."

"The great Samson Alagaratnam has been given the task of unearthing the main culprit and stopping him. If he can't do this fast enough, he's got to design counter-measures to neutralize the effect of the streetpapers."

"But what has this kind of thing to do with the Ministry of Culture? I'd have thought it was a routine police matter or, at most, something the Special Branch would be interested in."

She laughed, throwing her head back. But there was a bitter edge to her amusement. "Oh, Hernie, you poor, poor thing! Did you not realize that culture is a matter of security?" She straightened her face into a mock seriousness but her eyes continued to laugh. "Did they never tell you that on this island paradise of ours trade is a matter of security, education is a matter of security, health is a matter of security, how you wash your underwear is a matter of security. As Samson would put it, 'In which sand dune you bin hidin' yore head, honey-chile?'" She rocked back and forth on the settee.

I was quiet for a while, then asked, "How would he go about making the streetpapers ineffective?"

"Simple," she said. "We run our own streetpaper. Swamp the market with it. We'll make outrageous, impossible, dangerous suggestions. Create a bit of violence here, a bit of racial trouble there, and no one will pick up a page of typescript from the streets if you paid them to. It's easy." She patted my hand. It was a leisurely gesture and she maintained contact longer than was absolutely necessary. "That's where you, my little innocent, come in."

"Me?" I asked horrified. "What can I do about all this?"

"Write," she said. "Samson needs someone who can churn out words. You can." She was unsmiling, her face devoid of expression. She put her hand on mine and, this time, left it there. "You poor, lost boy. Relax. There's nothing you can do about it, anyway."

"But isn't that just what the person behind these streetpapers wants?" I asked. "Something that will keep up interest, maintain a sort of dialogue?"

"I see," she said. "You read the very first of the streetpapers. The one that appeared in the Orchard Road area on the evening of the 16th." She sighed. "No. We're not going to give them what they want. What we're going to do is discredit them. Produce such strong counter-currents that they are submerged. The people want streetpapers, the government will give them streetpapers. Ours."

"Aren't you going to try and find who's behind it all?"

"In due course," she said. She took her hand off mine and leaned back on the settee. The movement caused a wave of her body smell to crash against me. "Samson's in charge. And you know Samson. If he can't get the real cuprits, he'll find substitutes."

"Substitutes?' I asked, my voice rising. "What d'you mean by substitutes?"

"Scapegoats," she said, her face bland. "People we've wanted to get for a long time."

"Innocent people?"

"Sure. At least, innocent of producing streetpapers, but maybe guilty of other things."

"Other things like what, Anuita?"

"Does it matter?"

"This is crazy." I shook my head. "It's simply impossible to believe."

Her face softened and she was quiet for a while. Then she spoke, emphasizing every word. "Dear, sweet, self-centred boy, living in your lofty and ivory tower, believe me." She looked towards the bedroom door and dropped her voice a fraction. "Have you noticed that you are being followed?"

I would have liked to laugh at her, to dismiss the absurdity of Hernie Perera being trailed because he was politically dangerous but I remembered the dim, square headlight in my wing mirror. "Perhaps I have . . . But what on earth for?"

"I suppose just to give you a clean bill of health. I hope so." She shrugged, "Routine surveillance, we term it. One never knows though what that kind of thing can unearth. Anyway it's policy to know a little more about the people who work for us than they think we do." Her voice dropped further. "There's always two of them. One on a motor-scooter and one on foot." She touched my arm lightly with the tips of her fingers. "Whatever you do, don't . . . don't let on you are aware of them." She tried to smile but her facial muscles pulled in contrary directions and she looked as though she was about to cry.

"Why are you telling me all –"

"Clean and not so mean, that's your Sammy out of the steam," said Samson emerging from the bedroom. He held a fresh bottle of whisky, which he was opening. Under his arm was a sheaf of typescript. He put the bottle down beside its fellow and handed me the paper. "You take a gander at these," he said.

"Some pieces I dashed off. No fancy brushwork, man, but upbeat. Way, way upbeat. You'll dig it when you meet the beat. Just open wide, hang loose and let it grab you."

"Thanks," I said, taking the sheets.

"Soft, mood music mostly," he said, pouring himself a drink from the newly-opened bottle. "But note, and note well, that under the sweet sounds are facts, hard facts, realities every sod-arsed citizen must dig. Tough truths the wet, pussy-soft types avoid." His voice had risen and his eyes bulged. His breath came in short gasps. Then suddenly his shoulders slackened. He flopped into his chair and gazed longingly at the controls. "Sixty goddarned minutes and they just whiz by in this contraption. Maybe when Hern's gone, cock-a-doodle here and I can spend a few minutes in it . . . together." He laughed and rolled his eyes about in mock ecstasy. "But we got to chew the fat a bit before the *nuit d'amour* can begin."

"I'll go," said Anuita, getting up.

"Sit." He snapped. "Nail your sweet-moving tail to the seat and both of you hear what Sammy has to say. And hear good."

"You want to fly, right, Hern?" He banged the table to confirm I did, then continued. "And you want to fly high?" He banged the table again. "Now nobody, not a liquored-up single-winged mosquito, gets off the ground without our express, made-to-measure permission. You hear that, Hern?"

"Right," I said quickly, but too late to prevent a further thump on the table.

"And there ain't no way we can give permission to folk we don't trust, now is there? Now is there, you tell me, boys and girls?" A hideous look of self-righteousness crossed his face.

"We get all this high-fartin' talk about freedom for all fliers, right? You just take one teensy, cross-eyed peep at what would happen if we let every chickeroo with wings fly."

"What?" I asked.

"You'll get all the phoney Tonys who yack about press freedom, individual's rights and all that crap swinging in. There'll be yobos yelling for independent trade unions, lecherous lizzies bending arse-over-tit screeching women's lib, punks who don't know what sex they are let alone the colour of their hair knocking our fighting defence policy. We just have to let one little crack appear, boyyo, and the castle comes a tumblin' down."

"Oh," I said, contrite.

"Yeah," he snarled. "You allow that kindda crap in and you'll get shit under your fingernails and piss in your mouthwash." His face softened and he looked down into his glass sadly. "Yeah, man, if we let those screwballs loose they'll be jamming our networks with talk about world peace, protection of the underprivileged and cat's shit like that. Slime stinkeroo that will make us zoom to our doom." He dipped his finger into his glass then sucked it. He repeated the process and pointed his finger towards Anuita. She leaned forward dutifully and took it into her mouth. I thought I felt her shudder as she did.

I stared blankly ahead and asked, "I don't quite get how this concerns me, Sam?"

"Maybe you don't listen good, Hern, 'cause you sure don't hear good. The chief will want to know if we can trust this Hernie Perera. If we can be sure he won't turn out to be some kind of nut who'll skewer his arse over human rights or press freedom. We gotta be sure this here Hernie Perera is on our side, a guy who'll dip his hand into the bucket to hurl shit for us. Geddit?"

"You can vouch for me, Sam."

"Sure, boyyo, sure. But Sam's not everybody. There's dudes that need proof. Not just the numbers but live, swinging, humdingeroo acts to go with them."

"I really don't know what I can do, Sam. To convince your people of my good faith, I mean."

He leaned forward. There was a strange look in his eye, one I had never seen before. It took me a moment to realize it was amazement.

"You really got about as much knowhow as a nun in a whorehouse." He shook his head in disbelief.

It was the second time that evening that my naïvety had caused comment. I was about to protest when he raised his hand, silencing me.

"Right. Sammy wants you to jive with the group, so mammy's boy will guide yore feet, to the beat. Here's like it is. Maybe you know some big guy, some ride-over-'em-all dude in Benson's who's talking ungovernment stuff, some Mr Big who thinks he should be given a crack at the wheel, like. Now –"

"But the top-brass of Benson's don't confide in me, Sam. They don't talk politics to me . . ."

"There you trip again, fall on your arse faster than a whore on heat," he said, shaking his head. "You gotta get it out of them, man, sweat for it. You gotta tickle 'em to talk, Hernie baby. You find this cat, who don't like us, this big smasheroo who thinks he can do better, like, come the elections, then you scratch up the dirt about him. Maybe Mr Big likes sticking it into the office girls or, better still, the office boys. You give us the lowdown on the cat. If what Hernie gives us is not on our computer, Hernie's in."

"But what if I can't find anything?"

"Now, now," he wagged a finger at me, "we don't play with grousing-and-whining and I-can't-see-the-sun-shining types. What's more, Sammy's gotta lot of heavy loving skedooled."

He leaned across the table, put his hand into the top of Anuita's bathrobe and fondled a breast. She sat absolutely still. When he removed his hand, she leaned over, poured some whisky into a glass and drank it straight down. She did not bother to adjust the robe, which had fallen partly open.

"Now git," said Samson, standing up. "Even you gotta see that ladybird here's got a pussy-pie a-crackin' with heat."

I did not notice if I was followed as I drove home. I was too busy with my thoughts.

Both Sam and Anuita had seen me as an innocent, unaware of the way the system worked. This was not absolutely true. Cloistered in the furniture department of Benson's, I had managed to insulate myself from what went on around me. Now, forced by circumstances to throw in my lot with Sam and his people, I realized that my insulation was not enough to protect me from an awareness I found extremely disagreeable. I had decided to compartmentalize my life, to live in sealed rooms that had no communicating doors. But words made this impossible. They crept like mildew along the walls, spreading from one room to the other, connecting them.

As proof of my trustworthiness, Sam was asking for a betrayal. I could not uncouple that word from the myths of my childhood: the kiss in the garden, the thirty pieces of silver, the agony on the cross . . . Nor could I disconnect it from the degradation that results from viewing another person's life as a piece of merchandise.

I dislike moralizing, as it usually leads me nowhere, and quickily wearied of these thoughts, but I could not sleep. Rather than toss about and risk waking Sylvie, I picked up the manuscript Sam had pressed upon me. The typewriting was flawless. It had obviously come off a word processor. The first piece was called "Heat".

Heat. Seeped through the walls around him. From the floor below him. No. The floors below him. This was a high-rise. One of the first built by the government but still good. Good? Maybe just serviceable. No escape from the . . . heat. Clothes. Nearly all off. Sitting in sweat-stained chair. Staring out of window. Collapsing. Drying up. Collapsing. Staring at open windows opposite where other people sit. Collapsing. Sails without a breeze . . .

Not bad the flat, they said. Two bedrooms only but not bad. And cheap. You can make monthly repayments easily. Easily. No sweat, they said. Sweat. Running into eyes. Into groin. Stinging, stinging sweat. You work hard, they say. You study hard, they say. Get qualifications then get better job, they say. But how to study with sweat stinging your eyes. Use fan. Fan only turns the same heat round and round. Round and round. Must get air-con. With air-con can study. But where to find money for air-con? Study and get qualifications, they say. Then you earn more. Then you can buy air-con. They say.

So it went, on and on. I knew the kind of stuff that Sam wrote. I had hoped that reading it would put me to sleep. But there was too little in this to engage my interest. Too little to tire me and bring on drowsiness. I turned to the last page.

The heat of revolution moved our leaders. Hot they were against colonialists, communists, communalists, chauvinists, conservationists. Yes, how hot they were. No housing estates then. Just slums. Slums, everywhere you turned. Slums. Dark huts. No electricity. No water. Children living like pigs. With pigs. No running water. Just filth.

He looked out of the window and thought of the heat of the leaders. Heat of anger. Anger against the colonialists. Anger against the slums. He thought of the struggle. Their struggle. Marches in the sun, all dressed in white, untouched by heat. Their heat made them not fear the revenge of the communists. Their heat made them sacrifice themselves for the nation's sake. As he thought these thoughts, a warmth began inside him. Slowly, steadily. Increasing bit by bit. First the heat inside him balanced the heat outside, then it drove it away. Suddenly he felt cool. Very cool. Thinking of the heat of the leaders. Thinking of their struggles, he felt cool. No need for air-con, now.

I put the last page down with the rest.

Sam had began writing this kind of thing when we were in our teens. At university he had become the editor of several magazines for the express purpose of getting his work published. I began thinking of our youth, hoping thereby to summon some warmth for the man. Instead of pleasant memories, I remembered the time we had visited a brothel together.

We were on holiday. The brothel, in southern Thailand, was well-known for the vast numbers of girls and boys it employed and it boasted that it catered for all sexual tastes and perversity. We were obviously tourists and looked fairly inexperienced. The brothel-keeper, a kindly soul, asked us to make our selection from the dozen or so girls who hung about the waiting-room. They looked terribly young, but, nodding sagely, the man assured us that they were experienced professionals.

Sam picked the youngest-looking girl in the group. She seemed not much more than twelve, sweet-faced but terribly thin, her breasts making tiny points in her cotton dress. I remember her well, laughing, chattering, moving her little blue-veined hands about wildly, the bird-brisk gestures of childhood still part of her. Half an hour later she returned to the room screaming and stomping about. Tears streamed from her eyes, snot from her nose. It wasn't the tears I remember, it was her indignation. She screeched at the brothel-keeper in Thai, rage and weeping interrupting her tirade. He, poor man, tried to placate her with more money. She flung the notes he offered her on to the floor, then extracting from her bodice the money she had already been paid, flung this down as well. We could hear her angry chattering long after she left the room. I never dared ask Sam what he had done or had wanted to do that caused such offence.

Remembering the Thai child-prostitute I thought of Anuita: the radiant, fragrant skin, the unlikely orange lips, the heavy breasts under the bathrobe. The lust that stirred in me was quickly joined by compassion. I wondered what Sam would be doing to her? I was sure I had not seen the full repertoire of his mechanical chair and couldn't imagine the contraptions he might have in the bedroom. The prostitute could return the money and walk out, but what could Anuita do? Would she be able to return to her job as a messenger-girl or was she inextricably snared? Poor girl. Poor Anuita. Pity swelled in me. It included the Thai prostitute, it included myself. I too was a victim of Sam's. Once I was accepted, my loyalty proven, there would be no escape. I hadn't thought about what I would do to prove it. I could not think of someone worth betraying. Until I did, my bondage was deferred. This thought did not bring me any relief. I needed Sam's job. And somewhere in the back of my mind I knew I did have something to sell. I simply refused to look at what it was.

nine

I arrived at Benson's late.

The news of my resignation had quickly got around. As manager of the furniture department, I had kept a distance between the staff and myself and had always been excessively formal in my dealings with them. Now that formality was no longer necessary, I expected an easy familiarity to develop between us. This was not the case. Ahmad, particularly, had become not merely distant but distinctly cold. He treated me like a stranger, a customer almost, and once or twice I thought he was about to tell me the price of the piece of furniture I was looking at.

Chuang, too, seemed changed and was no more his bustling self. He drifted into the department several times in the course of the day but offered no suggestions as to how things could be improved. From time to time he touched a piece of furniture or a bale of fabric, the way one does the shoulder of a friend in trouble.

"Just gazing to and fro, Perera," he would say if he caught my eye, but he tried to avoid doing so.

He muttered a good deal under his breath and shook his head often as though in disavowal. There was something he wanted to tell me but he seemed unable to find the courage to do so.

Finally he came up to my desk, put his hand on my shoulder and said, "Perera, too sorry I feel about final breakdown." He shook his head. "I try and try but only get twenty thousand. Only twenty thousand dollars, Perera."

"Twenty thousand dollars for what, Chuang?"

"For you, Perera. That's all they release."

I was stunned. "For me? What for?"

"Several aunts," he said, nodding slowly.

"Several . . ." I began, confused, then realizing what he meant added quickly, "severance pay, yes. Very generous, Chuang. Thank you."

"No, thanks," he said, shaking his head. "Not good." He tapped his chest. "Heart say five-year service, fifty thousand; but no chance. Benson's make policy. Big recession, maximum twenty thousand. But no three-month notice. You can leave by new year and find good job, yes."

"When will I get the money, Chuang?"

"Banking already." He was vastly relieved at my gratitude and smiled. "Banking already, my friend."

I was delighted. I had never had access to any sizeable sum of money and there seemed to be so many things I could do with it. I turned these over in my mind: an electric typewriter, one of those fancy word-processing ones, the hi-fi equipment Sylvie had always wanted, perhaps a new car. I didn't want to make up my mind too quickly. I would savour all options before I decided.

When I got home, Sylvie told me that my mother had phoned from a motel in Kuantan, some two hundred miles away. My father had been haemorrhaging again and was getting much weaker. He was, however, obdurate and insisted on proceeding further north. Mother was confident that, given a bit of time, she could persuade him to turn back and hoped to be back in Singapore by Christmas.

As I listened to Sylvie I realized what I could do with the twenty thousand dollars. It was clear that my father had only few months to live. As soon as he died I could take Sylvie and my mother away on a holiday. We would go to England, which Mother had always wanted to visit. True, her view of England had reached her by way of Hollywood, but the very prospect of visiting the country where people spoke like Greer Garson and Walter Pigeon would be enough to distract her from her grief. I was about to tell Sylvie my plan when I stopped myself. It should come as a surprise. Sylvie was very attached to my father and would suffer almost as much as my mother would when he died. A pleasant surprise could be a most effective remedy for grief.

I said nothing about the money.

Deciding how I was to spend my severance pay reminded me that I would soon be without a job. I had not given much thought to what I could offer Samson and his friends in exchange for their patronage. I had, though I hated to admit this, a vague picture of the kind of thing this might be but couldn't bring it sufficiently into focus to identify what it was. This feeling of being unable to grasp what was already in my mind disturbed me all day and continued to do so as I fell asleep that night.

I called Su-May as soon as I got into Benson's the next morning. As I dialled her number, it crossed my mind that Su-May was in some way connected with what I had to offer Samson. Hearing her voice bubble with happiness at the sound of mine drove away all such thoughts.

"Isn't it lovely, Hern?" she said. "Lovely that the first voice I hear when I wake up is yours."

We had been lovers for a year but had never been able to spend a whole night together. I knew that this was something that saddened Su-May, but she never complained. She very much wanted to wake up in the morning to find me beside her, to have me make love to her while she was still half asleep. This, however, she considered Sylvie's right and something she only dared hint at occasionally. I too, had at times felt a need to wake up next to her. I said a little hurriedly, "I'm sorry it's only over the phone."

"Better than nothing," she said. "Ooh," she yawned languorously. She was stretching, pretending I was beside her. "You know something, Hern?"

"What?"

"Pete liked you. Liked you a lot really."

I should have been irritated by the remark. It was condescending and out of place. Instead, I was flattered.

"I'm glad," I said.

"So you'll come to lunch? Tomorrow afternoon, that is?" She sounded anxious.

"What's up tommorrow?"

"Dummy!" she scolded. "It's Christmas Eve and Pete said you promised you'd try. Try and have lunch with all of us. The kids and all, I mean."

"Oh, sure." I remembered Peter's invitation. "I'd love to."

"You lovely man." Her voice dropped. "Could we, Hern, spend some time together before we meet the kids?"

"You're quite the sexy little beast, aren't you?" I said. "Why don't we go up to Sheng's place for a couple of hours before lunch. We can really work up an appetite."

She giggled. "Will that be OK?"

"Sure," I said. "He's out of town till after Christmas." Then a darker thought struck me. "Will you be able to use your father's car? I'd rather not use my own." I didn't want the motor cyclist with the square headlight following me to Sheng's place or the house in Tampines which the Children used.

"No problem," she said. "I'll pick you up outside Benson's at ten o'clock."

"No, don't," I said. "Pick me up at the main bus terminal at Orchard Road."

"As you say, darling." Her voice was throaty and trembled a little, as it always did when she was excited. "I'll start thinking of you now. Imagining, like. I'm feeling things so strong that I may not need you tomorrow.

Anticipating a morning in bed with Su-May in her present mood was a sweetness that cleared my mind of other thoughts. It was a razor-sharp pleasure, breath-taking, almost painful; it could only be experienced in short bursts. Behind these twinges of acute and almost unbearable desire, I was aware of a more chronic, aching happiness. I did not have to think to know what had brought it on: Cornelius Vandermeer had returned.

Captain Cornelius Vandermeer goes back as far as my memory does.

Cornelius had, in the late 1930s, come to Singapore from Java. These were the years preceding the outbreak of the Second World War. There was in the air at that time the restless uncertainty that precedes major change. An era was ending. Perched on its edge, people avoided peering into the future or looking back into the past, preferring instead the perpetual present of frenetic parties and mindless merrymaking. In this mood no one inquired too closely as to where one came from or where one was going.

He was tall, grey-eyed and had skin that was honey-coloured but freckled. His father had, he said, been Dutch, a planter who had come to Java at the turn of the century. He rarely spoke of him but somehow people always thought of Cornelius as being a Dutchman. Perhaps it was the way he spoke. (He tended to say: "Yoost a minute.") Or it could have been the courtly European bows with which he greeted ladies. He talked much about his mother, who was Javanese (a princess, Cornelius claimed, and descended from the Sailendras). Nevertheless, no one looked on him as being other than a foreigner.

I never, of course, actually met Captain Cornelius. He was killed in the early 1950s, at about the time I was born. It was my mother, Clara Perera, who told me about him. That I came to know the Captain piecemeal over the years simply meant that I came to know him the better. I was able to think about and put together fragments of his life, question my mother about missing pieces, fill in interstices with conjecture, supply motives where none were apparent.

Clara was always happy to talk about him.

"Handsome he was," she said, rolling her eyes heavenwards and raising her palms in surrender. "So handsome he made your teeth ache and," she laughed coarsely, adding, "other parts too." She glanced at me slyly and, having satisfied herself that I hadn't understood the innuendo, continued, "A lean and bony man. And tall. Why, child, he was a full head higher than all the men around. Outstanding, really outstanding."

She screwed up her eyes and stared into the past.

"He had a long, loping stride, almost a run, which always carried him smack into the centre of a room. There he would stand and look about him with those pale grey eyes." She shook her head. "Strange, piercing eyes, the Captain had, and thick, sand-coloured eyebrows. He looked around him often and always over his shoulder as though he was surrounded by enemies. Perhaps Cappy was right, because all the men hated him. Not that he cared." Clara laughed, half-yawning to indicate the contempt Cornelius had for their hatred. "For every woman in the room was waiting for those pale grey eyes to land on her." She giggled and touched her cheek with the back of her hand.

I was about nine years old when this conversation took place and had asked, "If the men all hated Cornelius so much, why didn't they do something about it? Why didn't they all gang up and kill him?"

"Fight the Captain?" She snorted her contempt. "Why, none of those cowards . . . none of those pi dogs even dared look him in the eye. They always looked the other way, even when snarling under their breath and baring their fangs to each other.

"No," she shook her head, "Cappy loved life too much to be killed by a bunch like that, or by anybody else."

A great love of life was one of the outstanding features of Cornelius's character. The other, paradoxically, was his fearlessness when confronted with death.

When the war with Japan began, Cornelius joined the Singapore Volunteer Corps and was commissioned as a captain. His daring during the siege of Singapore was to become a legend.

"When the bombs and shells were falling, when we all stood paralysed with fear, choking in the dust and fumes, the Captain was everywhere." Clara's voice was animated, her eyes shining with admiration.

"A building is hit. It begins to burn. Someone says there is a girl inside . . . unconscious. No one moves. Then Cappy dashes in. The crowd outside waits. Parts of the building begin to collapse." She paused for a long while, her thoughts turning inwards. "He emerges, a body over his shoulder. It is the girl. Seconds, just seconds later, the building caves in."

"Do you know," she said, returning to the present, "that Cappy's thick eyebrows were burned away in the flames. When they grew back they were no longer sandy. They were dark. Which was all to the good. It made it easier for him to disguise himself as a local when this was necessary."

"Who was the girl, Ma?"

"There's no need to ask that question, is there?" she said, so irritably that I realized I shouldn't probe any further.

When Singapore fell to the Japanese, Cornelius hadn't surrendered with the rest of the British forces. He stained his face, donned native clothes and, keeping well away from the main roads, walked to the northern part of the island. The bridge connecting Singapore to the Malay peninsula had been blown up by the retreating British in their efforts to slow down the Japanese advance. It was impossible to get a boat for the crossing. Cornelius had simply waited for darkness and swum some two miles across the shark-infested straits of Johor to reach the mainland. When I asked what made him dare this, my mother had simply said, "There was no other way across."

At that time the resistance to the Japanese had yet to be properly organized. Cornelius slipped into the jungles and made contact with small groups of fighters, bringing them together, organizing, as my mother said, an effective guerrilla force.

"But he didn't know they were there, Ma," I protested. "He was setting out alone into the jungle, about which he knew nothing."

Clara shot me a withering look. "What makes you think that Captain Cornelius feared the unknown or being by himself?"

"He could have died in the jungle," I suggested.

"So?"

"I simply can't understand, Ma, how a man whom you say loved life so much could take such foolish risks."

"Yes, he loved life," she said, smiling to herself. "That's exactly why he lived it to the fullest." She turned to me, her face solemn. "Cappy used to say that he continued to enjoy being alive even when he was suffering intense pain. It never stopped being worthwhile. I'll tell you more about these things when you are older. Maybe you'll understand then."

She did over the years.

Throughout the Japanese occupation of Malaya, Cornelius had, disguised as a native, shuttled between the guerrillas in the jungles and their sympathizers in the towns, from whom he obtained both information and supplies. Once, making his way into town, he had fallen into a pit and injured both his ankles. Unable to walk or even stand, he had dragged himself through swamp and scrub, avoided several Japanese patrols and finally reached a small village. When found by the villagers, he was bleeding badly, covered in leeches and barely conscious. It was his enjoyment of life, Cornelius maintained, that had seen him through. On the edge of death, life had become sweeter and more precious.

"Maybe he was just a thrill-seeker, Ma," I dared suggest. "Enjoyed the kicks he got dicing with death."

She shot me a look of venom. "You," she hissed, "you're already fifteen years old and still you don't understand."

"How did he die, anyway?" I asked, my tone sceptical, mocking. "He was killed, wasn't he?"

"Yes," she sighed. "But no one knows the full facts."

The war over, Cornelius had become the manager of a rubber estate. He was then in his late forties. His erstwhile comrades, the communists, were waging a jungle war against the British. Rubber estates, the main reason for British interest in the Malay Peninsula, were constantly being attacked. Cornelius had married a Malay girl. His wife Midah was in her teens. Little was known about her except that, a few years before Cornelius's death, she had had a son. My mother did not know what had become of her after Cornelius was killed.

"Was the Captain ambushed, Ma?"

"Yes. By the Communists. By the very men who were once his friends."

"Why?"

"Who knows?" she said darkly.

"Surely his wife should."

"She knows nothing. Nothing about Cappy."

"But was she not with him when he died?"

"So they say."

"And she escaped. How?"

"Must have just left him and run away."

"Surely the Communist guerrillas could quite easily have killed her too. They let her escape, didn't they? They only wanted to kill Cornelius."

"I suppose so."

"But how could he have allowed himself to be killed," I asked, "this man who felt that nothing was worse than death?"

She stared at me morosely. "That Malay girl, that Midah, was no good for him."

"And you, Ma, would you have been good for him?"

"Maybe." She smiled, tilting her head to one side.

"Then why didn't you marry him?"

"It never came about for him to ask me," she replied sharply.

This was a typical Clara Perera evasion. It neither told me if

Cornelius Vandermeer was ever in a position to ask nor whether she would have consented if he had. At this point, my mother became extremely uncomfortable, twisting about in her chair, picking at her clothes, examining minutely the tips of her fingers. Then suddenly she pulled out a rather soiled white handkerchief and began dabbing her eyes.

"Ma," I said, as gently as I could, "you never really knew the Captain, did you?"

"Came as near to knowing him as to make all I've told you God's truth," she said with a just discernible sob. "Whether I actually met him or not doesn't really matter, does it?"

And she was right. I don't know the actual facts of Cornelius's life are all that important. He was more presence than person, albeit a complex presence: an admixture of anecdote and speculation, a tapestry woven on shreds of evidence, an enigma whose unravelling would be rewarded with hope. Sometimes I saw him as the archetypal colonial hero, a brigand like Drake or Clive preying on opportunity and turning it to their advantage. Sometimes he seemed like the winners of Victoria Crosses, walking glassy-eyed to their deaths, too stupid to be afraid. However, more often than not, Cornelius came across as a tortured soul, a man trapped in the conflict of his inclinations. Loving life, he must fear death, but he must never allow that fear to limit his experience.

Over the years he had come to me unannounced, remained as long as he chose, had gone when he pleased, leaving me always the sadder for his departure. Neither his advent nor stay were determined by anything I did. I had become quite fatalistic about his comings and goings, and at times I believed that Cornelius might himself feel likewise about the circumstances of his life. Born in Java, he would have been touched by both Hinduism and Islam and could easily have incorporated both karma and kismet into his thinking. The better I got to know the Captain, the less likely did this appear. If he was not directed by imperialistic purpose, activated by mindless reflexes, or swept unresistingly onwards by the slide of events, what was it that moved him?

I raised these questions when we were alone, late at night in the silence of my room, or as he followed me home from work.

Cornelius would smile, crinkling his once-sandy eyebrows. The smile did not offer an answer. If I pestered him too much, he would go away for a while. These absences were short and I knew temporary, but I was careful not to press him when he returned. But now I cajoled and bullied. I needed to know not just the facts of Cornelius's death or how he viewed that event but his thoughts and reactions when he knew that the end was close and unavoidable. I needed to know because my father was dying, helpless and terrified, clinging to a past that probably never existed. I felt sure that if I bothered Cornelius enough, I would discover some fragment about himself that would make my father's death less pointless and horrible. I wasn't seeking a blinding revelation that would once and for all dispel my doubts and fears. All I wanted was an imperceptible gleam, a forgotten flicker, an imagined spark with which to assure myself that darkness was not all there was. I was certain that Cornelius could provide me with this and, when he did, my father's death would be the easier. I also knew for the turn of events in my own life that I would soon be making some very major decisions. It is impossible to make big decision unless one has, if only in some small way, come to terms with suffering and with death.

ten

I awoke early on Christmas Eve and left the flat soon after. I wanted, for possibly the last time, to get in to Benson's before Chuang or any of the others. There was a hint of rain in the air and it was cool. Cornelius Vandermeer was very much with me that morning and I walked slowly, enjoying his presence and the prospect of rain. My enjoyment was, however, not undisturbed, and though I moved in a leisurely manner I looked over my shoulder several times to see if I was being followed. The streets were virtually empty and my fears seemed unfounded. It was difficult to believe that the two old men practising Chinese callisthenics or the ancient crone waving a sheaf of incense-sticks heavenwards were members of the secret police.

The furniture department was quiet and dim. I wandered about, smelling the leather and the fabrics, rubbing carpets against their pile, settling myself into armchairs. Then I sat at my desk, enjoying the stillness around me till Ahmad walked in.

"Mornings very quiet nowadays, Mr Perera," he said, trying but failing to keep a note of accusation out of his voice. Then, "You want something, sir?"

"Just looking around at a few things, Ahmad." I began shuffling the pieces of paper on my desk. "Tidying up, I guess."

The girls came in a little later, each nodding a greeting. Seeing me in my usual place, they smiled. I avoided thinking if it was surprise or hope that lit up their eyes, fixing my own resolutely, if blankly, on the invoices before me. I had enough on my mind without having to worry about my salesgirls.

Su-May was picking me up at ten. I had to be quite sure I was not followed to our rendezvous at the bus-stop, or worse, from there to Sheng's place. The last thing I wanted was to give Sam and his people the kind of information that would put me even more in their power than I felt I already was.

At 9.30 I began to walk casually around the furniture department, nudging pieces into place, arranging the odd drape. My wanderings took me to the doorway and I walked nonchalantly out into the foyer, which led directly to the main entrance of Benson's. There were several people on the sidewalk outside and it was impossible to tell who, if any of them, might be assigned to following me. I stepped out briskly. A man who was intently examining a shopping-guide looked up and started towards me. I stopped, examined my watch, shook my head several times and stepped back into the store. The man returned to his shopping-guide. I was sure that there would be somebody watching the back entrance as well so at 9.55 I let myself out of the building by the small side door to which I had the key. The side door opened on to a little alley which once separated rows of shop-houses. These had recently been pulled down and were soon to be replaced by shopping malls and a modern hotel. I stopped, in the middle of a vacant lot, and looked about me. There was no one around. Certain I was not being followed, I hurried across the lot, crossed a narrow lane and reached the main bus-terminal on Orchard Road. I had been there barely a minute when I heard Su-May tooting wildly on her horn and screaming out to me at the same time.

As she slipped the car into the mainstream traffic she said, "What's the matter, Hern? You'll get a crick in your neck if you go on looking behind you."

"Just like to know what's behind me, my love." There were no motor-cycles behind us. I put my hand on her knee and relaxed.

She accelerated into the fast lane and, putting the tips of her fingers on my thigh, said, "Can't wait for you, Hern. Sometimes I simply can't wait."

She drove dangerously, putting an added edge to the excitement of our being together. Once out of the main city area we travelled east, towards Changi and the coast, where the land flattened and gave way to a coastline dotted with islands. A few miles before reaching the coast, we turned off the main road on to a pot-holed semi-tarred track leading to Sheng's house. This was a modern bungalow which stood on its own, concealed by a small forest of withered rubber-trees, their productive years long past. Their barks hung loosely about them like the breasts of very old women. A tiny nameplate hanging askew on a gatepost said: N.C. Sheng.

I had come to know the man soon after I started with Benson's. Sheng travelled around South-East Asia buying textiles and handmade wooden furniture, which he supplied to large department stores.

One lot of fabric he supplied us had not been up to specifications. Instead of reporting the matter to Chuang, an action that would certainly have meant the end of Sheng's dealings with Benson's, I (convinced that the man had not intended to cheat) had phoned and told him of the discrepancies. These Sheng promptly made good. From that time on, he had looked upon himself as being in my debt.

"A trust," he said, "is born." The man was visibly moved. "Just like that which comes by birth to brothers. I hope some day you will use this trust."

I was not quite sure what he meant but was happy to use his house when Su-May and I needed somewhere to go. Sheng, a bachelor, and often out of town, was only too pleased. To Su-May and me there was something special about Sheng's house. There we made love undisturbed by the strange noises that filled Benson's when its occupants left. There we stomped about rooms accustomed to our nudity and were unafraid to leave traces of our presence in the toilet. There we had access to a kitchen in which Su-May concocted meals made edible only by the edge that love-making puts on one's appetite. At Sheng's we enjoyed snatches of domesticity, idyllic and impossible outside the confines of marriage.

Su-May bounced on the edge of the bed, her body dripping from the shower she loved to have immediately after making love.

"Aren't you going to cook me one of your special nutritious meals?" I asked.

"But, Hern, you said . . ."

"I said?"

"It's Christmas Eve. You said . . . you promised you'd have lunch with Peter and the kids."

"I suppose I did," I said. "Then I suppose we'd –"

"It's 'I suppose' time again," she said. She smiled cheekily, but her eyes were brighter than they should have been with laughter and she blinked before adding, "Let's go before we change our mind. I promised the kids too, you know."

There was an air of gaiety about the wooden shack in Tampines that was difficult to understand. The Children had made no effort at Christmas decoration, nor could I hear the carols unavoidable in the city. I did notice that the way to the house had been partially cleared of the dead leaves. I suspect this was the result of many people using the path that morning, rather than any deliberate attempt to tidy up the garden for Christmas. Looking through the large wooden window, however, I observed signs of tremendous activity: an event was being prepared for.

As we neared the door I became apprehensive. These, after all, were the people I suspected of carrying tales of my affair back to my father and, I had no doubt, they knew of my suspicions. There was bound to be bitterness or, at best, that gritty accommodation in relations we call compromise. Su-May must have sensed my uneasiness, for quite unexpectedly she slid her hand down the whole inside length of my arm and, taking my hand in hers, pulled me fiercely against her side. We walked in, leaning a little stiffly on each other, looking as though we shared a crutch.

"Not to worry, Hern," she said. "Safe you are."

The Children, despite their activity, seemed subdued. They greeted Su-May warmly but without the usual squeals and rib-tickling. I sensed in them a disappointment, as though they expected not us but someone else. Peter, however, was his usual self. He rushed forward as soon as he saw us enter and embraced the two of us together.

"Good of you," he said, "to come. So happy, Hern, you can give some of your Christmas to us."

He led us to the far end of the room, to a table laden with food: pots of curry steaming spiciness, elegantly dressed cubes of bean-curd, steamed prawns the smell of the sea still about them. There were also several loaves of home-baked bread, something rather unusual for Singapore.

"Yes," said Peter, noticing my surprise. "The girls insist on baking it themselves. A good thing, I suppose." He added, in a laughing whisper, "But only when they are successful. No table is strong enough to bear the weight of their failures."

Peter moved towards a small gas stove perched at one end of the table. Here he and a frail-looking girl were in the process of putting together a chicken stew. They quarrelled spiritedly about the order in which the ingredients should be added, the girl quite fierce, Peter pretending an annoyance that easily turned to laughter.

I moved away from them to a group of girls making spring-rolls. They looked up at me, half-smiling, openly flirtatious. I wasn't sure how I should react. Cornelius had been with me all along but had kept well in the background. I looked at him now, hoping that the Captain with his great experience in handling women would offer guidance. He avoided my eye. I moved away from the group towards the centre of the room.

All around me there was movement. Laughing, chattering, quarrelling, the Children went about their business. Beneath the bustle I sensed an expectancy. They were waiting for something and it wasn't simply for their meal or for the party to begin. There was in the air a tension, a terror almost, that all their bustle could not hide. From time to time, one of them would stop whatever he or she was doing to listen, an ear cocked towards the distance. Once a car passed near the house and everyone stood still until its sounds faded away.

Suddenly the frail girl who was helping Peter sang out, "OK, everybody, the food's just about ready."

"But Dorcas isn't here yet," said one of the Children.

"Should have been here hours ago," said another.

I looked inquiringly at Peter, who said, "Dorcas is my sister. She's out on a little errand." He smiled around him. "Don't worry, kids. She'll be here soon."

"Let's wait for her," a chorus suggested.

"Maybe Su-May will sing then," someone said.

"OK, OK," said Su-May. "Maybe my singing will drown the hunger music your stomachs are making."

I found a packing-case to sit on. The Children sat on wooden boxes, stools, small benches. They flopped on to the rough cement floor in small groups holding hands, touching each other, casually intimate. Su-May carried her guitar to the centre of the room and sat on the floor, tucking her legs under her. Her hair, which she had washed at Sheng's house, was now in plaits. This made her look younger, strikingly virginal: a Christmas Madonna. She strummed the guitar a few times then began singing. It was the same song she had sung the evening I had stood alone in the dark, wet garden:

"Oh, my loves have been many
But the loving was for One,
For the same light can shine in
A candle or the sun."

The last lines of the opening verse stuck in my mind even as she went on singing, continued to ring after she had stopped and put the guitar down on the floor beside her. The words seemed to have developed a peculiar relevance to my life and went round and round my head in ever widening circles, encompassing more and more of what I saw as experience. I sat still, not joining the patter of applause. Su-May came and sat beside me. The packing-case was narrow. She put her arm round my waist and drew us together. The Children on the floor looked up at us, smiled. They knew what she was saying. Peter joined them. I couldn't understand why I was unhappy. I looked to Cornelius. Again, he looked away.

"Now the Reverend," said a chorus of voices. "A song from the Reverend."

Peter protested, "You know I can't sing, kids."

"Go on, Pete," said Su-May. She wriggled even closer to me. I could feel her ribs flare out against mine as she breathed. "Do the one I taught you."

Peter looked around him, nervous. "OK. I'll try."

He moved to the centre of the room and picked up Su-May's guitar. He turned the instrument on its back and standing rather awkwardly began to beat out a rhythm on the wood:

"I come as a beggar
With a gift in my hand,
I come as beggar
With a gift in my hand."

He had a soft voice and sang in a tuneless monotone that was almost a chant. The absence of melody seemed to increase the impact of the words:

"The need of another
Is the gift that I bring,
The need of another
Is the gift that I bring.
By the hungry I will feed you
By the poor I'll make you rich,
By the broken I will mend you,
Tell me, which one is which?"

His song was interrupted by an extremely noisy vehicle entering the garden. Its engine, straining all the time, managed to wheeze, rattle and explode before sighing into silence.

"Dorcas! It's Dorcas!" the children shouted as they rushed into the garden.

Peter put down the guitar and walked slowly towards the door, his face strained, his normally delicate skin suddenly wizened. Su-May and I walked behind him. In the middle of the garden, perched at an angle suggesting it had come to an unexpected halt, was an ancient bright-green Morris Minor. The Children, screaming, "Dorcas! Dorcas!", had begun pulling out its sole occupant. A pair of beautifully long legs emerged, followed by a well-built girl wearing an extremely short skirt. She had a tiny nose, which squatted in the middle of a face that was almost perfectly round. Her hair was cut very short but still managed to look dishevelled. The most striking things about her, however, were her eyes. These were large, bright and darted about as swiftly as a serpent's tongue. There was, however, nothing evil or frightening about their movement. They were the friendliest eyes possible and flitted about only to spread their goodwill the more effectively.

"Dorcas," said Peter, his voice rising slightly, "is everything well?"

The big girl disentangled herself from the attentions of the Children and turned to him. "Fine, Pete. Everything went off

A-one." The worried look remained on his face and she added, "You're such an old lady, big brother." She slapped his back. "I'm late because of a bit of trouble with the car." She had one hand on Peter's shoulder. In the other she carried a large canvas bag. This was identical to the one Su-May took to work, except that the one Dorcas held must have been, from the way she swung it about, empty.

"Whenever you're on this kind of thing, I worry –" Peter began. Dorcas's hand leapt from his shoulder to his mouth, silencing him.

Following behind, I heard her say, "Did it all, Pete." Then, laughing: "Yes, Reverend, between Gabby and me, we sowed all the ground you wanted. Rock and concrete jungle as well. Almost empty, see? She swung the canvas bag in a huge circle. "Gabby had to rush off to his grandpa's. Says to say sorry."

"Did you find anyone taking a special interest in you . . . or Gabby?"

"Not a chance," she said slapping him on the back again. Then softening, added, "Like I said, Pete, we were very, very careful." She flung the bag on a chair and zipped it open. "All gone except for the few we kept to read ourselves."

Discoveries never really come as surprises. The picture exists in its entirety the moment we lock the first piece of the puzzle on to the second. The speed at which we realize this depends on our willingness to admit to the reality of what is displayed before our eyes. I knew, before Peter reached into the bag, that it would contain the latest issue of the streetpaper. I let my mind drift back and remembered knowing for a long time what the Children had been about. I knew when I moved Su-May's canvas bag across the bed and found it unexpectedly heavy; one is forever surprised at how light a single sheet of paper is, yet how much a bundle weighs. I knew it when a devious set of circumstances drove me to use the front entrance of Benson's and to discover the streetpapers Su-May had placed there. I knew it from the way I avoided thinking of Peter and the Children when Samson talked of the operation being run by "some cool cat and a load of kits". I knew all along, and couldn't deny this to myself as Su-May snuggled up beside me on the packing-case.

Peter dipped his hand into the bag and pulled out a copy of the streetpaper. "Our Christmas issue," he said, offering it to me. When I made as though to read it, he added, "No, not now. Read it when you get home." He folded the streetpaper and tucked it into my shirt pocket.

"I see," I said. "This Dorcas sows discontent rather than garments for widows."

"See, Pete," Dorcas said, nudging him. "Didn't I say when we first heard of him that he'd know his Bible pretty well?" She laughed. "I got the gift of prophecy, brother."

"I think you can see, Hern, why we were nervous of outsiders getting too close to any one of us."

"I see quite well," I replied. "You're not really a religious group. You're what the government calls a clandestine political organization."

"There's no diff between the two," Dorcas chipped in. "Political and religious organizations, I mean." She was breathless, her eyes brightening for battle. "You know the Bible so well, you should know how Christians have always been looked upon as subversives. Well, they still are. Here and everywhere. In the Philippines, in South America, priests resist tyrants, fight new Herods backed by legions in helicopter gunships." She spoke in a rush, allowing no interruption till she was out of breath.

"Dorcas," said Peter. "Enough." He hadn't raised his voice but there was no question of his authority. "We can talk to Hern freely . . . later. Now let's eat."

We moved to the table.

Singapore is an eater's paradise, known for the variety of its foods, for the novelty of taste sensations available, and its inhabitants are obsessed with eating. We scurry after nuances of flavour, seek out the texture that some new process has put into rice noodles, pursue down dark and dingy side streets new degrees of spiciness that some Indian cook has worked into his curry. But our savourings are joyless and we wind up disgruntled, missing always the vital, ingredient that brings fulfilment to eating.

Like most Singaporeans I know a lot about food. I noticed immediately that there was nothing special about the dishes laid out on the table. Prepared by amateurs, they were displayed without style. I knew from the way Peter and the frail-looking girl had put together the chicken stew that a lot of enthusiasm had gone into the cooking and the energy of this hung about the dishes like haloes. But amateur cooks remain, however enthusiastic, amateurs.

I was cautious and helped myself to a small portion of the stew. I was surprised at how good the food tasted and how each morsel demanded that I go on to the next. Before long I had dispensed with caution and was loading my plate willy-nilly with whatever was before me. I am neither a gourmet nor a glutton and was at a loss to understand my appetite. Perhaps it had been stimulated by the strenuous love-making Su-May and I had just enjoyed. Perhaps? I would try and believe that, try to deny that the vital ingredient in the enjoyment of food was fellowship: this fellowship that proclaimed itself in the smell of the bread, that impregnated the onion skins, had found its way into the stew and could be heard in the crunching of the spring-rolls the Children chewed.

Dorcas was beside me. She stood on one leg and leaned slightly on my shoulder, a plate in her hand.

"Eat well, Hern," she whispered in my ear, "so no one will notice how much I put away." She straightened herself to her full height. "It's a long way down for me and a whole lot of space to fill."

"Dorcas confessing her gluttony?" asked Peter, coming between us.

Su-May joined us wiping her plate clean with a piece of bread.

"You have enjoyed your food," said Peter, "but you are not happy." He looked at me intently, his head cocked to one side.

This was true.

I cannot remember enjoying a meal as much as the one I had just eaten. But the good fellowship and gaiety around did little to remove my discomfiture. While unhappy about the way in which Singapore was run, I was disturbed at the prospect of upheaval and uneasy in the company of people who proposed it. This was partly due to a natural conservatism. But there was a more important reason for it. In writing, I snatched images and sequences from my head, matched them against a well-ordered world and between the two concocted a reality essential to my well-being. Anything that threatened this process frightened me.

"I thought you were a bunch of Christian do-gooders," I said.

"Now I find I am mixed up in some sort of urban guerrilla movement. What the hell are you lot anyway?" I tried to sound light-hearted, bantering, but my voice had risen and I seemed to be addressing the whole group.

Peter spoke. "As Dorcas said, it is the way of tyrants to keep religion and politics separate." He paused for what seemed a long while before going on: "What is wrong is wrong. You can call the movement that seeks to right it whatever you wish."

"I thought you Christians had it spelled out for you," I said, affecting a smile. "Isn't there some injunction that requires you to render unto Caesar the things that are Caesar's and unto God . . .?"

"Caesar?" he said. "Caesar?" His voice was louder than I had ever heard it. His eyelid twitched as he fought to control the look of contempt and fury that was developing at the corner of his mouth. His skin had become slightly mottled and his nostrils flared. Peter spoke not to me nor even the Children but over our heads, his eyes focused into the distance, his face intense. In a flash, all my distaste for the man returned. I saw him for what he was, not just a demagogue but one who was Su-May's lover in the bargain, an irresponsible crackpot guru who had made a cuckold out of me.

The Children, Su-May and Dorcas included, had backed away to the sides of the room, leaving us facing each other, two men in the centre of the ring about to begin battle. Peter looked around him. With great deliberation, he placed his right foot on a packing-case, clasped his hands around his knee and, this done, turned his head upwards to look steadily at me. His movements were precise, balletic, designed to intimidate.

"People driven by fear," he pronounced, "cannot say where Caesar ends and God begins."

"So we are back to the old streetpaper business about Singapore being a police state, ruled by terror."

"Fear is a strange and mysterious thing," he said. "To begin with, it's dazzling, painfully bright. A fierce and unavoidable force. Then we grow used to it, make ourselves excuses and find room for it in the secret places of our lives. Yes," he said, chin and raised for an audience that was yet to be his, "we are indeed a flexible and accommodating people. We swallow our pride, we swallow our self-respect not with difficulty, not as though it were broken glass, but smoothly, like shark's-fin soup.

"When we have done that, we no longer see our fear. It is hidden inside a new name. We talk of facing realities and think of ourselves not as cowards but as hard-headed practical people." He laughed – to himself and at me. "Yes, my friend, even as I talk, you see the truth of my words."

This was correct. Peter's speech had much the same effect on me that the streetpaper had had. It hypnotized me. Compelled me to believe. Subdued the tiny, protesting voices of reason that rose within me. One broke away from the rest and I heard myself ask, "How is it I see no signs of this terror you talk so glibly about?"

Speaking in a large oracular voice he said, "We are all blind to sights that hurt our eyes." He took his hands off his knee and spread them out before him, appealing for agreement. "Think of the times, my friend, when rather than stare at injustice we have shielded our eyes and called it bad luck. When, rather than accept naked hate in somebody, we refer to his touchiness." He stopped, dropped his hands and laughed. His voice became low and he seemed to be talking to himself. "Yes, self-reliance is a disregard for everyone but yourself; and the callousness to climb to the top on the faces of your rivals is called a healthy competitive spirit. It becomes worse and worse, for truth and justice are looked on as foreign values designed to corrupt our people and upset the productivity of our state."

He raised his voice and looked steadily at me. "Of course, friend, you don't see the terror because with the terror is provided the means of hiding it from ourselves, the means of making it invisible and our shame bearable. When selected women are ushered into breeding camps and the poor are sterilized, whispers of fascism are drowned in loud talk of encouraging social development, of correcting population imbalance. Oh, no, we're not afraid to voice our disagreement – if there were some place where we could safely make our voices heard. No, we're not afraid to speak up. We're not intimidated by the vast, uniformed, and even vaster, un-uniformed, unidentifiable police-force. We're not frightened by the rumours of what happens to people who do speak up. Oh, no, it is not fear. We choose to bite our tongues and remain silent in the interest of our nation." His hands dropped to his sides and his shoulders sagged.

"Apart from your streetpaper, how," I asked, "do you propose to change all this?"

"I don't really," he shrugged, his face no longer intense, "know." The strength seemed to have left him. "Though the streetpaper seems to be going quite," he looked over his shoulder to smile at Dorcas, "good. I thought that, perhaps, we could some time – at culture week, like –" he shook his head as though already dismissing the idea – "we could get people to make some kind of protest sign."

"A demonstration?"

"Nothing," he shook his head, "big. A gesture at a parade or concert."

I laughed, "Some kind of clenched-fist salute?"

"Too strong, man, and nowadays getting a bit square, like," said Dorcas, stepping up to us.

As the tension between Peter and me subsided, the Children moved closer. Surrounding us now, they were back to being their old noisy, laughing selves, jostling, interrupting each other.

"We thought of something new . . . peaceful, like, too," Dorcas continued. "Just raising both arms . . ."

"Hands open," someone began.

"Palms upwards," someone else added.

"Like the gesture of surrender," explained Dorcas.

"But not a surrender at all . . ."

"More appeal . . ."

"Asking for support maybe . . ."

"And when is this . . . this appeal going to be made?" I asked.

"Whenever the national anthem is played," said Peter. "There will be hundreds of shows and concerts during Culture Week. The anthem will be played at all of these."

What he planned was now clear to me. It was about six months to Culture Week and, during this period, the streetpaper and its offshoots would be used to generate resentment against the government. People would be reminded of all the occasions on which the ruling party had been vindictive, callous, arrogant or just incompetent. Apart from encouraging people to expose such situations and report them in streetpapers, no action would be proposed. This would bring anti-government feelings to the boil.

Just before Culture Week, streetpapers would suggest that some overt demonstration of disaffection was necessary: a gesture to show that people were not afraid, a sign not merely of their discontent but of their willingness to protest. Once initiated, defiance would escalate. The first meaningless gesture would be followed by more specific ones: walk-outs at the appearance of dignitaries, flooding post-boxes with unstamped mail, sighing in unison when government advertisements were shown in cinema. Later there would be strikes, riots. . . .

As Peter spoke, his eyes brightened and he began to pant slightly. "We will undertake no acts of crime or sabotage. Just," he smiled grimly, "defiance. The David in all of us standing up to the oppressing Goliath."

"And," I said, "once things are under way, the protesters will find a political leader in Peter Yu."

"Tell, tell, Pete," said Dorcas, laughing wildly. "I didn't know you aimed to be a political hotshot."

Peter laughed too, holding his head to one side, fragile and boyish again. He said, "I am not a politician. Believe it or not, I have no wish for power."

"Then why take all the risks?" I asked.

"A difficult question, Hern," he said. "I tell myself that I can sow and not want to reap, but that's not quite true." He looked over his shoulder and Su-May stepped forward and stood beside him. "The truth is, I won't be around for much longer."

His voice had dropped to a whisper. It was obvious that he was determined to inject as much drama as possible into what he was about to say.

I couldn't resist taunting him. "Don't tell me you've got a fatal disease and are not long for this world. I thought the pallor in your cheeks was due to lack of sunlight; now you are going to tell me you've got leukemia –"

"No, Hern," Su-May interrupted. "It's something we, Peter and me, have been planning to tell you for a long time."

"Let's the three of us go into the garden for a chat," said Peter. He smiled at the group around us and added, "Time for grown-up talk, kids, so you lot can get on with the clearing up."

I remembered the last time I had been in that garden. It had been dark and wet then. Su-May had offered me tears and a kiss, which I had read as that of betrayal. Looking back on events, I tend to think of Rex Zhu's visit to Benson's furniture department as the start of my misfortune, the tiny tremor that warned of the collapse of my life. Perhaps I was wrong to think so. Perhaps it was Su-May's warm, tear-salted kiss in that dark, damp garden that signalled the beginning of my end. Though it was now day and the garden looked different, rain was clearly in the air. It was starting to darken and heavy, black clouds moved lugubriously across the sky while light, grey ones scampered across their faces. Little puffs of wind ruffled the leaves that had been dried and swept into neat piles ready for burning. The wooden bench on which we had kissed was no longer wet and Peter led us towards it. He indicated that I sit but I shook my head and we stood around awkwardly, waiting.

Finally I asked, "When you say you'll be gone before anything happens, I take it you were talking of leaving the country?"

Peter sighed. The look of weariness that crossed his face bordered on pain. He took Su-May's hand and mine in each of his before lowering himself on to the wooden seat. He could have been an old man blessing a young couple, sanctioning a relationship.

"Some people, Hern . . ." he began, then shook his head and started again. "Some of us can only be happy when we are involved in the lives of others." He looked miserable but went on. "It is not that we are good or kind . . . or even thoughtful people. It's a need we have, a craving to put things right. To relieve pain, help the oppressed, overcome –"

"And producing your streetpaper was one way of satisfying that need?"

"Yes, one way. A small way."

I laughed. "Provoking people into dissatisfaction and rebellion is helping them?"

"Yes," he said very softly. He looked a little dreamy and there was in his eyes the beginnings of that faraway look. "Yes. The first step in the cure is to bring the disease to the surface, applying a poultice to the abscess so the pus can show itself." He snapped his head upwards and the dreamy look left his face. His voice rose as he said, "I don't want to talk about that. I want to tell you our plans. Like I told Su, you must hear them from us, directly."

He said this steadily, looking up at me, his eyes holding mine. An icicle entered my heart. I shivered internally, the way one does when looking down a precipice.

"Your plans? Yes, tell me your plans."

"There's a hospital in Africa." His face was composed. He spoke slowly, choosing his words carefully. "A little place run by missionaries. They need help. All the help they can get. Medically trained help, I mean."

"Trained?" I said, my voice high with challenge. "Su-May's a nurse, but you, you're just an agit –"

"I'm a trained physiotherapist, Hern." He allowed his face to lapse into a smile.

"So you're going out as a . . . team?" I was surprised enough to make this a question.

"First we thought of New Guinea," said Su-May, joining the conversation. "But Pete felt it was too close to home. Crazy, we were. Even thought of South America." She was bubbling over, eyes shining, hands fluttering about in excitement. "Real loonies, Hern." She put her forefinger against her forehead and made a twisting movement. "Then I heard about this place in Tanzania. A young doctor at the hospital just got back from working there. So much to do, he said. So off we'll go."

"Marvellous," I said. "Simply marvellous."

"Great, yah, Hern," she said brightly, and began to chatter about the equipment they would have to take with them and how they would acquire it.

I was shocked, not merely by their plan but by Su-May's insensitiveness to the effect this would have on me. Two hours ago she and I had been making love. She had kissed me many times and in many places, displaying an ingenuity that never failed to surprise and excite me. Now each of those kisses had become a gesture of betrayal, itemized and unique, personalized reminders of her treachery.

I stood beside them, stricken not merely dumb but immobile, an animal resigned to stillness at the point of the abattoir's bolt.

Oblivious of my distress, of my presence even, the lovers continued to make plans. At thirty I was an old man, left out, a nuisance. Someone to be derided, pitied, ignored. Strangely enough, I knew the feeling well. My mother, Clara, had a passion for seeing movies not once but again and again. As a child she had often taken me to an unfashionable cinema, which specialized in reruns. In darkness and on an uncomfortable seat, I had learnt how stupid old men in love become. I remember *Carrie* and *The Blue Angel*, I think of *Limelight* and *Pygmalion*. My eyes begin to smart. I did what I always do to stop my tears: I frowned slightly, screwing up my eyes and at the same time staring into the distance.

From the house the sounds of shouts of laughter were followed by silence. Then a group began singing "Mary's Boy Child".

Pete said, "Let's get back to the kids."

Su-May nodded and stretched out a hand towards me.

I backed slightly to stay out of her reach and said, "I suppose I should be getting home."

I hoped she would notice the turn of phrases and be touched by memories. She didn't. Her body moving slightly to the rhythm of the music, she said, "Stay, Hern. Stay. The party's only just beginning."

"I'm afraid," I said, hoping once again to catch her attention with what she always regarded as my old-fashioned speech, "I'll have to run."

"Don't run," she laughed, and I was grateful. "I'll drive you to where you can catch a cab."

"There's no need to," I said, holding up a hand. Still staring into the distance, I shook Peter's hand solemnly and managed, after a tremendous effort, to touch Su-May lightly on the cheek. Then I walked away.

The house in which the Children met was surrounded by a maze of winding lanes, anonymous, and leading purposelessly one into the other. My mind was a blank as I wandered among these. When I finally decided that the best thing to do would be to get home, I realized I was lost. Not knowing the direction in which the main road lay caused me to panic. I took a road which ended blindly and another which led to a fenced garden policed by unfriendly dogs. The sky, which had earlier been overcast, was now rapidly blackening as dark, low-flying clouds moved swiftly across it. I knew that once these had blown over it would beome a pale luminous grey and the rain would come pelting down. Not too far away I could hear thunder, prceded by that snap of silence which is the moment of lightning. The air was heavy and damp but contained a hint of burning like that which lingers around freshly-fused light bulbs. An unnatural smell. Unnatural and menacing.

Betrayed by Su-May, taken in by Peter, I was now being threatened by the elements themselves. As I struggled up a road with a steep uphill gradient, I felt abandoned and unloved. I needed to believe that someone worried about me; worried that I would be cold and wet in a storm, worried that I would be struck by lightning. The road wound haphazardly, making unexpected bends and doubling back on itself. I had no idea of the direction in which I was going and my progress was slow. A silence began to settle around me and I knew the storm was gathering for its opening onslaught. More than ever did I need a woman whose anxiety for me bred the kind of love that swelled in her chest till it threatened to choke her. There was no such woman in my life. But I was not alone. Cornelius was with me. The good Captain, however, was of no use in situations like this. I would have to look after myself and, realizing what this involved, I avoided his eye.

Of course, I had known all along that it would come to this. Just as I had known all along that Peter and the Children were responsible for the streetpaper, as I sensed betrayal in that dark, damp garden when Su-May kissed me, as I saw control of my life snatched from my hands the morning Rex Zhu had come into the furniture department of Benson's.

I am increasingly conscious of living in an eternal now, an unending present that makes tense meaningless. The events we see in sequence are with us all the time: an enormous canvas upon which we dare not gaze. Instead, we snatch glimpses of it and with piecemeal impressions impose sequence and a sense of time upon our lives. Had I dared look, I would have seen the solution to my problem instantly. I struggled round yet another corner and, to my surprise, found myself on the main road. The first, fat drops of rain were beginning to hit the ground like bullets when an emtpy cab drew up beside me. I must call Samson Alagaratnam as soon as I reached home, I thought, getting into the cab and pulling the door shut after me.

eleven

"Did you get caught in or out of the rain?" Sylvie asked as I walked through the door. She sat on the floor surrounded by the bits and pieces necessary for wrapping Christmas presents. She was crouched beside the Christmas tree, legs tucked beneath her, a tiny pair of scissors flashing as she cut wrapping-paper into the exact size needed for each gift. Lit intermittently by the lights from the tree, her hair and eyes took on an afterglow that I well remembered seeing on my mother when she had wrapped our Christmas presents. Mother never used to do the tree or set up the presents till late on Christmas Eve. Leaving things to the last moment heightened the excitement and increased the drama of the occasion. This was exactly what Clara Perera wanted. She would let me watch her but with her body positioned to prevent my getting a good look at what was beneath the wrapping.

"Surprises are the sweeter for being so," Clara would mutter, moving herself around the better to obstruct my view of things.

From time to time she would turn and face me, and her eyes would shine as though lit from within.

When Sylvie had moved into our lives she had at first assisted my mother, imperceptibly doing more and more over the years. Sylvie had taken over the task completely at about the time Mother had begun to need reading-glasses. The change was so subtly effected that only the most careful observer would have noticed it. Sylvie simply adjusted herself a little more around the tree and Mother moved back a bit.

The two women do not resemble each other physically and yet, as I looked at her from the doorway, Sylvie could well have been Clara: the quick movements of the hands, the shifting round to conceal what she was wrapping, the suspicious way she raised her eyes to meet mine. As I watched her a strange thing began to happen. An ancient spirit seemed to enter Sylvie's body. Instead of my beautiful wife, I saw before me an aged woman. True, the woman was still Sylvie but it was a Sylvie grown old. Her skin was pinched and papery, her cheeks were slack, her mouth collapsed into itself. Her hair seemed to have greyed in the multicoloured lights of the Christmas tree. The eyes she turned towards me had lost their luminosity and her hands, now withered, worked with the jerky, uncertain movements of the elderly. I looked at her with an aching pity. Sylvie grown old would wrap Christmas presents without eyes to watch, perhaps without someone to give them to. Waves of tenderness washed over me as I stared at her crouched over paper and tinsel and tape; tenderness not for the beautiful woman there before me but for the old lady, the Sylvie of the future. As I thought of this person my heart quickened, my mouth dried. A warmth fluttered lower and lower down my body and became the familiar throbbing of lust. It was strange how this lust I felt for the crone of the future was couched in protectiveness and was the more insistent because I knew I would never in reality feel or satisfy it.

"Well, which was it?' asked the bright-eyed creature beside the Christmas tree.

"Which was what?"

"Did you get caught in or out of the rain?" she repeated, turning her head upwards.

"A bit of both," I guess." I dabbed at my forehead with my handkerchief.

"You're very clever anyway not to come in till after I'd wrapped your gift."

I was truly back to the present and remembered what I had to do.

"I must call Sam, to discuss a few things."

"Do that," she said, "but from your room, so my gift-wrapping doesn't crumple your thoughts."

The phone rang for several minutes before Sam picked it up.

"Hey, Hernie-Bernie. What's the breeze on Christmas Eve?" His voice was slurred and, before I could answer, continued, "Sammy here's full of grade-A Scotch and in just three hours some tight-arsed Thai chick, sugar-lined front and back, is a-gonna be full of Sammy. It's one hour to take-off time, man, so all aboard, put out your cigarettes and unfasten your chastity belts."

"Sam, there's something very serious I've got to talk to you about."

"Will keep, man, will keep; but this king-sized hard-on Sammy's got for Christmas gotta find itself some skin-tight, honey-smooth wrapping, pronto."

"I know who's producing the streetpaper, Sam. The names, Sam."

"You're sure a shining dude, man, but those names ain't gonna cure the kinda problem Sammy's got between his legs, what's interfering with his walking. Look, man, I can hang my suitcase on it."

"But you still want the information?"

"Sure do, but when I get back from Bangkok. The revolution ain't gonna burst like a Christmas cracker, man. Drop down to the ministry slow and easy like on the 28th. Come up and cheer Sammy with your news, while he cools his raw and bleeding tool."

I replaced the phone and flopped into bed, all energy gone from my body.

Earlier in the afternoon, as I struggled to get out of Tampines before the storm broke, I was aware of the act of treachery I planned, and realized the kind of retribution it would bring down on Peter and his group. I tried to see my actions as inevitable, part of an already existing picture that any pair of correctly focused eyes could see. Deep inside me I knew this was not quite so. And after talking to Sam, I realized that disavowel of the consequences of my actions was impossible. With responsibility, I embraced guilt.

I knew Cornelius was in the room and I summoned the energy to look around it. But the Captain was wily. He kept in the tail of my eyes, his face averted. There seemed nothing to do except let the darkness press down upon me while the viscid sweat of despair glued me to the sheets.

Some hours must have elapsed before Sylvie turned on the lights.

"All packed, stacked and ready for the reindeers," she said brightly. "You going to give the good Lord a shock on his birthday by coming to midnight mass?"

Sylvie attended a newly-built church, light-beamed and airy. Instead of dark corners it had large windows ringed with stained glass, which filled it with brightness in a variety of colours. The fount was a stainless-steel bowl supported by telescoping cylinders of the same material. Sounds of the world outside, traffic from the motorway and voices of children from the nearby housing estate drifted in throughout the mass and gave it a continuity with the world outside. I would have liked to accompany Sylvie. Perhaps in her church it would have been possible to have my guilt acknowledged and my despair lightened. Then I remembered. At Christmas the church would be filled with young people wearing old jeans like new skins. Some of them, strumming guitars and jingling a variety of instruments, would make up the choir and would provide a medley of light-hearted carols and pop songs with vaguely religious sentiments. I could face my guilt in the darkness of my bedroom with only Cornelius for company; I could ignore it when I was dealing with Sam's cynicisn. It would be unbearable beside the fresh-washed, shining faces of these children.

"No, Sylvie," I said. "You go. I won't upset mother church tonight."

The ringing noise went on and on in my head. It wasn't solid enough to be the sound of church bells nor shrill enough to be a fire-engine. It was a tiny tintinnabulation, the sound of the little bells used in the mass or the ringing of a small musical instrument. Not something I should have difficulty sleeping through, I thought, rolling over. It seemed hours later that I felt Sylvie shaking my shoulder.

"Well, sleepy eyes," she said. "That was Ma."

"What was?"

"The telephone call that made you roll over."

"Oh." I sat up.

"They got back late last night. Pa's in a terrible way and Ma wants us over as soon as we can get there."

We got there some two hours later.

The house was more depressing than ever. In daylight the curtained living-room with its ill-matched contents seemed even gloomier and more desolate than I remembered. Yet, there was about the gloom an unpleasant air of expectancy, and realizing why this was so depressed me further.

My mother met us at the door and gestured us to silence. "He's dozing in the bedroom," she mouthed. "Say you dropped in for Christmas, not because he's sick. He never liked to be a nuisance."

"Why are we keeping this quiet?" I whispered. "And why are we talking as though Pa was already dead?"

"If your father were dead," Clara hissed, "there would be no need to whisper. As it is, he's barely conscious." She waved us to follow behind her.

My father lay in the centre of the large four-poster bed, his hands folded across his abdomen. He was dressed in white silk pyjamas and was propped up on pillows with white slips. The sheets were white and he was half-covered with a white flannel blanket. Around the bed were arranged three chairs, two near its foot and one near its head. On a bedside table was an unlit white candle, a crucifix, several old photographs and curios my parents had picked up on their travels. On the pillow beside my father was a musty-smelling leather-bound Bible. Draped across his head was one of Clara's lace silk handkerchiefs, soaked in eau-de-cologne. My mother motioned Sylvie and me to the chairs at the foot of the bed while she lowered herself into the one at its head, so that she looked not at us but directly into my father's face. It was obvious that Clara Perera had set up the props for a death-bed scene and I wondered if she planned Bible-readings or oath-takings for my father's last moments. I coughed and she flicked her head in my direction with so swift a movement that the venomous look I shot her missed her eye completely. I heard Sylvie murmur softly, a warning and a reproach, and turned my attention to my father.

His skin, wizened and mottled purple, contrasted sharply with the smooth whiteness of the sheets on which he lay. His lips were a blackish-blue and shiny, the way bruises become. His nails, too, appeared darker than they should be though they were clean and had been freshly manicured by Clara, no doubt, in anticipation of any close-ups the death-bed scene would require. We sat still and stared at him while he slept, unaware of what was going on around him.

He seemed far away. I hoped he was reliving his childhood. The smell of cologne from the handkerchief on his forehead must have touched his nostrils and reminded him of his mother. My grandmother was a large woman who always wore voluminous skirts that smelled slightly of mothballs and strongly of cologne. On her hands, however, there always lingered the aroma of curry. Perhaps the curry-flavoured hands comforted him now, brushing back the hair from his forehead or the tears that some boyhood pain or rage had brought to his eyes. Perhaps the musty smell of the leather Bible returned him back to the excruciating boredom of the catechism and the terrifying excitement of his first communion. Perhaps Clara, sitting close, exuded some special odour that only he could recognize and which carried him back to the delights of their honeymoon on the east coast.

His folded hands were quite still and I wondered, hoped even, that my father had died in a cascade of memories. I looked at his chest. It did not appear to be moving. A faint rustling sound appeared to come from him, but I was not sure if this was his breathing or the echoes of my own.

I stared into his face. His eyes were sunken so that his lids were stretched tight over the eyeballs. Behind these lids I could see the globes moving. Suddenly his eyes flickered open. They were bright with fear and his hands clawed the air with the kind of energy that only terror can produce.

"Where, where, what . . . Clara . . . ?" His voice, hoarse and rasping, ended in a pitiful whine. Then he began to weep.

My mother's face stiffened. She stared straight ahead, her mouth pursed but firm, her chin turned upwards. Clara Perera was ashamed. Fred, her brave, noble Fred was not only refusing to enter into the spirit of the death-bed scene, he was blubbering like a baby.

Sylvie looked down a while, then turned to me.

There was nothing I could do. My father knew he was dying and was afraid. I could not think of anything to do or say to help him.

My mother turned stiffly round to me, her eyes looking through me, but joining no less in Sylvie's appeal. I looked around the room, not quite sure what I would find to tide me over the embarrassment of the moment. Out of the tail of my eye I saw Cornelius Vandermeer. The Captain smiled. I shrugged and turned my palms upwards, appealing. Cornelius's smile widened and he shrugged too, disclaiming the possibility that he might be of use in a situation such as this. Why not, I asked across the room? Had he not been near death several times and had he not finally died? Who was better placed than the good Captain to tell me what to do? I begged for a tiny crumb of advice, some minute indication as to how I might proceed, but the Captain merely smiled and shook his head.

It was then I decided that I would begin writing the story of Cornelius Vandermeer; that I would pin his life to paper, and in the process remove him from mine. I was reluctant to do this. The Captain had for such a long time participated in the goings-on of my life that it was difficult to imagine him enjoying a circumscribed existence on a few pages. My father's dying was but one of the several things happening to me. I knew that in Cornelius's life I would find answers to some of the others.

Sylvie and I got home in the late afternoon. As soon as we were through the door, she said, "Don't let the light shine too brightly in your eyes, Hern. I can see a typewriter reflected in them." She punched my middle. "Go on and do some typing. You need a break."

The room in which I work faces east. By late afternoon it is cool and fairly dark. The shadows that formed around me were imprecise, no outline relating to object, but they were real enough. As I sat there staring at my typewriter and doodling on the sheets of paper beside me, I could see Cornelius Vandermeer gliding about in the corners of the room. The Captain was not too happy about becoming something finite and tangible. It meant that he would enter into one big decison in my life but would be denied participation in all the others that lay before me. I caught his eye, then avoided it. I too was reluctant to relegate him to a memory that had existence only on a page.

Nothing I wrote about Cornelius, however, seemed to come out right. Long before dawn, I pulled the covers over my typewriter and made my way to Sylvie's side. I hoped, but without much optimism, that in her quiet breathing, little snores and all, I might find the answers to the problems that beset me.

twelve

The two days following Christmas were perhaps the worst of my life. I spent them between my parents' home or sitting long hours alone in my room. My father alternated between periods of fretful coma and febrile lucidity. For hours he would lie in bed, his eyes closed, tossing a little and picking at the bedclothes, then he would suddenly sit up, eyes bright, his body quivering with excitement and say, "Remember, honeysuckle-bunch, that song Dada used to sing with Mama when we were little?"

Clara would move to the top of the bed beside him and Fred would do his best to sit upright. Then he, in a rasping air-hungry baritone, and she in an uncertain contralto would begin singing "Trees". They gave each other sidelong glances at the sexual innuendoes the song contained, and reaching the last line a little out of step with each other would end in an unnerving discord.

Throughout this play-acting, Sylvie managed to keep a look of mild but fixed approval on her face. I did my best to ignore what went on. Watching someone die was embarrassing enough. These impromptu side-shows made it painfully so. Clara was more distressed than I was. The crucifix, candle and Bible were there as she had arranged them but they looked discarded, the props of a movie the producers had scrapped. Uncoupled from her own fantasies, she was forced to participate in the terminal meanderings of Fred's mind. I felt a twinge of pity for her.

"And this, Clara bunch," he said with spurious vigour, "remember?" And he began singing "Pale Hands I Loved Beside the Shalimar". He turned to Sylvie. "Come on, old girl, give us the benefit of your dulcet tones."

Sylvie joined in, her voice at first tentative, a little tremulous, then gaining in strength. I nudged her, to indicate I was leaving. Without altering a note, she nodded me out.

Back in my room I looked at all the bits and pieces I had written about Cornelius over the years. Separately they seemed good enough: interesting anecdotes, cameos of character. But there seemed to be nothing I could do to make them cohere, still less coalesce. There was no matrix I could find that would make every fragment not merely connected to, but an essential part of all that existed around it. I realized that before my story could come together something would have to take place in my own life. I knew what it was but refused to look at it directly. From the little peeps I dared take, I surmised it concerned betraying Su-May and the Children and was, in an inextricable way, related to my father's dying.

I phoned Sam as early on the morning of the 28th as I dared. The sweet-voiced Anuita said that Samson would be at meetings all day. I explained that it was something he wanted to speak to me about.

"Why not drop by later in the evening?' she asked.

"Wouldn't you and Sam rather be alone after this long break?"

She laughed. It was a coarse laugh, thick and unwieldy. "No. After one of his trips Sam usually needs a few days to get his bits and pieces in place again."

I arrived at Sam's flat a little after nine. He was in his chair. He began to say something but his entire person was shaken by vibrations of near seismic proportions and speech was impossible. He held up a hand in explanation, indicating as he did the bottle of whisky before him. After about ten minutes he turned off the machinery.

"Needed that more than I needed my balls blowed in Bangkok," he said, pouring himself a drink. "You got the sweet music for Sammy's ear, the kind his drums are a throbbing for?" He sipped his drink. "All specifics must be recorded and filed before further action can be effected. Remember that, daddy-o."

"About the steetpapers, Sam, I think –"

"Shitpapers, man," he interrupted. "You know, Hernie baby, they got those things a-coming so fast they are as thick as turds littering our streets. This ain't no paper chase, man, it's war. Total war. You tell Sammy all you know, so we can clean the shit off the streets and make this city sweet-smelling again."

I told Sam. I told him of how Su-May and I had met and of the beginnings of our love affair. I told him of Peter Yu and the Children and of my discovery of the first streetpaper on the evening of our reconciliation. I told him of Peter's intentions of encouraging displays of defiance during Culture Week.

"And this mangy cat and a litter of kits thinks he can shake loose the whole operation. Does he really think that the entire apparatus of government will become his because he puts out a few badly-typed subversive memoranda?"

"No, Sam. Peter Yu is not interested in political power himself."

Sam's eyes bulged with disbelief. He leaned forward, swallowed a large amount of whisky and set his chair in motion. After a few minutes he stopped it and said, "Guess there's somebody the cat's grabbing the nuts for then?"

"Not that I know of, Sam."

"Just a shazmaroo of trouble for its own sake?"

"I think Peter Yu feels that once people see defiance is possible, better organized groups will think of coming in."

"Ah geddit, ah shore do," said Sam, relaxing. "This cat just starts the patter of drumbeats. When the main rhythm begins, once the show is really on the road, he steps up front, natural leader, like."

I shook my head. "I think he hopes to leave the country in a few months, Sam, and," I couldn't help the catch in my voice, "he's going to take my Su-May with him."

Sam laughed, leaned forward drank some whisky and slapped me on the back. Then, as though this was not assurance enough, he did it again.

"He ain't goin' no place but one, Hernie baby. Our A-One, top-secret, fully-modern, electronic, staffed-by-specialists detention-centre. You done Sammy boy one God-almighty favour right now.

Till you sprung your sweet little lips apart, the world looked darker than the inside of a nigger's arse. Now all's strobe light and flashing signs." He paused. "But actions must be concerted, directives clearly controlled. And for this piece of action Sam's yore honeyman, Hernie baby. Now don't you go a-worrying. We'll soon have you movin' in the groove you loove. You and your May-May."

"Su-May," I said.

He inclined his head, an apology, and went on. "We gotta get the whole scene going, man. Pick up some of the old hands, grab the odd fellow-traveller, get some of our in-house commie groups to sing new tunes, a bit of persuasion here, a bit of persuasion there and hocus-pocus, what've we got: a brand new television spectacular." Sam giggled and bounced around his chair without having to turn on the mechanism. "We'll have them yowling at prime time, competing to tell us more."

"Sam, by persuasion you don't mean any kind of torture? I can't stand the thought of Su-May being beaten up . . ."

"Fisting faces, man, you crazy. Ain't this modern Singapore? We got electricity, boyyo, and," he laughed, "refrigeration. I'll let you into something, Hernie baby," he shook his head. "Once we stick a cat's wick into an iceblock it rarely lights up again. And for encores there's strobe flash lightning, slowburns, ultrasonic disrupters. You name it modern, and we've got it. All electronic and fully computerized."

"But Su-May, Sam –"

"Don't get your underarms soggy, baby. You'll get a chance to let her see the light before the main action gets under way."

"You promise, Sam."

He poured some whisky into my glass and more into his, "I'll drink to that, Hernie. And you know, Hernie, what Sammy drinks to stays as straight and firm as an Arab dick in a Filipino arse."

We drank, me sipping slowly, Sam in large gulps. As we did, Anuita entered the room. She was dressed in jeans and a nondescript T-shirt. Her hair hung in bedraggled clumps and the life had gone out of her mouth. She pulled up a little stool and sat distant from us.

"What news?" she asked bleakly.

Sam ignored her and spoke to me. "We've had whispers, Hernie, that this group of yours plans a big razzmatazz for the new year. Mass release of streetpapers. So much shit-paper around, the city's gonna look like a public latrine in a cholera epidemic. We want to rope in your bambinos on New Year's Eve, Hern. Their shit-sheets on them, their fingers still sticky, so we can smell whose pants they've been into.

"Meanwhile we get the chorus ready." He looked at Anuita and nodded several times. "Back-up groups with pre-recorded tunes, statements, photographs, media boys ready with all the background jazz. But no whisper of all this, Hern. Not a whiff of a fart. And," he leaned over and prodded me in the chest, "you are the only sneak of a leak. Geddit, Hernie baby?"

Anuita spoke, her voice very quiet, "Sam means that if for any reason our trap is sprung before we are ready, we'll know who did it."

"And," said Sam smiling contentedly, his eyebrows raised, "we'll know whose balls we can shove into the juicing machine instead. You run along, man, and don't wet your underwear as you drive. Just paste a sticker to your head reminding yoreself that New Year's Eve is D-day."

Back in my room I returned to working on Cornelius. I had taken the step I had feared thinking about and now the Captain's story should begin to resolve itself. There was some urgency about things. My father clearly had not long to live and I wanted things sorted out with the Captain before Fred Perera died. Not that there was anything even vaguely similar about their lives. It was not parallels that I sought, nor finding events in one life which, when transposed to another, would become significant. Fred Perera was a platitudinous fool, used to striking poses as a schoolteacher that barely fooled even himself. There was very little in his life that, when it was over, would matter to anyone at all. Cornelius Vandermeer, even if he was a composite creation of Clara and Hernie Perera, born of incestuously mingled fantasies, was made to be larger than other men. I would have to find in Cornelius's life something of relevance to Fred's. Heroes have a duty: they have to make the prospect of the minotaur a little less daunting and to provide us with the thread, however insubstantial, that makes our journey through the maze less meaningless.

Cornelius, however, rejected the role. He lurked in the corners of my room, smiling enigmatically. I couldn't tell whether he was being evasive or just laughing at me. In desperation I began to wonder if the good Captain had ever been in a position to help me with my problem. After all, he had found himself in the midst of a war about whose rights and wrongs he knew little. In the course of this, youthful impetuosity, as often as plain stupidity, had earned him a reputation for courage. The war over, the Captain, middle-aged, was forced to live up to a reputation he could not remember acquiring. No longer did danger cause his muscles to tighten or the blood to rush to his head. Instead it dried his mouth and turned his bowels. What then made Cornelius choose death when escape was still possible? Perhaps his legs, softened by fear, had simply refused to support him any longer and the body's ultimate subjugation to terror had come to be seen as an act of courage. I looked around for Cornelius but he had moved into the darkest corner of the room. Only his pale grey eyes were visible and they were as revealing as the mist that joins sea to horizon at dusk.

I woke early, after an uneasy night, and decided to go into Benson's. Ahmad's coolness had by now become surliness. He pretended not to hear the questions I asked, and when he could not avoid doing so, answered in truncated monosyllables that were barely intelligible. The girls were a little kinder but did their best to indicate that they would be happier if I kept my distance. Nevertheless I believed that sitting at my desk, surrounded by the familiar smells of the furniture department, I had the best chance of unravelling the intricacies of Cornelius Vandermeer's last moments.

I arrived to find Anuita examining the carpets that were on display. She was wearing a grey suit, which had masculinized shoulders, large enough to conceal even her uncompromising curves. She wore court shoes of patent leather and on her shoulder was slung a handbag of the same material. Her hair was elaborately coiffured into whorls and was held in place by a pair of large clasps. She studied the carpets through a pair of thick-framed spectacles. It was difficult to believe that this was the same girl whose warmth had, but a few nights ago, moved me to such a pitch of desire.

She waved me to her and, noticing my surprise, laughed and said, "Yes, sir, this is the battledress they like us to wear, and Anuita is never the girl to say no."

"Compared to what I saw in Sam's place, these carpets are pretty poor."

She leaned nearer the carpet and, rubbing its pile with her fingertip, said, "I didn't come to talk about carpets, Hern," The jokiness had gone from her voice, which had dropped almost to a whisper. "I came to talk about last night."

"Last night?"

"Hern, sometimes I think you make out to be dumber than you are." Her eyes narrowed severely behind the spectacles. "Sam's going to make the most of what you told him."

"I don't see what real harm he can do, Anuita. I'll be the first to agree that the Children of the Book are misguided, perhaps even criminally so. But the most one could do with types like that would be to fine them or impose some minor deterrent sentence."

"Oh, Hern," she said. "Do you purposely make yourself stupid to avoid seeing certain things?"

"You are not making yourself very clear, Anuita."

"Let me spell it out for you then." She looked over her shoulder to make sure Ahmad and the salesgirls were out of earshot before continuing. "Because of your . . ." she paused, "assistance, Sam has been able to locate the persons behind this streetpaper thing. He could simply expose them as a gang of loony kids and leave things at that. But that would not be good enough for the men who control us. They demand more than that."

She shook her head and said, "Did I say 'they'? I'll say 'we', because I'm as much a part of this whole thing as anyone else. What they . . . we will show is that this whole effort is part of a massive conspiracy involving several people, including, of course, the Communists."

I burst out laughing and said, "Anuita, this is some kind of monstrous joke –"

"My dear, dear Hern, there's nothing funny about any of this." She slid her hand across the carpet and touched mine lightly. "Sam and his boys have been hard at work all night sorting out the different groups, formulating evidence, and, in the case of people already under detention, extracting more comprehensive confessions. We work very hard you know."

"I can't believe this . . ."

"Believe it, Hern," she said, snapping round to face me fully. "In forty-eight hours, by Saturday morning, we will have pulled in all the requisite people, extracted the necessary statements, prepared the documentary and other evidence we need. By mid-morning this will be in the hands of the local newspapers and television people, so that when the arrests are made late on Saturday night the media will be prepared. Sunday-morning editions will carry a story . . . fully explained."

"What happens then?" I felt myself shiver slightly as I asked the question and wished that I had not, to achieve the effect of winter, dropped the temperature of the department so much.

"That depends on what exactly they hope to accomplish by the exercise." Her face was quite impassive and the hand with which she stroked the carpet was steady. "If they," she smiled, "*we* wish to implicate large groups of people, even set aside a few confessions for later, then interrogations will be prolonged and intensive."

"In this case?"

She shook her head. "I'm not too sure. But I suspect that Samson is out to prove he can implicate anybody he wants to. This is something for which he is highly paid. If you look at it from his point of view, this," she smiled weakly, "is really his big chance."

"But what in heaven's name is the object of all this?"

"Object?" She looked genuinely puzzled. "Really, Hern, you continue to surprise me. If you can make a case for there being an ever-present threat to the island's security, then we have a free hand in using any measures we wish to overcome that threat. The greater the number of people potentially involved, the freer the hand one has in dealing with them."

"Is there such a threat?"

She threw up her hands. "That depends on from whose point of view you look at things. Right now, Samson can make that threat seem just as large or small as he wishes."

"What can I do to get Su-May out of this mess?"

"Nothing." She thought for a bit and added, "For old times' sake, Sam will probably give you a chance to talk to your lady friend and persuade her to incriminate as many people as she can. On the understanding, of course, that this will encourage the authorities to go easy on her."

"What if I advised her to leave the country?"

"Between now and Saturday?"

"Yes."

"Samson would like nothing better. He'd arrest them at the airport. Criminals, caught making getaway. What further proof would he need?" She shook her head. "And if they did somehow manage to get away, Sam would still have you, and I need not emphasize that he would quickly forget any sentimental feelings he has for you. Try to remember that, Hern." She touched my hand in farewell. "No, there's nothing you can do. Concede."

She was offering the only kindness that was possible: despair.

I arrived home to find a note from Sylvie informing me that she was at my parents' place and would probably be spending the next few days there. This suited me well. I wanted to have the flat to myself, and Cornelius.

It had finally dawned on me why I was unable to write about the Captain's last days. I had had, for some time, the feeling that the events of my life had been taken out of my control, that a path existed along which I was tracing some pre-ordained course. This was correct. I had allowed circumstances to jostle me along, absolving myself from responsibility. However momentous might be the consequences of my movements, I had not acted but reacted. I was not unlike the tectonic plates floating on the face of our planet, grinding against each other to produce mountains and earthquakes, altering the shapes of continents but unable to do anything about the process that moved them. When I betrayed Su-May and the Children to Sam, I believed I had finally taken back control of my life. This was not true. All I had done was to follow convenience one step further. I now saw that to be genuine, actions must be at variance with convenience, possibly even inimical to survival. It was this understanding that separated the creature of choice from that of chance.

Cornelius kept close to me all the while, smiling, sitting on the edge of my desk as I typed. Often he came round to read what I had written. Mostly he approved, sometimes laughing aloud at some peculiar circumstance of his life which he had failed at the time to find amusing. Only occasionally did he frown and shake his head. I would stop typing and he would indicate the sentence or juxtaposition of words that did not meet with his approval. I argued with him. The life might be his, the words were mine. He would smile and ask me to proceed. I would, but before long found it impossible to continue. Cornelius would laugh, nod towards the heavy blue pencil I used for deletions, and I would begin again.

So we worked for two days.

We both knew that when the story was completed Captain Cornelius Vandermeer would have left my life for ever. The thought saddened us. The Captain, however, dismissed my expression of regret with a little grunt and a shrug of his shoulders. In elucidating his life fully, I was taking control of my own. Losing the Captain was an essential part of the process that would free me from the mutterings of prophets and the formulations of sooth-sayers. I had chosen it to be this way.

Early on Saturday morning the story was finished and I put together the pages of "Dutch Courage". The dawn chorus was beginning and Cornelius had gone. Near the end he had realized that concern for the well-being of others is the only defence we have against terror and death. The Captain had learnt this from the circumstances of his life; I, by fabricating them. The pages of "Dutch Courage" lay before me, a blueprint for what I had to do. I began reading them to confirm I had got their message right.

dutch courage

Cornelius Vandermeer was afraid. He had been from the moment the lights went out. The houseboy was quick to set up the lamps and candles. These provided an uneasy illumination in which shapes flickered and changed and the line between light and shadow was unclear. But it wasn't this muddy, intimidating light that worried Cornelius. It was knowing that the generator had broken down three times in a week. That terrified him.

"Ah, yes," said Father Noonan. "For you, my friend, a reprieve," he indicated the unfinished chess game on the table between them. "and for me, a chance to sample a wee-bitty more of your excellent whisky." He laughed throatily and added, "Truly an act of God."

The priest finished in a gulp the remains of his drink, reached for the half-full bottle and poured himself a generous measure. The sun had been down several hours but the air had yet to cool. Both men were perspiring freely.

Noonan pointed the bottle in Cornelius's direction and said, "Drink up and have a bitty more yerself. Do you good. Help keep out the cold." He laughed noisily, slapping his middle.

Cornelius shook his head. He would have liked more whisky but did not want to pick up his glass. Even in the poor light the trembling of his hands would have been obvious. He didn't want anybody, not even the Father, to know how frightened he was.

Noonan put down the bottle and turned slightly away from Cornelius to peer intently at the chessboard. Suddenly this seemed to occupy his entire attention. He ho-hummed, sighed several times and viewed the chessmen from various angles. He seemed to have lost all interest in his companion. Confident that the priest's attention was elsewhere, Cornelius seized his glass with both hands, lifted it shakily to his lips and downed it.

The priest, a large man, appeared even larger in the white cassock he wore. He was hunched over the chessboard and his body was twisted away from Cornelius. Without moving or altering the tone of his voice, he said, "There are no demons in the dark, my friend, and even if there were, surely they would hold no terrors for you." He looked up from the chessboard and grasped Cornelius's wrist with a large hairy hand. "Talk about what troubles you, man."

Cornelius would have liked to tell Noonan, rather than have the priest find out for himself. He yearned to talk of how insidiously his fear had begun and grown, of how it had eaten him up bit by bit till none of the old Cornelius seemed to exist any more. The process was a peculiar one. He remembered all the events of his life but the life itself had become alien to the person who now inhabited his body. The young Cornelius, his Dutch father and Javanese mother dead, had left Batavia for Singapore in an unseaworthy Chinese junk. As the vessel bucked and heaved in pitch-black waters, Cornelius remembered being aware of an excitement, pleasurable but not frightening. War broke out shortly after his arrival in Singapore. As Captain Vandermeer of the Singapore Volunteer Corps, he was too busy leading his men to be intimidated by the shock of bombs or the whine of bullets. When the island fell, he remembered his heart pounding, strong and joyous, as he blackened his face and hair and took the dangerous journey north to the jungles of the Malay peninsula. Here, it was rumoured, there might be the beginnings of a resistance. That was the way it had been. Why now this sagging of the heart, this buckling at the knees, this preoccupation with the moment of death?

Midah had something to do with it, and Asif too.

She had been eighteen and Cornelius fifty when they married. Asif, now four, was nearer in age to his mother than Cornelius was. He could hear them in the back room, Asif babbling away in Malay, then chortling at his mother's reaction to his words;

Midah gurgling, and making noises of pleasure she did not produce when Cornelius made love to her. He listened to them in the sinister quiet of the generator's silence.

He would have liked to tell Noonan all this and should have. Instead he said, "Damn, that generator."

The priest leaned across the table, tipped up Cornelius's face and stared into it. "It's a blinding brightness that pursues you in the dark. You feel like an animal trapped in a car's headlights, squirming and ducking, but the light stays with you. You shut your eyes but somehow it's got in behind your lids."

"What on earth are you talking about, Father?"

"Terror, son. Your terror." The words spoken, the priest slumped into his chair. "The fear with which you, Cornelius Vandemeer, the Captain Vandemeer, are so unfamiliar." He chuckled and sipped his whisky. "My, my, my, you must feel like a Hottentot in an igloo."

So Father Noonan had guessed. No, knew. Had probably known for a while now. Cornelius checked the relief that threatened to wash over him. He must control it till he was ready for it. Delay would make it the sweeter.

As a boy, Cornelius had lived in a house some five kilometres from the sea. Every afternoon he used to run to the beach along dusty mud roads, baked hard and hot by the Javanese sun. By the time he reached the coast his feet felt as though he had walked on live coals and his body, depleted of sweat, was febrile and trembling. Before he reached the sea he had to run up a hill that sloped down to the beach. From its top the ocean looked blue and cool. But the boy would not dash down into it. Burning, he would wait till in the distance he saw a great wave forming. Then, timing it carefully, he would run down the slope, splash through the shallows and plunge into the heart of the wave so it carried him ashore. His relief was the greater for his patience.

Cornelius waited.

The priest poured more whisky into his glass. "To be sure," he said, "disquiet of the heart is not the easiest thing in the world to hide."

Cornelius shrugged, "You know more about such things than I do, Father," he said, and waited.

"Right on, right bang on." He sipped his drink. "And what's nearer the heart of the matter is how familiar I am with the humiliation of men." Cornelius looked up sharply and the priest smiled. "It's the confessional I be referring to, my friend. Makes us priests thick-skinned about other people's shame. So you can sing your heart out, son, and Father Noonan here won't be thinking any the worse of you."

Cornelius took the plunge. His voice was a little shrill and unnatural, the words staccato, coming in uncertain bursts, but as he spoke, they began to flow more and more easily till they washed over him.

"This is the third time, Father, not the first or second, but the third time the generator has broken down this week."

"Things that happen in threes," said Noonan, his heavy shoulders twitching slightly with laughter, "are evidence either of divine intervention or sabotage."

"This is sabotage, Father. I know it. Each time, the breakdown appeared to be due to normal wear and tear. A slipped fan belt the first time, a loose spark-plug, the second. But I have no doubt that it's sabotage, Father."

"There were other signs pointing to sabotage, I suppose."

"None at all. The fence round the perimeter of the estate has not been cut, neither has the lock of the shed housing the generator been tampered with."

"Then surely, Cornelius, you are inventing the demons to justify your terror. The arm of coincidence is long. Accidents happen. Misread instructions of the Almighty, I consider them."

"No, Father." Cornelius shook his head. He was talking easily now and picked up his glass with a steady hand. "Not only do I know it's sabotage, I know who's behind it."

"Good God, man, if it's one of the workers on the estate, simply unearth the wretch and get rid of him. Goodness knows what hold the Communists have over him."

"It's not one of my workers," said Cornelius. His voice had become so soft that it carried just across the table. "Pour us more whisky, Father, and I'll tell you."

The bottle was almost empty and, swivelling backwards on his chair, Cornelius pulled open a wooden cupboard, from which he extracted a fresh bottle. This he placed on the table.

Then in the same soft voice he continued:

"When the British surrendered in 1942 I didn't give myself up. Couldn't see myself being led meekly into a Jap prisoner-of-war camp. So I stained my skin, donned native clothes and, travelling only at nights, made my way to the northern part of Singapore, where I crossed the Straits and got to the Malay peninsula."

"Story goes that you swam the Straits, shark-infested or not."

"It was no big feat," said Cornelius.

He remembered how dark the water had been and how it had reeked of burning oil. He had heard about sharks and had carefully blackened his body to avoid attracting them. He swam a gentle breaststroke all the way, disturbing the surface as little as possible and keeping his head well down. The sea was full of debris: the remains of craft the British had scuttled, floating metal objects which could have been oil-cans or mines. Twice his legs got entangled with half-submerged sheets of tarpaulin. They felt like the hands of dead men clutching at him, trying to drag him down. They must be Japanese, he had thought, posthumously continuing to serve their Emperor and their cause. But he had thought this whimsically, without fear. With a pang Cornelius remembered that there had been no doubts then, no thoughts of death; only a confidence that he would reach the mainland, join the resistance, carry on the fight.

"Anyway," Cornelius continued to the priest, "I made contact with the anti-Japanese forces in the jungle easily enough. The Communists were, of course, the backbone of the resistance."

"In the band with me was a young lad called Peng. His family were small-time farmers who had been murdered by the Japs. Peng, who had hidden himself in a pigsty, had seen his mother and sisters repeatedly raped before they were butchered. He was to become the most daring of our group and in those days," Cornelius laughed bitterly, "I wasn't short of guts myself." He smiled to himself. "The two of us got up to all sorts of stunts. Must have had the Japs wondering if they were up against humans or some kind of demon."

"An excess of derring-do always confuses the enemy," said Noonan. "I remember a prank or two during the troubles in the old country which had the English wondering if the devil himself was not in league with the Irish. But carry on, carry on. . ."

"I can't recall how many times Peng saved my life or I his," Cornelius looked across at Noonan. The colour of his eyes had deepened and the lines on his face had relaxed. "You know, Father, I actually came to look upon Peng as a son. I was young then and when I thought of a son I thought of a slightly younger version of myself. And Peng was the ideal age." Cornelius sighed. "I taught him as much as I knew about jungle warfare and though we were low on knowledge we were high on improvisation. Peng was ingenious and cheeky.

"Have you ever wondered what the real object of sabotage is?" He did not wait for Noonan to answer. "No, the destruction of a bridge or cache of arms is unimportant. The dismantling of the enemy's composure is what really hurts. By sabotage, you inform him that you have access to his most secret and secure places. You convince him that his strongholds are no longer fast. And you must do this subtly, Father. It must be a realization that he makes for himself. He must discover the evidence and come to see his own weakness." Cornelius's eyes narrowed as he looked into the past. "There must also be an element of mystery as to how you achieve your effects, a touch of magic. That always heightens the terror." Cornelius paused and looked directly into Noonan's face. "I taught Peng all this, Father."

"And?"

"He now uses my own methods against me."

"Ah, a situation full of interesting possibilites. Bursting with them, I'm sure. But in itself," he looked sideways at Cornelius, "a situation that is by no means novel. Son challenges father, pupil master . . . Oh, Lord, don't look so hurt, Cornelius. It's been happening since time began."

Cornelius stared straight ahead and went on with his story:

"With the war ended and the victory parades in London over, Peng said he was staying on in the jungle. The fight for freedom was not over, he maintained. In fact it had only just really begun. The British imperialists, of whom I was a lackey, would have to be driven out of the country. Peng said – a little sadly, I think – that the day might come when we would confront each other in battle, and whichever of us allowed sentiment to affect his judgement was doomed.

"That day has come, Father."

"Are you sure," said the priest, his face expressionless, "that your anticipation is not creating this phantom?"

Cornelius shook his head. "The first time the generator failed it was because a fan belt had snapped. It hadn't been cut, mind you, but the belt didn't look worn enough to break. The second time we found a spark-plug had come adrift. Of course, it could have been shaken loose by the vibrations of the generator, which is ancient and rattles rather a lot. But I'm sure that's not what happened. The wire fence surrounding the estate had not been cut, nor had the lock on the door of the shed housing the generator been touched. Yet I knew in my bones that the machine had been tinkered with. How, I ask myself? Magically, by demons? No, Father, I'm sure these weren't accidents. I see Peng's signature on them."

The priest let a hairy paw fall on Cornelius's forearm. "You taught him to write. I reckon you'd read his hand best."

"This fear of mine, Father, it's not of fighting Peng or of dying. It's to do with Midah and Asif. I keep asking myself what would become of them if something happened to me."

Noonan picked up his glass and carefully put it to his lips. Then he took three large gulps of whisky very slowly, swallowing the first and allowing it to go down before beginning the second. The third down, he carefully replaced the glass on the table. He achieved the effect of having crossed himself. Before speaking, he carefully wiped his lips with the sleeve of his cassock. "Cowardice, my friend, has many disguises. But its most popular cloak, worn till threadbare, is that one is not afraid for oneself but for someone else." Noonan sighed. "What a grand alibi for gutlessness, an alibi that increases the standing of the coward . . . No, my friend, better to confess your terror than to hide behind that kind of lie."

Cornelius said wearily, "Perhaps you're right." He sipped his whisky. "I know you are not afraid. You ride your little motor-bike, day or night, drunk or sober, wherever you wish, your white cassock making you an easy target. You are an Irish priest, you may hate the British and think of yourself as revolutionary, but as far as the Communists are concerned you are white, an imperialist dispensing opium to the people. Nevertheless, you are not afraid." Cornelius paused and let his shoulders sag forward. Then suddenly, as though wishing to provoke a response too instinctive for insincerity, he snapped upright and said, "It's your faith, isn't it, old man? God-almighty belief in an after-life . . ."

"Oh, no, my friend," said the priest, looking grave, then smiling quickly. "It's not faith. Not unless you have the Joan of Arc kind, the brand that makes you fireproof. For ordinary fellas like Patrick Noonan faith in the after-life offers as much protection as a spider's web in a thunderstorm."

"What helps then?"

"Dutch courage."

"Whisky, Father?"

"No." Noonan shook his head. "I'll try and explain." He picked up his glass, reminded of it by Cornelius's question, changed his mind, and put it down. "Every time I get on my wee machine and belt about these jungle roads, I'm scared. But after a bit I get to wondering how I'm going to squeeze a few dollars out of the moneybags I'm visiting without promising to save his soul or sell him mine, so that I'm too busy to bother about what's waiting for me round the next corner."

"And these thoughts keep you from being afraid?" Cornelius's voice rose a little in surprise.

"Most times. That and the problem of keeping my machine on the road. You know what sort of condition I'm sometimes in, man." He slapped his thigh and finished his whisky. "And I have thoughts of the orphanage."

Noonan rarely spoke of the orphanage but it was with him always. The wooden shack with its corrugated-iron roof and in it the children: bastards of the village girls who had gone to the city to find work, the younger daughters of large families,

abandoned as babies, the orphans of farmers killed by the
security forces or the guerrillas. In fact, any stray that he,
Patrick Noonan, happened upon. He never spoke about them, his
family, these children, though he could see them right now,
lying on their canvas beds, tossing in their sleep, slapping at
mosquitoes, laughing or crying in their dreams. He saw them as
clearly as he did when, before going to bed at night, he would
stand, sometimes a little unsteadily, at the doorway of the shack
and look on the children who were his benediction.

"No, my friend Cornelius, I've no secret information about
the after-life to keep me going. I'm too bloody busy chasing my
tail in this one to pause and ask the Almighty what happens
when the dancing's over."

There was a knock on the door and a young Malay sergeant
stepped into the room. He nodded to the priest and formally
saluted Cornelius.

"Captain, sir, somebody's cut the wire fence near the
generator."

Cornelius could feel his muscles tighten and begin to quiver as
the man spoke.

A high fence, topped with barbed-wire, enclosed the living
and production areas of the rubber estate. Its inner perimeter
was patrolled hourly by two heavily-armed constables.

"Any damage to the generator shed, Sergeant Amat?" asked
Cornelius, struggling to keep the trembling in his knees from
showing in his voice.

"Generator shed still locked, Captain," said Amat. "Detail
for inspection outside, sir."

"How many men, Amat?

"All in all, four, sir."

"Four," said Cornelius, his voice high-pitched and quivering.
"You get four more and I'll meet you outside in five minutes."

He stood up and straightened his loose khaki tunic. His
gunbelt hung on the wall. He took it down and put it on outside
his tunic. Seeing Father Noonan staring at him, he said, "Easier
to get your gun when you wear it this way." From a wall
cupboard he extracted two hand-grenades, slipping one into
each of the large side pockets of the tunic. The actions were

automatic. He never left the house without his gun and grenades. He patted the gun as he made towards the door.

Noonan stood up before he reached it and Cornelius said, "You're not coming, Father."

"Oh, why not, Cornelius? A dash of excitement will go well with all the whisky I've been drinking. And the old legs stiff with the booze unless I prance about once in a while to remind them that there's life before death."

Cornelius laughed. "All right, Father, but keep well back and get your head down if there's any shooting."

There were more than eight men outside and Amat explained, "Four extra, Captain. Doing nothing so come to join in the fun."

The twelve men, like Amat, were in their late teens and had difficulty in keeping their voices down. They were excited about being on a mission with Cornelius. He could hear loud whispers of "Kapitan Belanda". It was strange, he thought, that after all these years, they still talked of him as the Dutch Captain. The thought did not upset him. Something else, however did. Under the gun-oil and insect repellent, Cornelius could smell the excitement pouring from their bodies, with their sweat staining their tunics and the air around them. It was an odour sharp and unpleasant. The more so because Cornelius could remember the times he had been able to smell it on himself. Remembering, he felt anger against the youths around him. What damn fools they were, he thought. So anxious for an engagement with the guerrillas. If they did meet a party of Communists, several of the jabbering group behind him would be dead. Why on earth, he wondered, were young men always in such a hurry to enter that unending tunnel of darkness?

"Yes," said Noonan, intruding but not contradicting his thoughts. "All in such a hurry to jump on the bandwagon to the grave. Houseman was wrong, you know."

"Who was he, your friend Housman?"

"A poet," said the priest, and began to recite in a soft voice.

"Here dead we lie because we did not choose
To live and shame the land from which we sprung.

Life to be sure is nothing much to lose;
But young men think it is, and we were young.

"Yes, he was wrong," Noonan continued, "as wrong as those who look for God in their navels are wrong. It is not the young who fear death. It is the old, though in His infinite wisdom the Almighty has given them a whole lifetime to prepare themselves for the event."

Cornelius remained silent. They were walking briskly now and would soon reach the perimeter fence. The knot that formed in his throat had begun to tighten and, as it did, it sent tremors into his legs. Had Father Noonan not been with them, he would have found some excuse to postpone the expedition until morning. With the priest present and aware of his terror, there was nothing he could do except move along the dark narrow paths that led to the fence. The men were quieter but he continued to hear excited whispers of "Kapitan Belanda". In the distance he could see, dimly lit, the line of workers' huts, hear the sounds of women's voices, smell faintly the woodsmoke. He thought of Asif and Midah, safe in the bungalow. He thought of them not with relief but a vague, angry envy. The knot in his throat became a hard lump and his legs began to seize up. There must be some reason to turn back . . .

"Look . . . here, Captain," said Amat, darting forward and shining his torch at the point where the lowest two wires of the fence had been cut. The cuts were exactly one above the other. The higher wires had been neither stretched nor displaced. This was clearly not the work of a wild animal.

"See this side, sir," Amat said, directing his torch to the low scrub outside the fence.

A path had been beaten through the scrub, the low bushes deliberately flattened. The path ended neatly at the breach in the fence. Cornelius had no doubt that this was the work of Peng. He was probably nearby, watching them, studying Cornelius's reaction as he recognized his signature. Had not Cornelius himself taught him to be at hand, to see the effect ones's tricks had on the enemy? There would be more signs; Cornelius was sure of that.

"Turn off that bloody torch, Sergeant." He tried to snap out the command, tried to put an edge of anger to it. What came out was high-pitched, almost a squeak. He breathed deeply a few times and in a more level voice asked, "Is the generator shed damaged?"

"Outside all fine, sir," said Amat, leading them to the shed.

With a pen-torch Cornelius examined the door. The bolt was in place and the large padlock appeared untouched. He let the beam play along the side of the shed and around. Nothing appeared to be disturbed: the little fuse-box, the large outlet cable, the potted plants lining the path leading to the door. Yet, the very air of normality was sinister, a ploy to make the surprise that awaited them inside the more shocking.

From his pocket Cornelius extracted the key to the padlock. There were only two keys to this. One hung in his office. The other he carried on his person. It was an old padlock and had a peculiarity. The key had to be turned twice and angled to one side before the mechanism would work. The lock opened to his manipulations and the bolt of the door slid back smoothly. Nothing seemed to have been tampered with. It was clear that Peng and his comrades had got into the shed by way of the roof. Cornelius began to do things quietly. He walked on the balls of his feet, his breathing became slow and measured, his movements definitive, economical. The men behind him had become absolutely still. Drawing his revolver from his belt, he motioned Amat forward. The sergeant moved to one side of the door. As he did, he unhitched the bren-gun from his shoulder and released its safety lever. With a sideways movement, Cornelius kicked open the door as he and Amat fell to the ground on either side of it, their guns covering the exit to the shed. The door slammed open with the violence of a thunderclap, making the silence that followed the more difficult to bear.

There was just enough light for Cornelius to see Amat lying prone, his bren still at the ready. The group on the ground behind him were a uniform mass, which moved slightly as the men changed position. Father Noonan's white cassock was clearly visible in their midst.

He rolled over to Amat. As he did, he realized that the side on which he had landed hurt. He knew he would hesitate the next time he had to fall. Terrible, this business of ageing. The terror and the justification for terror the body provided. He touched Amat's shoulder lightly and together they began to crawl forward. Their caution was unnecessary. The shed was empty, its roof undamaged. At first nothing seemed to be out of place. Then he saw it. Just at the point where it left the shed, the main cable had been neatly severed. In the light of his torch, the fresh-cut copper wires surrounded by heavy black insulation glinted at him like Peng's teeth when he flashed his most impudent smile.

Cornelius returned to the generator shed the next day. It was afternoon and the estate snoozed under a blanket of leaden-grey cloud that trapped the heat, making effort difficult and somehow pointless. He found Peng in the shade of the wooden structure. The lad wore a nondescript khaki uniform which had no markings of rank. Only the red star on his cap identified him. He lay face-down, rolling a cigarette. He heard Cornelius but didn't turn until the cigarette had been fashioned and lit.

"You recognize the style, master, as you must, for it is but an imitation of your own." He smiled cheekily at Cornelius.

"How many years has it been, young fella – seven?" As he spoke, Cornelius noticed that the years showed, if only slightly, in the tightening around Peng's mouth, the roughening of his cheeks. His eyes remained bright. Dancing and mischievous. "All this is not some childish joke . . ."

"Those without childhoods have no time for childish jokes."

It came back to him then, Peng's habit of speaking in short generalizations. He smiled because he remembered Father Noonan with uncharacteristic loss of insight once telling him: "Beware of aphorisms, they are the devil's tongue." Cornelius had a feeling that Peng and the priest had much in common.

To Peng, he said, "So there is a reason for these little tricks."

"To risk one's life without reason is to act no differently from a lunatic." He rolled over on to his back and continued to puff at his cigarette. "Yes, master, I have a purpose."

"Why come to me?" said Cornelius. "After all, I'm only –"

"The manager of a rubber estate and an imperialist running dog," said Peng. "While I am –"

"A guerrilla soldier and a liberator of the people," said Cornelius.

They laughed. Briefly, but without bitterness.

"We need something from you, my Captain."

"Arms?"

"No," said the young man. "Things that reduce the damage of guns and the jungle."

"Medical supplies?"

"Yes, master. Penicillin, sulpha-drugs, pain killers, iodine, bandages, dressings, tablets for malaria, tablets to purify water . . ."

"The estate has only a small supply of these things, Peng."

"But you are expecting a big consignment soon. A whole year's supply. Right, master?"

"You seem to know a lot about us, Peng."

He grinned. "Know your enemy. You taught me that, my Captain, long before I read Mao."

"But what makes you think I can simply give you a year's supply of drugs meant for the estate?"

"You don't give me anything, my Captain. You just tell me when and how the supplies are arriving and I will arrange to take them."

"Ambush the transport, you mean?"

"We have no other way, my Captain."

"You tell me why, my young and daring comrade, soldier for freedom and all that, why I should do this? For money? For old times' sake?"

"To offer you money, master, would be to offer you an insult. And I don't think you have forgotten what I said about sentiment when we parted. No, master. I offer you security. Not peace but a truce." He sat up and looked at Cornelius intently. "Age makes the blood cold, master. These days you shake at the thought of battle, but it is not eagerness that makes your muscles quiver." Seeing he had scored, he laughed out aloud, flashing his teeth in boyish delight. "You give us the drugs and I'll promise you safety."

"Meaning?"

"You tell me, my Captain, just how the drugs are to be delivered. The exact route, the times, the number of armed men guarding the consignment. You tell me this and I will promise that our people never bother you again. You and your family can live happily and without fear." A strange look crossed Peng's face. It took Cornelius a while to recognize it as envy. Peng was a young man and some of his needs could certainly not be catered for in the jungle. "Yes," he continued, "your Midah is a lovely girl, but then you imperialists always took the best of our womenfolk for yourselves."

"I'll have to think over your proposition, Peng."

"I'll be back in two days."

"Why, Peng? Impatience was never one –"

"The jungle is not kind to our soldiers. The fight cannot go on while wounds fester and rigors are uncontrolled. My Captain . . ."

"Yes, Peng."

"Your secret is safe with me. But think of this when you make your decision: untested cowards can share graves with brave men." He half-raised his right hand, palm forward, in the salute that comrades-in-arms have used from time immemorial. "Stay well, my Captain."

Automatically Cornelius's hand began to rise and he was about to offer Peng the other half of the salutation, but stopped himself in time from saying "Go well", and instead muttered, "I'll see you around."

The next two days were the worst that Cornelius had ever spent. His fear, now tangible, was no less easy to bear. He jumped at little sounds, was irritable with Asif, slept poorly and burst into sweat for no reason. It unnerved him that Peng knew so much, not only about what was happening on the estate, but about his personal life. He reminded himself that intimidation was the stock-in-trade of the "fifth column", as guerrilla fighters used to be called. Even as the expression crossed his mind, he could recall telling Peng: "A few facts and a bit of guesswork is all you need. Then drop a hint here and there that nothing is secret from you and their fears will do the rest."

"I know," Peng had said. "The fortune-teller used to fool my mother like that."

These memories did not stop Cornelius waking in the night convinced that Peng had an accomplice on the estate.

Peng looked different when he met him two days later. He seemed to have gained weight. Then Cornelius saw that the young man's khaki tunic was stuffed with strips of an old army blanket. His face was flushed, his movements jerky and erratic. *I must really be getting old,* thought Cornelius, *not to recognize malaria, the oldest and most undiscriminating enemy of all who fought in the jungle.*

He watched the boy shiver and said, "Hang on, I'll dash back and get some quinine from Ah Cheong." Ah Cheong was an old and drunken male nurse who dispensed medicines for the estate and looked after its medical supplies.

Peng shook his head, "No," he said. "Just tell me how the consignment of medicines is arriving. If from the north, by which route. If it's from the south, we have no problem. There's only one road up."

"It's coming from the north. From Kuala Lumpur, through Tampin."

"Armed escort?"

"None really. Just the driver and one armed guard."

"Times?" Peng's overly bright eyes darted about aimlessly, but he was registering everything Cornelius said.

"The lorry gets to Tampin by ten in the morning. We expect it to arrive here by two . . . three at the latest."

Peng's body had begun to shake violently. Cornelius remembered the paradox of shivering in the muggy, mid-afternoon heat while your comrades sweated in it, an inconsistency that made the fever the more difficult to bear.

"G-good. You s-stay away f-from the estate. S-stay away the whole d-day. Your f-family t-too."

"Let me get you the quinine, Peng."

"No." He smiled, something of the old sprightliness returning to his face. "I'll wait till Friday. I can wait two days." He smiled again. "The revolutionary soldier who can't wait finds that death can't either."

As he walked back, Cornelius felt that something was wrong. It was a vague unease, a disturbance so gentle that he wondered if he felt it at all. It involved something Peng had said. Something that would, in the old days, have made his nose itch and his skin prickle. But the special sense that in battle separates the survivors from the slain had lost its sharpness. It had become imprecise and useless. He remembered what it was much later, when it was too late to matter.

In a way, he would have liked Peng to have the consignment. But this was impossible. Once he acceded to the request, more would follow. There would be demands for more drugs, food supplies, arms and God knew what else. As long as Midah and Asif were around, the possibility of blackmail was endless. Peng would squeeze everything he could out of the situation, till Cornelius, ridden with guilt or remorse, would try to be the man he no longer was and attempt something foolhardy. No. The only certain protection for his wife and son would be to get rid of Peng and his guerrillas permanently. He would report all that had transpired to the British security forces based in the nearby town of Gemas. Cornelius was not happy about the course (he refused to look upon it as betrayal) he had to take, a course that would certainly result in Peng's death. He knew that the security forces often mutilated and displayed the bodies of guerrillas as a deterrent to those aiding their cause. There was no doubt that he still retained a considerable affection for the lad but even the image of Peng's body, dead and disembowelled, did not cause him to change his mind. His options were clear. If he gave in to Peng, the course of his life would be determined by the struggle between the guerrillas and the security forces. If he didn't, he would have to accept the responsibility for the lad's death.

Having made the decision, Cornelius felt more in control of his affairs. His fear of death, however, did not go away. He lay awake at night, sensing everything about him acutely, his body unwilling to fall asleep, to relinquish consciousness even temporarily. It was too good to give up: the moonlight filtering through the window and making cool elegant patterns on the bedclothes; the undulations of Midah's body as she slept; the

infinitely varying harmonies coming from the nearby jungle.
Nothing could justify an end to this sweetness nor distract him
from the certainty of its passing. As though endorsing his
thoughts, Midah murmured, turned, and still half-asleep,
gathered him into her arms. They made love, but even when it
was done and his head rested against her breasts his mind was
still troubled. It turned again and again to the terror of the
moment when one knew that death was unavoidable and close at
hand. He raged at the thought of such a moment, but could
think of nothing that would make it less agonizing.

Early the next morning Cornelius made his way to the long
whitewashed building that housed his office and the estate
dispensary. Ah Cheong, the old male nurse, was asleep on a
bench in a small back room, the smell and effects of alcohol still
upon him. It took Cornelius several minutes to rouse him.

When he did finally succeed Ah Cheong jumped to his feet,
albeit unsteadily, and with the fussy, energetic manner sobering
drunks assume said, "Yes, yes, I know. I did not forget medical
supplies arrive today. Yes, Captain Cornelius, I remembered.
Got the shed behind the dispensary ready for them. Come and
see for yourself. All ready." Then, catching sight of Cornelius's
blank expression, he said, "Oh, no. Trouble. Don't tell me,
Captain – ambush. All lost to Communists. Shame, shame.
Nothing safe. Not even medical supplies."

"Ah Cheong," said Cornelius wearily. "Even though you may
still be drunk you know very well that our supplies always
arrive on Friday, which is tomorrow. It's a holiday but do
remember to keep a few workers in to help you unload."

"Memory gone. Old age," said the drunk, striking his head
several times with his knuckles. "Thank goodness. God is great.
No ambush."

"There were some vague rumours about that kind of thing,"
said Cornelius. "I'm driving down to Gemas to arrange for some
protection. Perhaps we'll even set a trap for the guerrillas."

Ah Cheong nodded grave approval.

The trip north to Gemas took less than an hour. The drive
was an easy one and left Cornelius's mind free for his thoughts,
which were far from happy. His death fear, now a chronic,

background disquiet, was joined by a sharper worry, which was in some way related to his encounter with Ah Cheong. Again, he was reminded that he had lost that extra sense on which he had, so often in the past, depended for survival.

A contingent of British security forces was based on the outskirts of the town. Captain Roberts, the officer-in-charge, was happy to see Cornelius and even happier with the information he brought. He told Cornelius that in recent months the guerrillas in the district had not only been more active but also more daring. They had booby-trapped armed convoys on trunk roads, and on two occasions he had found evidence suggesting they had actually been inside the British encampment. It was a relief to know that they would soon have the man responsible for all this. He assured Cornelius that it would be a simple matter to have a few heavily-armed men hidden among the supplies and in radio contact with a larger group, out of sight, but following close behind.

Roberts smiled grimly to himself and continued, "It promises to be a fine old party, and if I were you, Sir, I'd get my missus out of the way tomorrow. We'll be doing a public body count on the estate when it's all over, and that ain't a sight for a lady." He grinned, adding with relish, "It really ain't, sir.

"And another thing –" he was a bit uncertain about the title but decided to use it – "Captain . . . keep all this tight under your hat, sir. Never know which one of these chinkos and nignogs is a sympathizer, or even actually working for them."

The disquiet that had nagged Cornelius all morning became acute and an icy hand gripped him between the legs.

"What's the matter, sir?" said Roberts, his face suddenly concerned. "You're shivering, sir. You look like . . . like somebody's walking on your grave." Then, realizing that the Dutchman might not quite understand, he explained, "As though you've had a premonition, sir. Something awful, like."

With difficulty Cornelius pulled himself together, assured Roberts he was all right, refused his offer of a cup of tea, and drove over to Father Noonan's orphanage.

The priest was in a field behind the building, teaching a group of ragamuffins how to sow maize. He carried a large rusty bucket containing a combination of dung and compost. Kneeling on the ground, he mixed a handful of the contents of his bucket into the earth, implanted the seeds, patted the earth around tenderly and marked the spot with a small dried twig. When this was done, two eight-year-olds, carrying between them a bucket of water, struggled forward. Noonan scooped water from the bucket and sprinkled it over the implanted seed as tenderly as he would at a baptism. A group of younger children following behind "ooh'd" and "ah'd" in appreciation of the priest's efforts.

"See, my wee ones," he said, "you must put them to earth lovingly, the way you would a brother or a friend. Then they never die but become something new." He sighed and squatted on the ground, rinsing his hands in the bucket the eight-year-olds carried. With a muddy hand, he wiped the sweat from his face and neck. "But now we must stop. Father is tired and hot." The children gathered round him protectively, some wiping the sweat from his body, others attempting to fan him with their hands.

Noonan disengaged himself from their attentions and the two men strolled back to the orphanage to sip warm beer on a verandah. After a while, the children began to come in from the field. The priest looked at them and said, "It's the tiny shadows of these wee ones, not the mighty church, that shields me from the blinding light of terror."

Seeing how Noonan coped with his fears did little for Cornelius. Listening to Midah's quiet breathing in bed, he felt that his attachment to the woman and their child, if anything, increased his fear of death. The icy hand that had first gripped him when he talked to Captain Roberts was still with him. Midah's warmth and nearness did nothing to lessen its hold.

He left for Gemas again on Friday morning, this time accompanied by Midah and Asif. Cornelius drove slowly. There was no rush to get out of the way, since the consignment was not due till early afternoon. Steel louvres had been fitted to the windscreen and sides of the old Vauxhall to ensure it was bullet-proof. These made the interior of the car dark and cool, something Cornelius normally liked. Today he felt as though he was driving a hearse.

The friendliness of Salamah, his mother-in-law, loud and cheerful, did little for his mood. He was irritated at how much she and Midah had to chatter about, and jealous that Asif, with his grandmother around, ignored him altogether. Things got worse as the time for the ambush neared. Instead of eating lunch, he stomped around the table glaring at the food. Normally he enjoyed Salamah's cooking but today even its smell revolted him. He put off phoning Captain Roberts for as long as he could, but shortly after 3 o'clock called him.

"Supplies got through safely, guv," said Roberts. "No hide nor hair of the Commies in sight."

"You mean there was no ambush?"

"Right the first time, squire," Roberts replied. "The comrades must somehow have got wind of our plans."

"But that's impossible," said Cornelius, holding down the fear in his voice.

"Walls have ears these days, sir. But not to worry. We'll get them the next time round."

It was dark when they left Salamah's house. Asif, as usual, had refused to be parted from his grandmother. Normally Cornelius would insist that he return with them, but today he was too preoccupied to argue and so let the child stay behind.

Something had gone terribly wrong. He would not be able to work things out till they were back at the estate and there, he hoped, he could discover exactly what had gone amiss. Somehow Peng had found out his plans. Cornelius was uncertain as to what the young guerrilla would do when he realized he had been betrayed. Whatever his next move, Peng would surely make it soon. It was a good thing that they had left Asif with his grandmother. This meant there was one less person to worry about in an emergency. Perhaps he should have let both Asif and Midah stay in Gemas, at least until Peng and his band had been dealt with. The thought of a bed without Midah in it and a house without Asif's noisy chatter made him ache with emptiness. Yet it was something he would have to accept if Asif's future was not to be endangered. He had great plans for the boy. When he was older, he would send him to school in Kuala Lumpur, or even Singapore. He could see him growing up, a Malay with a touch of white, the perfect hybrid in a country where orchids flourished.

Midah appeared to have fallen asleep and Cornelius drove in silence. He turned off the main road on to a gravel one leading to the estate. He had barely driven a hundred yards along this when his skin began to tingle. Some fifty yards away, his long headlights had picked up a mound of fresh earth on one side of the road. He knew exactly what this meant. Further along, perhaps just out of the reach of his lights, a trench would have been dug across the road and carefully covered. Cornelius knew too well how efficient this kind of trap was. He had taught Peng how to design them. The guerrillas would strike the moment the car's wheels landed in the trench, while the vehicle was askew, its occupants stunned. As clearly as he saw the trap ahead did he see who on the estate had been Peng's accomplice: Ah Cheong.

It was stupid not to have worked this out earlier. Ah Cheong had easy access to the key to the generator shed. Cornelius had spoken to him not only about the consignment but of the planned ambush. Now Cornelius remembered what had disturbed him after he spoke to Peng. The young guerrilla knew without Cornelius's telling him the day on which the medical supplies were due. "I'll wait till Friday," he had said. "The revolutionary soldier who can't wait finds that death can't either." Only Ah Cheong knew the supplies arrived on Friday. Yes, thought Cornelius, he was really getting too old for the whole business. Just because the man was English-speaking, old and a drunk, he had trusted him. Age and language did not guarantee loyalty, and drunkenness was a cover for all sorts of things.

He braked sharply to let the engine stall. Midah awoke with a start and began to murmur. Cornelius put a hand on her knee to silence her. He knew what he must do and he must do it before his mounting terror immobilized him. He pulled gently at the starter so the engine turned over but did not fire. Peng would be puzzled by the car's breaking down a few yards in front of his trap. It would not, however, take him long to realize what Cornelius was up to.

"Midah," he said, in as controlled a voice as he could, "there's an ambush ahead. Move across to the driver's seat." She sat frozen and he pulled her roughly across the brake and gear levers towards him. "I'm going to get out and run across the headlights." He felt sure that Peng would not fire on the car once he, Cornelius, was out of it. Not until he had finished with Cornelius anyway. "Once I've crossed your headlights, turn them off, and reverse all the way to the main road. Then get to Captain Roberts and the British soldiers for help."

She began to protest, but he silenced her. "Don't worry. I've been in worse situations than this. I'll hold on till you get back."

She moved into the driver's seat. (After all, her husband was Captain Cornelius, and everyone knew how good he was at handling trouble.) Cornelius felt for the grenades he had put into the pockets of his tunic and patted his gunbelt before slipping out.

His heart was pounding unpleasantly and his whole body trembled. He was sweating profusely, yet felt unbearably cold. It was ice water that ran down from under his arms. There was a dampness about his crotch and he wondered if he had wet himself. More important, he wondered if his knees would support him as he ran across the headlights exposing himself to Peng, offering his own body as an alternative target to the vehicle.

He began running across the line of the headlights, weaving and bobbing as he did. His gunbelt felt unnaturally heavy and the grenades banged painfully against his sides. Neither offered him any comfort. He thought of Asif, a Malay boy with light-grey eyes, singing pantuns with his grandmother, of Midah cooing to her son and gurgling with pleasure. Thinking these things, his run became more oblique, and he was a target for a longer period.

There was a burst of gunfire from his right. Something slammed into his body, a little below the left shoulder, throwing him to the ground. There was no pain, only a momentary electric shock which ran down his arm making it numb and lifeless. The moment he hit the gravel road, Midah turned off the headlights. He heard the car start and begin to reverse. He rolled over and over towards the bushes at the side of the road, changing directions as often as he could. The dead left arm made things difficult, slowing him down. He drew his revolver and fired in the direction the shots had come from, moving as he did between shots. There was a vague aching in the side of his chest and he felt a bit weak. The sweat continued pouring down his body but on the left side it was now warm and strangely sticky. He managed to get on to one knee and, with some difficulty, extracted a grenade from his pocket. He pulled the pin and hurled it in the direction of the gunfire. He had forgotten how much he disliked the metallic taste of the pin.

In the background but very distinctly, he could hear the sounds of the car reversing.

He began rolling to his right. Midah would probably marry again. She was young, beautiful and randy as a rattlesnake. He laughed at the thought, and his heart went out to her. Her husband would accept Asif and treat him like one of his own. He was sure of that. The Malays were always terribly kind to children whatever their origins. The boy's light eyes would, however, take some explaining.

He fired several times into the darkness. There was no answering fire. He knew exactly what was happening. Peng was, after the flash of the first grenade, letting his eyes get accustomed to the dark. Once this happened, his night vision would be as good as most people's in broad daylight. Cornelius had never failed to be amazed by it. "I have eyes like a bat," he used to say and they would both laugh at his elaborate joke. He took out the second grenade, controlled his nausea as he extracted the pin, and hurled it into the darkness. The flash would keep Peng night-blind a little longer.

The silence following the explosion accentuated the high revving sounds of the car engine. He wondered if Midah would tell Asif about his real father, the legendary Captain Cornelius Vandermeer. Perhaps Father Noonan would. The priest might even tell the boy about how Cornelius had lost his courage and then recovered it, after a fashion, in the last moments of his life. It was strangely peaceful, thinking of this future he was not going to share.

There were tiny flashes of light in front of his eyes and a little blood began to bubble into his mouth. It was salty and had a metallic taste which he found preferable to that of the grenade. His left side was now very wet and Cornelius knew he was dying. He could feel the blood seep out of his body and soak the earth around him. The unending darkness was almost upon him. He should have been afraid but he was too busy listening to the sounds of the car, fading as it carried Midah to safety.

thirteen

I showered, shaved and let myself out of the block of flats through a basement exit used exclusively by cleaners and lift-repairmen. There was no one about and after walking a short distance I found a public telephone.

Sheng was surprised at the earliness of my call but not at the kind of help I required. It would be no problem, he assured me, to sneak two people out of Singapore. He did not seem particularly interested in why they wanted to leave the country. I said their reasons were political, but when I began to explain the background to the whole business, he interrupted me.

"I'm only transport man, Mr Perera. So no need to know too much. But you must take care. Very great care. Your friends also. Very tricky, the Special Branch nowadays." He then gave me elaborate instructions on what the three of us were to do.

I phoned Su-May at the hospital. She seemed less surprised by my revelations than I expected.

"Yeah," she said, "Pete warned us about this. Said sooner or later they'd squeeze some rat's tail, like, and he'd squeal."

"But, Su-May, you don't seem to understand. It's I who told Samson. I wanted to stop you going away. Wanted to keep you for myself."

"No sweat, Hern. Pete and I were going anyway, and soonest bestest."

"Can you inform Pete discreetly?"

"Just a down lift ride from my ward to his physiotherapy

department, and we have our way of getting the kids to scatter."
She laughed. "Any other orders, master?"

I told her, as Sheng had instructed, that they were to leave the
hospital separately, dressed in street clothes. They were to make
sure they weren't followed and, using public transport were to
rendezvous at Changi Point, at the eastern corner of the island.
From here they were to take the ferry to Pulau Tekong, an island
some two miles distant. The island had a single coffee-shop where
Sheng and I would meet them around six in the evening.

"Carry very little but don't forget your passports."

"Not to worry, Hern. We always carry our passports . . . in
case."

I was surprised, almost disappointed, by Su-May's lack of anger
or bitterness at my betraying her and the Children. But there was
too much I had to do to dwell on this for long.

I got to Benson's before anyone else. It was officially my last day
at work and I made out I was examining everything in the furniture
department for the last time. At exactly ten, I presented myself at
the bank on the first floor and withdrew the twenty thousand
dollars I had received as severance pay.

The manager, who had personally to authorize such a large
withdrawal, laughed and said, "You're certainly all set up for a
marvellous New Year celebration, Mr Perera."

"Why not?" I said. "You only get sacked once by Benson's." He
laughed but less comfortably as he handed me twenty one-thousand
dollar notes.

This done, I slipped out of the side entrance of the store and soon
joined the mass of expectant people who wandered up and down
Orchard Mall on New Year's Eve.

At one of the larger shopping-centres, I found a money-changer
who was prepared to convert my twenty thousand Singapore
dollars into American money. I was nervous about this part of my
plan because such a large transaction would almost certainly
attract attention. The money-changer was an elderly Indian who
recorded the serial numbers of the notes, then examined them by
hitting each one against his table and holding it up to the light.

As he went through this ritual I began to worry about the course
on which I was set. Failure would mean not only the arrest of

Su-May and Peter but possibly of Sheng and whoever was assisting him. I looked around the little shop. I was its only customer and those passing outside seemed innocent enough, pausing only momentarily before moving on. Finally the old Indian was satisfied and counted out nearly nine thousand US dollars. These he slipped into a large brown envelope.

The encounter with the money-changer increased my anxiety. It was barely noon and Sheng had said I was not to turn up at his home until 5 p.m. "Don't stay still," he had advised, "and don't do anything that makes you look suspicious." So I traipsed from shopping-centre to shopping-centre. Up escalators and down escalators, across basements and through underpasses. Every loitering shopper became potentially one of Sam's minions. They must be looking everywhere for me by now. Would not my being closeted for two whole days with Captain Cornelius have given them enough cause to think I had bolted? And if they believed this, would Sam not have raised a general alarm, given orders for me to be arrested on sight? I tried not to enter shops because my doing so without buying anything would certainly constitute suspicious behaviour. I stood at several windows, attempting to look nonchalantly at their contents while studying the reflections of the people who passed beside me. If anyone stopped, even for a moment, I hurried on. Finally I took a bus ride out of town, then back in again, and several short taxi rides. It was nearly 4 o'clock before I caught a bus going towards the east coast. After travelling for an hour on it, I alighted and caught a cab. About half a mile from the turn-off to Sheng's house, I stopped. The driver looked surprised, for there was no habitation in sight. I winked at him and grinned, hoping he would read this as meaning I had some clandestine appointment with a lady friend. He gave me a tightly-controlled smile and hurried off. He seemed to think I was mentally deranged.

I arrived at Sheng's sweating profusely and obviously flustered.

"You are looking too nervous, my friend," he said. He poured me a little brandy from the bottle out of which he had been drinking. "A little Dutch courage before we make a move, yah."

I don't know if it was the title of my story or the brandy that did it, but by the time we boarded the tiny launch at Changi Point I felt much more in control of myself. The boat was manned by three young men whom Sheng referred to as godsons ("That means I'm the godfather"), though they looked too much like him not to have been blood-related.

As soon as we had tied up at the ancient and unsteady-looking pier at Pulau Tekong, Sheng instructed the lads to get on with the minor repairs necessary for the deep-sea fishing trip they were to make later in the evening. We found Su-May and Peter Yu in the coffee-shop that had been erected on wooden slats at one end of the pier.

Peter's eyes looked red-rimmed, as though he had been crying. It took me a moment to realize that this was simply the effect of the sea and the sun on his delicate skin. "Hello, Hern," he said, extending a hand. "So good," he nodded several times, "of you to go to all this trouble to help."

I wasn't sure whether it was a sneer or a note of triumph in his voice. The prophet proven right is, after all, entitled to both.

Before I could decide on how to respond, Sheng took over and said, "You, young fella, go down to the boat and help the other three get things fixed." Peter left promptly. "I go and talk to island friend, but only for a little while."

When we were left to ourselves, there seemed to be little I needed to or could say.

I began to apologize, but Su-May put a hand over my mouth, "No need, Hern," she said. "You only forced us to do the thing we were putting off doing." She giggled. "So that's the good Samaritan Sheng, whose house I know so well. What plans has he made for us?"

"The boys will take you up to Mersing, which is about a hundred miles up the east coast. From there you catch a taxi and keep travelling north till you reach Kota Bahru. From Kota Bahru it's only a short hop across the border into Thailand. Make your way to Bangkok, from which you can fly to any place you wish. Africa, I think you –"

"Tanzania, Hern. To a mission hospital on the slopes of Mount Kilimanjaro. But how do we . . . ?"

I gave her the large brown envelope filled with US dollars.

She opened it and her eyes widened. "We only expected a cut of thirty pieces . . ." she began, then, seeing the hurt on my face, added, ". . . but you've gone and robbed Fort Knox for us. Thanks, Hern." She squeezed my hand.

"Time's up, time's up," said Sheng, and things began to happen very quickly.

The three lads and Peter were revving the boat's engine. Su-May and I stood at the edge of the pier, Sheng some distance away. She held the inside of my arm and leaned heavily against me. One of the lads from the boat waved, Su-May turned and offered me her cheek, which I kissed chastely.

"I suppose . . ." she began.

"I suppose too," I said.

Then she was in my arms, kissing me wildly, the salt of our tears mingling in our mouths.

Someone offered her a hand but she jumped into the boat unaided and stood looking at me, a little girl in jeans and track shoes, her hair held in place with a rubber band, her shoulder bag swinging wildly as the boat lurched forward.

I stood watching the launch disappear. The sun had gone down, and the sea and sky were becoming a uniform, darkening grey. Dusk was whittling at the outlines of the islands that form a ring enclosing Singapore. Gradually these became black, shapeless masses merging one into the other. Between them, however, I could just make out pale, slightly shimmering patches. I knew what these luminous areas were. They were the channels leading to the open sea.

At Changi Point, Sheng suggested that we should travel separately and saw me into a taxi before going in search of his car. I gave the driver my parents' address and leaned back.

In the darkness of the cab I began to wonder whether or not it would be possible to structure all that had recently happened to me into a longer story, perhaps a novel. Generally I am against fiction that is based on fact. Authenticity has no literary validity. Nevertheless, recalling events from the past and using them, even in the order in which they occurred, was not something that automatically disqualified them from becoming worthwhile fiction. After all, both literature and reminiscence are commemorated in words and it was words I would use to fashion my memories. I have noticed more and more how stories, which are my reflections, have come to illuminate my life, and I did not find it impossible to envisage the reverse happening. Such a process had a distinct advantage: I would no longer have to fabricate events; I could simply abstract them from memory and decorate them with my fancies. Thinking back, I could discern a definite plot in the events of the past few weeks. Perhaps a fact would have to be twisted, a phrase turned, to meet the demands of my narrative, but this presented no problem. Stories must, however, rush towards their ending, and I was convinced that the conclusion to mine lay with Sylvie and my parents. I asked the driver to hurry. By the time the cab drew into the driveway of my parents' home I was selecting situations and touching them up for later use.

The house was in darkness but my mother let me in at the first ring of the bell.

"Where in goodness' name have you been?" she hissed. "Not even bothering to turn up for Sylvie's good news."

"What good news?' I hissed back.

"About the baby. What else?" She treated me to a smile. "Due in August, the doctor thinks, but the first you'll know of its arrival will be when you hear it bawling at night." She laughed coarsely. "Just like a man. Stick it there and think your job's over."

For a wild moment I thought that Sylvie had got herself artificially or, worse still, adulterously, inseminated. Then I realized she had lied to make my father happy on his death-bed and had been clever enough to see that the lie would fail unless it took in my mother as well.

"Well, Ma," I said, contrite, "you know how I am about these things."

"Don't I just," she said. "You go in to Pa right away. He's been waiting to congratulate the father-to-be."

My father lay in bed looking physically no better than when I had last seen him. As soon as I entered the room he attempted to sit up, his hand reaching towards mine. The effort was too much for him and he fell back gasping hungrily for air.

"I'm afraid, my dear chap, Mohammed will have to come to the mountain for the congratulations I believe are in order."

I sat on the edge of the bed and extended my hand, which he grasped and pumped with all the energy he could muster.

"Thanks, Dad."

"Oh, no," he said. "The boot's on the other foot. It is I who owe you thanks."

"Oh, go on, Dad . . ."

"Well, going on is what I will not be doing for very much longer I am afraid. But your news . . . yours and Sylvie's, that is, has really brightened my last days and made it somewhat easier to shuffle off this mortal coil."

"You've got ages –"

He held up a finger. "No, my boy. We didn't begin with lies, we won't end with them." He paused, gasping. His lids fluttered shut and I thought he had fallen asleep, but after a while he opened them. "I have one request, only one, about this infant that I am destined never to see. Will you grant it?"

"Of course, Pa. Anything."

"In the matter of names, I would like you to consider two. If it's a boy, will you call him Clarence, which is the nearest I can get to Clara?" He stopped for breath and swallowed several times. "If it's a girl perhaps you would consider Frederica, after yours truly." He attempted a courtly nod but his head simply lolled over. When he had pulled it straight, he continued, "I am absolutely certain that half the world is going to call her Ricka, but Ricka Perera sounds an excellent name to me."

"To me too, Pa."

He managed to take both my hands in his but the effort was so great that again he dozed off.

When his eyes opened, he said, "You know, old chap – or perhaps you may not have been quite cognizant of the fact – you've been a truly wonderful son to us." He made a tiny gesture and my mother joined us on the other side of the bed. "Yes, indeed. Quite a paragon. All that man and wife could want of their offspring." His voice broke a little.

I have always regarded my father as a long-winded, somewhat pedantic phoney, forever adopting poses, working from a book of rules he neither fully believed in nor had read too carefully. As I grew up I had learned to avoid conflicts with him, not because I feared their outcome but simply because I knew that they would reveal some yet greater insincerity of his character. I had learnt to accept and tolerate him, but I cannot remember ever having loved him. That he loved me and regarded me in the way he did came as a complete surprise. The eyes he turned to me were full of a love that warmed and comforted me. The feeling of being loved is ultimately indistinguishable from that of loving. I leaned closer to him and he smiled a little.

"And now your generosity really overwhelms me. I know how you feel about children and I have yet to experience the depth of affection that has moved you to make the kind of sacrifice you have elected to make." He held up a hand to forestall my protest. "I am not a religious man but I say from the fullness of my heart that my cup runneth over." He smiled. "And all because of you, Hernando."

There was something missing in my reaction to what he had just said. I wondered what it was. Then I knew.

For the first time in my life, I didn't baulk at the use of my full name. In fact I rather liked it, though my father rolled it around his tongue, extracting from it a spurious Spanish cadence. He smiled at Clara and she nodded as though to reassure him that tangos never lie.

He turned his face to mine and I looked deep into his eyes. In their depths I could still discern the terror, but Fred Perera was not going to let it be seen. There was now too much at stake. Clara was going to talk to her grandchild of its grandfather, tell it tales of his courage and of the noble way in which he had met death.

"I'm going to ask you to go soon, old chap. With the new child on its way, there are a whole lot of things your mother and I have to get sorted out."

I should have leaned over and kissed him, but such a gesture would have seemed unnatural. So I straightened up and shook his hand formally, in the manner prescribed for gentlemen.

He smiled approval. Then I went to the other side of the bed and kissed my mother.

"Don't worry, Mum," I said, "I'll let myself out and catch a cab on the main road."

I remembered only as I reached the bedroom door. "Happy New

Year, you two," I said, half turning. Clara had moved further up the bed. Her head was on my father's chest and her arms were round his body. She was making quite sure that if Fred Perera died that night he would die in her arms, ensconced in the memories dearest to him.

Neither of them returned my greeting.

Waiting for a taxi I became aware of an increasing desire for Sylvie. This reached such proportions that when I finally arrived at our block of flats, getting out of the cab became an embarrassing business. Of course, we would have the child. Fred Perera may have lived a liar, but he wasn't going to die one.

Sylvie noticed my condition as soon as I entered our bedroom and said, "Is it love, long-time-no-see or Happy New Year?" Her short nightdress had ridden up and she didn't bother to pull it down. "Who cares anyway? Just come over here, darling."

"I'll have a quick shower first."

"It's New Year, Hern. Come over and kiss me, then you can have a shower," she giggled. "By the looks of things, a cold one is what you need."

She kissed me first with her eyes, allowing her lids to flutter against mine, then with her chin, the dimple on hers brushing mine, then on the mouth. The kiss quickly became a violent embrace as my hands wandered over her body while she, without any break in contact, tried to relieve me of my trousers. I had just decided that a shower would be an unnecessary interruption when the doorbell rang. We would have ignored it but the rings were long, repeated, and accompanied by a thumping on the door.

"Stay on hold," I said, adjusting my clothes. "I'll go and chase it away."

Three men stood at the door, a large Indian whose muscles were just beginning to turn to fat, and two much younger Chinese who looked like gymnasts.

The Indian spoke. "My name is Singham," he said "B.S. Singham. Assistant Superintendent of police. We want a word, just a brief word. We crave your indulgence to obtain some clarifications." He shook his head before I could mine and carried on, his manner simultaneously obsequious and intimidating. "But we must insist."

"Can't it wait till the morning?" A picture of Sylvie in her short nightdress flashed before me. "I'm rather busy . . ."

Before I could finish, Singham and his gymnasts had shouldered their way into my living-room and bolted the front door.

"Are you one Hernando Perera?" asked Singham.

"Yes. But as I said . . ."

Singham hit me in the stomach. I doubled up with pain and nausea and began to sag to the floor. The two gymnasts held me up and Singham hit me twice more before they let me fall. I had never experienced physical violence and my reaction to it was not rage or fear but a surprise so total that it immobilized the workings of my brain. When my mind started functioning again, I did not think of crying out or hitting back. As I lay on the floor, retching, my first thought was: *I'm being assaulted, I must send for the police.* I struggled to sit up. One of the gymnasts put his boot against my mouth and began to push down hard. I heard a crack and an excruciating pain ripped through my brain. I thought I had been shot in the head till I realized that the salty, metallic taste was blood, and the loose, hard objects rattling in my mouth were my front teeth.

"Get up, you bastard," said Singham. "We're taking you in for interrogation."

fourteen

I have lost all sense of time. Day and night have ceased to exist. Blinding lights alternate, meaninglessly, with pitch blackness; freezing cold follows scalding heat. At some times, the silence is so complete I think I have gone deaf; at others, the world is filled with a high-pitched whine that seems to come from inside my head. Only pain is constant. I have learnt that it can come from anywhere but is worst when it springs from the places that previously gave me pleasure. There are marks on my body I can't explain. They don't worry me. Nor am I bothered by the excrement I find clinging to my person. I have become quite unashamed. I scream, wet myself, vomit, let loose my bowels and burst into tears without caring. I doubt my tormentors understand that torture is a self-defeating process: it destroys dignity and thereby removes much of that which makes suffering unbearable.

I don't think of my family often, though I once did dream of Sylvie. At least, I think it was a dream, and quite a strange dream too. We sat close to each other but in separate glass booths and conversed through telephones. I couldn't touch her but I could see her clearly enough. Sylvie looked old. Her hair was a streaky grey. The skin of her face was pinched and papery. She looked sad. I would have liked to have stroked her cheek to cheer her up. I lifted my hand and touched the glass between us.

"It's a pity we didn't have that child, Hern," her voice on the phone said. "Makes things incomplete."

"Incompleteness is essential to unending perfection," I replied. "Think about it. It cannot be otherwise."

"You're right, Hern," she said. Then, her eyes lighting up a little, added, "Right as rain, as Ma would put it." I smiled widely to show her I still could. As soon as I did, she cried, "Oh, God, Hern, what have they done to your teeth?"

Then there was this loud buzzing noise on the phone. Sylvie seemed to be crying and banging on the glass when they came to drag her away, and the dream ended.

My guardians are young gymnasts, so beautiful that they must have come from another world. They do whatever they have to do to me with consummate grace and in tune to harmonies I cannot hear. I think of them as participating in a cosmic dance from whose mysteries I have been excluded. But they dance without enthusiasm. Their eyes are opaque, meaningless pools, and the longish, black hair curving around each of their pale faces is a halo from which all luminance has been removed. I suspect my angels are damned to despair. Perhaps I am to blame for this. I heard one of them complain, "Nuts, that's what this guy is. Look at him grinning like an idiot when he should be yelling his guts out." He may be right. I could well be mad. But it is just possible that I know something they don't.

There is a green hill far away. Its grassy slopes are gentle and rolling and some distance from becoming the steep, snow-covered sides of Kilimanjaro. Where the grassland gives way to the rain forest, the air becomes cool, and here a well-worn trail leads to a line of hospital buildings. Peter Yu works in a room at the far end. He looks darker and more robust than I remember him. All morning he has been straightening crooked children, and the sweat pours from him as he teaches a paralysed man to walk. Su-May has spent the morning on a verandah in front of the hospital, vaccinating new-born infants. Now she turns her attention to their mothers. She seems to be scolding a teenage girl who carries a baby on her back and clearly has another in her belly. She waves a packet of contraceptives under the girl's nose and gesticulates angrily. Instead of being penitent, the girl laughs, throwing back her head and opening her mouth wide. The women around join in. The reason for their merriment becomes obvious when Su-May stands up. She too is pregnant. Though her middle is swollen, her arms and legs have remained thin. Pot-bellied and spindle-limbed, she resembles the starving children she has come to help, I think. She must have overheard my thoughts, for she looks in my direction and smiles. I smile back, reassured of the underlying goodness in the nature of things that is an inexhaustible source of wonder and warmth.

I turn and grin at the angel of despair who hits me across my mouth. But the blow falls painlessly, for I have become, miraculously, toothless.